Ron Stonebear Shields

"Zed's Path"

Vision Quest
BK 2

Dedication:

"Zed's Path" Vision Quest, is dedicated to my father, Billy F. Shields. At the time of this writing, he is 93 years old. He is a vanishing breed...one of the last of the remaining veterans of World War 11.

He served proudly for 21 years in the US Army, but he's served God since he was 17 years old. Recently, he and I were able to visit Webb Baptist church in Webb, Mississippi, where he was baptized as a young man. It was a blessing to both of us to make that journey.

He has had significant health issues and 2018, has not treated him kindly. Broken back, pneumonia, ambulance rides and in and out of the hospital, but through it all, he has been a staunch supporter of my writing efforts. His moral character influences the behavior and speech of my characters in this book. I write hoping to please him and I have. I think he's my biggest fan and he's also a frequent contributor of ideas that are within the pages of this book.

He is one of the finest examples of manhood I have ever known. He doesn't lie and he doesn't cuss and he likes that I don't feel the need to do that in my writing.

He's been with me in my darkest hours and never wavered, not once. I never had to look to see where my father was. He's had my back since I was born.

If God, gave me a box of puzzle pieces and told me to put all the bits and pieces together to make the perfect father, I would end up with him, because all of his pieces fit. Nothing missing, or out of place. Just like the character 'Zed' in this book, my father has followed a path in his life to do only good.

Dad, this one's for you with love, respect, and gratitude.

I am deeply grateful to Roberta Vlier for her encouragement and support. She is a fine editor and friend and a great source of help and inspiration.

The cover photograph was generously provided by my talented friends at Doublesmith Photography; Dale and Robin Dressler Smith

Check out their Facebook page Wild Horse
& Landscape Photograpy

DISCLAIMER:

Neither the author nor the publisher shall be held liable or responsible to any person or entity with respect to any loss or incidental or consequential damages caused, or alleged to have been caused, directly or indirectly, by the information or programs contained herein. No warranty may be created or extended by sales representatives or written sales materials. Every company is different and the advice and strategies contained herein may not be suitable for your situation

Chapter 1

Sheriff Debbie used the tip of her crutch to push the glowing log further into the fire. We were sitting behind Wanda's cafe sharing a bottle of merlot and thoroughly enjoying gazing at the night sky. The stars were so incredibly brilliant. A city dweller might well be stunned to see what they had been missing living under city lights. She had her broken ankle encased in a walking cast and was resting the injured foot on a bale of hay. I was within pouring distance of her and both Lucy and Dimmit had a ringside seat with their noses a whisker away from touching.

It was one of those times you look back on in later years and realize it was special and momentous. Right then, it just seemed nice and peaceable. We went from talkative to enjoying long spells of relaxed silence in a natural flow.

Debbie sighed, and turned her head towards me, and I saw the glint of the fire sparkling in her eyes. I giggled a little. After all, it was our second bottle, and I am a man that can get a little tipsy just smelling the cork. Nope, I don't drink much because old Capt. T. taught me it was easy to get into trouble from drinking too much, but required creativity to get into trouble from drinking too little.

"Zed, you ain't a real sailor, are you? Based on my considerable experience in upholding the law, I would suspect you of giggling while intoxicated. I would arrest you, but I would have to get up on my sore leg, so I'll let you off with a warning this time."

"Now, pass me that bottle. I'll do my own pouring while you enjoy a timeout. I have things I feel like saying, and I need a pair of ears attached to a working brain to listen to them. I have words running around my head like a hamster spinning on her wheel. I figure if I open the gate and let my thoughts run loose, maybe they'll line up and make some sense."

"You up for that Zed, can you listen to me talk until my hamster gets worn out?"

I started to answer her, but she immediately cut me off. "Hush, I ain't through, matter of fact, I don't need you to say nothing; just listen while I ramble around and let these word critters run free. If you can do that, just nod your head, OK?"

I smiled to myself and suppressed another chuckle and nodded my head in her direction, giving her a tip of my cowboy hat. I was getting good at the hat tipping business. I had practiced in front of the mirror the way a girl practices making duck lips. I had it down pert good, like a native of Wyoming, born and raised. I never got the hang of the duck lips. I grinned remembering how it looked plumb silly on me.

"Zed, I am watching your eyes and all of you is not here, and I need you to focus."

I got myself collected and simply nodded my head this time.

"I am going to start speaking and I don't know where it's going, or even if enough of it will come out the gate to make any sense.

I've always been a big gal, bout the biggest anywhere I've been, and I never was ashamed of that. I wasn't fat and I didn't make myself big.

It's simply the way I am, and as my Daddy use to say, *'God made you exactly down to each solitary hair on your head just how he wanted you to be.'* He said in the eyes of God, I was perfect."

"Later on as I grew, I realized I was not only bigger, I was also different in other ways from most other girls my age. I never gave two hoots about dolls or dressing up in my momma's clothes. I did like to clomp around in my daddy's boots with his old sweat stained cowboy hat riding down around my ears."

"I played with the other girls my age but I was happiest off with my daddy, either hunting or fishing or tending our herd. I was the only child, and my daddy took up a powerful amount of time with me. Zed, he was a good man, as good a man as that old desert rat you've adopted for a daddy. Yep, he was that kind of man, kind and patient, and a natural born teacher."

"He was big too, bigger than me by three inches even after I got my full growth. His name was John, and you know that old song, what's the name...give me a second?"

She paused and took a long sip from her cup and glanced off into the embers glowing brightly, and you could see her memory was located.

"It was "Big John" by Jimmy Dean, and it had these lines in it. *'And everybody knew you didn't give no lip to Big John.'* That was my daddy right to a T. He was kind and patient, but you sure didn't give him no lip; not man nor beast, and that sure as the dickens, included me."

"Daddy is the one that taught me how to box and wrestle and he knew a lot about Jiu-Jitsu too. He told me he had been a hand to hand combat instructor in the Army, and served as a Military police officer in Tokyo, shortly after the end of WWII."

"Zed, I idolized my daddy and worshipped the ground he walked on. The most scared I've ever been is when I told him I was gay. I was so frightened he wouldn't love me anymore and I was shaking like a leaf right down to the depth of my soul when I told him."

"You know what Zed, that giant of a man had tears rolling down his cheeks and he hugged me so tight I couldn't breathe." He said, 'Baby, I've known for a long time, probably longer than you. Do you remember when you were younger and questioning why you were bigger than the other girls? Do you recollect what I told you then?'

'I do remember it like it happened this morning, because I told you, God made you just the way he wanted down to each and every hair on your head. Everything about you is the way God intended.'

'Don't you ever be ashamed of who God wanted you to be, and don't you never take no lip from anyone trying to disrespect who and what you are.'

"God knows how I loved that man, and how much I miss him almost every day. I know people say that all the time, but I mean it. There's not a day goes by that I don't think of my momma and daddy.

"Here, let me show you something, and you ain't gotta say a word, just look."

Debbie unfastened her wide watchband and extended her upturned wrist to me. Right where you would put your fingers to take someone's pulse, she had a small blue tattoo. It was just numbers on top of one another...10-08-23 and 04-05-28.

"You know what that is Zed?"

I shook my head no.

"That's my momma and daddy's dates of birth. Daddy is 10-08-23 and momma is 04-05-28. Every morning, I kiss my wrist before I put on my watch and I pause and say a quick prayer and thank God for giving me such good parents."

"I've talked about my daddy, but my momma was quite a woman too. She could ride and rope with the best of them. She wasn't a big woman at all and looked almost tiny standing next to my daddy."

"I was as tall her by the 4th grade, and probably outweighed her by 25 pounds or more, but she was rawhide tough. She was a better shot than my daddy and she passed that skill on to me."

"Both of us could outshoot him by the time I was a ten years old, but that just made him enormously proud, and he bragged on us, and bet his friends that we could outshoot them.

"By the time I was 14 years old, my reputation for marksmanship was so well known that no locals would try me. The only bets we could get were limited to strangers passing through."

"I probably am giving the wrong impression of my momma. I can see her now with her blonde hair streaming behind her and her sweaty face caked in Wyoming dust astride a lathered mustang, but I can also see her all dolled up with her hair gleaming and wearing a fancy dress."

"Oh Lordy, she was a pretty thing, probably the prettiest gal around, and Big John laid claim to her early on in high school. Didn't either one of them ever date anyone else, not even when they were broke up from time to time. Two mighty strong willed people found they each had to do some adjusting to accommodate one another."

I started to say something and caught myself in time. Debbie needed this ... to let her words flow without interruption.

"You know Zed, I couldn't have been raised in a happier home. It was a blessing I wish all kids could enjoy, but it was also almost like being raised in a bubble as far as having a true awareness of how others lived."

"I grew up sheltered and naive almost until I got into high school. I thought everyone had wonderful parents, just like me. It was almost a shock to learn about kids who came from homes where daddies beat on mommies and sometimes the children too."

She paused for a moment and reflected back, "I think I started coming into an awareness of how cruel the world could be when my best friend Dorothy was almost killed. Her own daddy shot her, killed her momma and then killed himself. I could not imagine another human doing that to another. Not the way I was raised, in a house filled with love and balance."

"That's what I admire so much about my mother and daddy. They had such a fine balance to them like their marriage was a dance choreographed in heaven."

"Dorothy didn't die, and she eventually recovered physically, but she never made it back emotionally. Being an orphan with no kinfolks around to take her in, they sent her off to an orphanage in Laramie."

"Zed, I never saw Dorothy again and she killed herself before she was 18 years old. I have often pondered, did what she seen and survive condemn her to a life of suffering? Maybe, it would have been a kinder fate to have died in that blood-soaked ranch house."

"Learning how cruel we can be to each other was a shock then, and even after all these years of witnessing humanity at its lowest, it can still rattle my cage."

Debbie poked the fire again with the tip of her crutch and sparks leapt into the air and she turned to me, "Hold up your cup, I figure you've been in timeout long enough."

I nodded my head gratefully. Amazing how dry your mouth can get just listening. Besides, I didn't want to stop this flow of this one-sided conversation. She poured me full and I realized she had opened a third bottle.

Lordy that woman could drink and all it seemed to do is make her more talkative. She topped off her cup and corked the bottle and sat it on the ground and leaned over and rubbed Lucy's ears. "You know I love you, don't you, you big eared beauty?"

8

Dimmit gave me a sharp tilt of his head and fixed me with an inquiring look, as if to say, 'Cat got your tongue?' I did my duty and leaned forward towards Dimmit, and almost fell on my face spilling half my cup of wine in the process.

I looked up embarrassed and Debbie had me fixed with a grin on her face. "I never knew you sailor types were such lightweights."

I tried to regain my dignity by telling Dimmit he was a spotted he-devil, but a peach of a dog. Seemed to mollify him some and he licked the spilt wine off the grass and moved closer to Lucy. He's a cunning rascal.

"Like I was saying Zed, before your downward dog yoga lesson interrupted my flow of words, I have spent years and years reflecting on the evils of man and I ain't excusing women from that equation either."

"I have known some women as vicious as any man that ever walked and twice as dangerous. We had a woman up near Dubois that buried four husbands and she didn't raise any suspicions at all until the 5th husband got sick and they tested him positive for arsenic."

"They dug up the previous four husbands and every durn one of them had more arsenic in them than Napoleon Bonaparte. She murdered them all, and she looked like a sweetest little lady anyone could ever imagine.

They called her the Black Widow of Wyoming, and I suspect there may be plenty of bodies underground that have been buried over the last 100 years or so that have enough arsenic in them to keep a crime lab busy until judgment day."

Debbie smiled, "Wouldn't surprise me none if some of them weren't completely justified."

"Zed, you tend the fire while I get something from my cruiser. You've drunk and spilled all the wine and I am far from getting all these words out of the corral. I need something to lubricate my throat.

"I have an unopened bottle of Jameson that is perfect for drinking under the stars by a flickering fire with a good companion that's smart enough to keep silent."

As she arose, Lucy started to get up with her and Debbie quickly said, "No baby, momma will be right back."

When she got out of earshot, I took a sip and snickered, mumbling to myself, "No baby, momma will be right back." Dimmit looked up at me and grinned, I swear he did. Lucy gave us both a disapproving look, so I got up and added some wood to the fire.

"Looks like a long night watch ahead boys and girls, but tomorrow's Sunday, and we can sleep in, unless my favorite dust devil is spinning out of control."

Dear precious Wanda had been a virtual dynamo of a wedding planner ever since the day after the rescue of little Katy. She was like a train steaming down the tracks. You either had to get onboard or get out of the way.

She was sprinting toward the altar like it was the finish line of a life-long race and in a way I guess it was, with Charlie as the grizzled trophy.

I heard Debbie slam the door to her vehicle and she made her way back to the fire holding a bottle of Jameson aloft that glittered from the reflecting flames.

"Zed, I see you are an unusual man that listens and knows how to tend a fire. I'm in a mood for flames and sparks shooting into the night sky. Do you ever want to lay your head back and howl at the moon?"

She gave me a wink, and let loose a howl that sounded so authentic, Dimmit bristled up and howled with her. Lucy soon joined in and I couldn't help myself.

I leaned my head back and howled with them. There wasn't much of a moon, but you have to make do with what you've got. Sometimes, you've just gotta let loose and let a little wild spill out.

The upstairs door above the cafe came open with a bang and Charlie came out in his underwear, red ones, in case you're wondering, and shouted down to us

"What in tarnation is wrong with young folks these days?"

"Don't you know old folks approaching their nuptials are like nitroglycerin aboard a horse drawn buggy on a bumpy road? Me and Wanda were deep in thought trying to count how many cocktail weenies wrapped in bacon we needed for the wedding and since you invited half the civilized world on live TV, we had just about decided there weren't that many little weenies in all of Wyoming."

"Figured we would have to import product from Kansas. Uncle Bob always said he never saw so many little weenies in his life until he got to Wichita. He said it was the weenie capital of the world, bar none."

"Say, is that a bottle of Jameson these old eyes spy? You know Zed, I ain't much of a drinking man, but after two hours of discussing cocktail weenies, I could do with a pull from that bottle."

"Just hold your horses, and I'll be down faster than Dimmit can eat a donut." In just minutes, Charlie joined us wearing his cowboy hat, boots, an unbuttoned shirt and his red underwear.

"Aren't you a little underdressed Charlie?"

"Shucks, this ain't a formal occasion and my pants were lying too close to where Wanda is busy calculating my upcoming life of indentured service.

"Besides, ain't neither one of you intrigued by my manly appearance and if you're nice to me, I might even show you my war wounds."

Debbie was taking a pull from the bottle when Charlie said that, and she snorted whiskey through her nose and began to howl. Of course, Dimmit and Lucy joined in and I felt obliged to make it a quartet.

Charlie, being experienced in matters of this nature wisely rescued the Jameson from Debbie's grasp and took a snort. I saw his Adam's apple go up and down three times before he pulled the bottle from his lips. He may not be a drinking man, but he showed me he sure wasn't a rookie. He had obviously met Mr. Jameson, or some of his kinfolks a time or two back in his younger years.

"Now, if that don't hit the spot and make a man forget about cocktail weenies, he's a terminal case and might as well pick up and move himself to Wichita, the Weenie Capital of the World. I'm going to have another sip, but this one is purely medicinal."

"Lots of snakes where we are headed and this is preventive medicine, just in case I get fanged by a deadly Arizona Gaboon Viper."

Debbie had regained control of herself and asked me, "Have you ever heard such nonsense in your life? There are no Gaboon Vipers in the whole US of A, except in zoos."

"Well now, Sheriff, how do you know they ain't planning an escape right now? A sip of Jameson is worth a whole IV bag of anti-venom, and I can't take no chances at my age."

Charlie took another healthy swallow and passed the bottle to me. I immediately handed it to Debbie, because my chair was already moving like I was I was bucking an outgoing tide in a dingy.

No sir, I'm not much of a drinking man either, and the merlot had done a number on me, and I was pickled, or as Consuela would say, peekled."

A log fell into the fire shooting glowing embers high into the sky and the flames flared up lighting up our faces. Everyone had an external glow and an internal one as well. One of those perfect moments you look back on in life and wish it could happen again in just the same way with the same exact people.

A span of happiness and contentment to be treasured in years to come of a perfect moment of bliss. Charlie voiced his opinion that he reckoned he would have to fetch his own bale of hay to sit on seeing how one of us was an invalid and the other was a sailor too drunk to walk.

I grinned at him and took a sip of merlot that was beginning to taste more and more like purple Kool-Aid.

Charlie went over to Dimmit's pen where the hay was stacked. The same pen that darn sure hadn't kept Dimmit from escaping, and I suspect any Gaboon Viper worth its name could accomplish a jail break even faster.

I yelled at Charlie, "Watch out for Gaboon Vipers, they like to hide under hay bales and are attracted to the smell of Jameson and they are instantly angered by old cowboys wearing red underwear.

The Sheriff just informed me that three men over age 60 had been bit already, so they are riled up something fierce and ain't discriminating."

"Quiet down Zed, you get momma bear down here from her nuptial configurating, and she sees me drinking in my drawers, you'll get to see a dust devil that even a Gaboon Viper couldn't hold a candle too."

He sat his bale of hay down besides Debbie within easy bottle passing distance. "This night air feels mighty fine against my bare skin. Kind of makes me feel all tingly. You know, I might just be a nudist at heart. Yessiree, I imagine my battle scars would be quite a topic of conversation at a nudist colony."

"I couldn't testify to it in court, but I've been told my scar looks like Marlon Brando's face. Here, take a look see."

And before we knew it, he pulled down the right side of his drawers exposing a buttock with a sizeable scar that looked remarkably like Marlon Brando.

I lost it then, falling out of my chair, roaring with laughter, and rolled around on the ground.

My intoxicated brain tried to come up with the proper social media remark that would fit the situation. Rolling On The Ground Laughing When He Showed His Butt Off … ROTGLWHSHBO. Kind of unwieldy and I doubt it ever catches on.

Debbie lost it too, and the hounds had to join in because of all the dog breeds, there are no bigger party animals than Dalmatians and Basset Hounds. There was all kinds of consternation going on, both dogs howling like they were getting paid a bonus for enthusiasm, me rolling on the ground snorting grass and dust up my nose and Debbie bellowing like a tuba.

Charlie implored us, "You've got to hold it down." He looked up at the windows and begged us, "If she comes down here, you two are going to see a rare nocturnal dust devil and they don't come no worser than a dust devil in the dark."

While Charlie was looking up at the window, I was looking beyond him, and saw the aforementioned dust devil approaching at ramming speed.

Her housecoat was flapping and she had Charlie's britches in her hand. Charlie saw right where I was staring and he turned around and I could actually hear him gulp.

"Charles Bowden, have you lost your ever loving mind, out here with a lady without your pants on?"

"Aww honey ain't any ladies, just me and Zed and Debbie and these two old dogs."

This time, I gulped loud enough for everyone to hear. I don't know much about how to talk to women, but I knew you don't say there *'ain't no ladies'* when two of them are standing right in front of you.

Especially when one of them is armed, and the other one, that I thanked the good Lord, wasn't armed with anything more lethal than a pair of Wrangler jeans.

She was giving old Charlie a good verbal thrashing, but I saw a twinkle in her eye that I had seen before.

Her eyes flashed in the firelight and I realized she was having fun pretending to be mad. I don't know if I've ever remarked on how beautiful Wanda is.

She's got to be in the neighborhood of Charlie's age, but she could pass for being a young forty, even in bright sunshine. She was pretty enough to turn any man's head.

I had no doubt she could have had her pick of men, but she chose Charlie, and once she made her pick, she never looked elsewhere.

In some ways, if you didn't know Charlie and the caliber of man he was, you might think they didn't belong together. He was grizzled and wrinkled, and had been rode hard and put up wet.

Wanda, on the other hand, was fresh and unblemished. She looked like the Queen of the Red Desert. A discerning eye could look beneath the surface and see they were a natural pair and belonged nowhere but by each other's side.

They reminded me so much of Captain T and Momma T, way back in Bayou La Batre. They carried on the same way and teased each other unmercifully, but the love they had for each other was as bright as a flawless shiny.

"Charles, take your pants and go around the corner and put them on and fetch another bale of hay, unless you want to sit on the ground with Zed.

"Hurry up now, while I help this drunk sailor over to this bale. It's quite apparent that all of you need an adult minder that knows how to behave properly when Marlon Brando makes a cheeky surprise appearance. So by right of being the only one currently sober, I am commandeering Zed's chair.

"Anybody drunk enough to fall out of a chair don't need to be sitting on anything higher off the ground than a bale of hay."

"Debbie, if you'll pass me that bottle, I'll show you how a lady drinks." Debbie passed it over, and Wanda turned the bottle up to her lips and drank deep. She didn't have an Adam's apple to gauge how many swallows she took, but way more than Charlie had.

I was impressed, or at least I think I was impressed. Things were a mite fuzzy by that point.

Charlie came dragging up the other bale of hay and said, "How long have you been listening to us sweetie?"

"Long enough to hear your nonsense about Gaboon Vipers and the danger of nocturnal dust devils."

"That long, huh?"

"Honey, you know I think you are a plumb peach of a woman, you know I do. I don't know what came over me. I had cocktail weenies coming out my ears and my brain just balked on me and threw me into a pile of stupid."

Debbie picked up her crutch and poked Charlie with it, "Don't be forgetting there's another lady here you need to be apologizing to."

"I reckon I know that. I'm not completely stupid, so Miss Lucy, I offer you my sincere and humble apology for conducting myself in an inappropriate manner."

Debbie stood up like a towering grizzly, but she also had a twinkle in her eye, and she said, "Unless you want me to slap Marlon Brando plumb silly, you had best be amending that apology to include one other name."

"Aw Sheriff, you know I didn't mean a thing at all by what I said. I think you are a plumb peach of a woman too, I most surely do. You are just about the biggest old fuzzy peach of a woman I have ever laid eyes on."

"Hold on ... I see right away what I just said might not be taken in the spirit intended. By biggest, I mean more abundant. Yes sir, that's what I mean alright, you are abundantly peachy and not so fuzzy most folks would even take notice."

Charlie took off his hat and slapped it against his leg making dust and hay fly into the air. "Doggonit, I messed it up again. You reckon I could have a little swallow to wet my whistle while I call up the proper words to apologize more correctly?"

Wanda shouted, "Give him a drink Deb, and let's see how far he can dig a hole for himself, this is just getting good."

Debbie handed over the bottle, and Charlie gratefully took two decent Adam's apple bob's worth of liquid courage. Charlie rose to his feet with some difficulty and removed his hat.

He bowed to Wanda, Debbie and Lucy. He then placed his hat over his heart and commenced speaking in his cultured alter ego.

"My dear ladies, all of you exquisite examples of the female form, both human and hound, it has been most correctly brought to my attention that I have been remiss in delivering words adequately conveying my remorse for my ill-chosen words spoken unthinkingly a short while ago.

"It pains me down to the deepest chambers of my heart that I have caused offense to three of the finest examples of feminine pulchritude I have encountered in my earthly sojourn."

"I call you all peaches, which in my estimation is the finest example under heaven for a desirable fruit. A peach to me is the epitome of excellence. One cannot exceed a peach in either flavor or texture. Nothing feels better in the palm of a man's hand than a peach. No berry or cold skinned apple can approach the comfort of a peach.

"A peach, whether big or small, is the richest bounty that can fill the hand of man, even if it requires both hands to grasp the blessings given unto him.

"I, Charles Bowden, most humbly beg you to forgive this unworthy scoundrel. I deserve it not, surely I don't, but it is the earnest plea that I be forgiven of my transgressions."

With that said, Charlie again made a formal bow that would have been admired in palaces from Versailles to Buckingham.

Wanda looked at Debbie, and they both burst into uproarious laughter and Debbie punched me on my arm and I fell off my bale.

I was getting comfortable being 'grounded,' but I found myself holding on to the grass to keep from slipping away. The dry desert seas of Wyoming seemed to be storm tossed and the ground seemed like a good place to ride out the storm. It was not to be.

Debbie picked me up like I was a bag of dry leaves and planted me firmly back aboard the bale. "You hang in there sailor boy, I am ready to herd some more of these words of mine out into the open air and let them run free."

"I was just about to tell Zed about the time I realized I was gay, when our little therapy session was interrupted by none other than Marlon Brando in a pretty pair of red panties. Such an appearance would stop the flow of conversation even at a San Francisco costume ball."

"I've never been much of a fan of Marlon Brando. I always kind of thought he was an ass, and I have seen nothing tonight to dissuade me from that opinion.

"I had asked Zed to be quiet and just listen and he did just that. I don't expect such discipline will be possible now that we are faced with an unruly crowd of heavy drinkers, so join in, if you feel a need, but Zed might just keep his remarks confined to head nods and shoulder shrugs."

I looked over from my rocky hay bale and said, "Debbie, you are just a big old fuzzy peach," and I gave her smile so big that it made me realize my face had gone numb. I couldn't make that smile end at a decent interval.

Smiles have a societal time limit before they become unsettling and make folks nervous. I was in default smile mode and unable to break the smile connection on my own. Dimmit rushed to my aid and bathed my face with his wet tongue.

That broke the spell and I broke into laughter, and Dimmit thought it was a game, and he began prancing around me giving me play bites and fierce growls. I had upgraded my operating system from default smiles to default border-line hysteria.

My belly was shaking and I was snorting, both in and out like a laughing hyena. Plumb disgraceful, but like I said, I ain't much of a drinking man. Genuine laughter, especially the out of control variety is as contagious as the flu.

Little tiny giggle molecules were in the air and they soon infected everyone in the circle. You know that hiccup sound some folks make when they laugh?

That's how Sheriff Debbie was laughing, like the braying of a donkey and just about that loud, and Charlie was a snorter like an old boar hog, and Wanda was one of those that put their hand over their mouth and kind of vibrate all over.

Nuttiest bunch of folks you'd ever expect to see under a star swept Wyoming sky. Definitely one of those memories you'll look back on one day and remember when the world was plumb perfect.

That September night would be long remembered...at least the part I might be able to remember.

Debbie turned her face to the glowing coals after we all finally gained control of ourselves, and my gaze followed hers.

There is something so primeval about a fire. The way it captures your eyes and draws them closer until you begin seeing the coals winking like clues. They can lead your mind, into your own special room inside your brain that is seldom visited during normal consciousness.

It is as close to true meditation as some folks will ever come. I have found lots of answers in my life, from losing myself in the fire and letting my mind coast.

I've done it while listening to waves crashing on the beach or to the sounds of beating drums. Funny how fires and drumming are a ritual with so many cultures around the world.

It was around such a fire in the country of Laos, while sitting with some of the hill people, that I experienced an epiphany that changed the direction of my life.

While listening to the steady rhythm of their drums, I saw their shiny teeth blackened from chewing betel nut smiling at me and reflecting the flames. I became mesmerized by the glowing coals and I found myself at the entrance to that door in my head that's seldom open.

The drumbeats seemed to be urging me to reach out and open the door, and in my head, that's what I saw myself doing ... reaching out, opening the door, and stepping in.

It was a bright and welcoming room with rows and rows of books. The books were labeled ... Thoughts ... Beliefs ... Regrets ... Purpose ... Expectations...

And so it went. This was the real me ... both good and bad, that no one else ever sees. I saw the books titled 'Mistakes' and 'Faults' were in volumes.

They were like a hymn books in church pews lined up book after book. I looked at one thin volume labeled 'Purpose.'

One tiny book labeled 'Purpose' and shelves of books titled 'Mistakes' and 'Faults.' I opened the cover of my 'Purpose.'

The first page had these words only; *'Your purpose is to do good.'* That was it, nothing more on the first page.

The next page gave some guidance. *"Your soul has a map of your path in life and your path is connected to your heart. As you travel your path and learn your purpose, your heart and soul will guide you.*

'If you stray from your path, your heart will hurt, and lose its connection to the soul. If your heart is hurting it's because you've gone astray and left your path.'

That was it for page two ... short and sweet, but it rang loud and clear with truth.

Page three was the shortest of all, and the end of my book of 'Purpose' read in bold letters ... **'STAY ON YOUR PATH.'**

I am not sure where my mind went after that but my heart began to hurt as memory after memory of mistakes and faults flashed through my brain until I thought my heart would burst.

It felt like it was beating to the sound of the jungle drums that seemed to be making the air vibrate with a shimmering intensity.

All the books of 'Mistakes' and 'Faults' suddenly turned to dust. Just crumbled and fell into nothingness.

That was my epiphany. I could start from that moment with a clean slate and do good from then on. My bookshelves for' Mistakes' and 'Faults' would be wiped clean.

I resolved at that moment that's what I would do. It was not an instantaneous and miraculous conversion by any means. Since then, I've put some more volumes of 'Mistakes' and 'Faults' back on the shelves.

It's like breaking a bad habit or behavior ... it takes practice and learning to forgive yourself and scramble out of the briar pit, and get back on your path when your heart starts hurting. The brain is a sponge and it will soak up anything you expose it to, and it takes in the negative and the positive with equal acceptance.

No cover charge, no dress code, and no bouncer at the door to guard against unworthy thoughts coming in and making themselves right at home.

I had to become a bouncer for my own brain, as silly as that may sound. It's totally up to me, to see what is allowed in, and what gets turned away. If you are not on guard, your mind can turn into a garbage dump quick, and if you let it hang around too long, you get accustomed to the smell.

I make a mistake every now and then, and let a negative thought or belief get in, because it came cleverly disguise or it is written so deceptively well that it seems like it just has to be true.

Once those thoughts get in there, they start causing chaos in the neighborhood and by the time you realize your mistake, they are like roaches to get rid of.

I am learning to get references from my soul and it frequently tells me to go learn for myself what I've allowed to happen. Seems part of my path, and a part just as important as staying on it, is to seek the truth. That's a sizeable chore these days and I get fooled regularly. Then my heart hurts and I learn that I have not learned at all.

I stopped searching for the truth when I found something to my liking, and called it the truth. I can be fooled but you can't fool my heart and soul.

Maybe my heart, but my soul and heart are a team and have each other's backs. That's the kind of places your mind can take you when you allow it to get lost in a fire.

Try it, and see if you can find that door in your mind, and find your own book of 'Purpose.' Your's might be as thick as an old family bible, or it may be as simple as mine.

Just to do good and stay on my path. Sounds so easy in theory, but incredibly hard to do in this world today.

I fail regularly and when I do, it is sometimes major. Those big mistakes in my life were the most demanding teachers and also my greatest lessons. The things you learn birthed in pain and despair tend stick with you.

No pain ... no gain, might well be my motto. Pain is a difficult and thorough teacher. It takes no prisoners and allows no excuses. You accept it and learn, and adjust your attitude, or you can wallow in misery and curse the unfairness of your life.

It's up to the one in charge and you can take control and climb back on your trail and move on with your purpose, or be lost in the confusion of life's distractions that tries to entice you away into an existence that is purposeless.

Debbie broke her trance with a noticeable effort after having been lost in such deep contemplation of her own. She began speaking in a low voice that carried well.

"I guess I was around eleven or twelve, that time period when little girls start discovering their bodies and their minds start thinking on things for the first time. In my little circle the big interest and subject of burning fascination was kissing."

"No one had kissed a boy yet, and there was some kind of unspoken competition about who would be the first of us to lay claim to that title. The problem was, not one of us had any inkling how to start. We practiced on the mirror in the girl's bathroom at the school."

"Some got real enthusiastic and put on lipstick and left marks all over the mirror in colors from Pink Coral to Decadent Scarlet.

"The janitor despised us, and left a hand-written sign taped to the mirror. It read, *'The only thing I can use to cut this lipstick buildup is toilet water from the boy's bathroom'*.

"That put a real damper on the mirror make-out sessions. Matter of fact, it ended like flipping out a light switch. The curiosity did not die and one girl suggested we recruit Cynthia's little brother Bob, as a practice kissing dummy."

"We approached Bob, as a group, and revealed our plan expecting he would be an eager volunteer. Nothing could have been further from the truth.

"He was horrified and ran screaming to his treehouse and he pulled up the rope threatening to dump a basket of 'horse apples' on any girl that tried to shimmy up the tree trunk."

"Zed might not know this, but 'horse apples' ain't a fruit, and despite the dire warning, a gal named Sally tried to climb that tree and she promptly got bombarded with a cascade of 'horse apples' about her head and shoulders.

"It look like she got pelted with about half a bushel, so we knew Bob was still well armed against further intrusion from any amorous females.

"We withdrew and came up with an alternate plan. We decided we would have a slumber party at one of the girl's homes and we would learn how to kiss by kissing each other. That idea was at first met with nervous shock, but that was soon replaced by curiosity and anticipation.

"Cynthia immediately said there weren't no way they could do it at her house because Bob would be too scared to come into the house with all us girls present.

"Sally jumped in and volunteered her house. Any girl willing to risk a bushel basket of 'horse apples' dumped on her head to snatch a kiss from a reluctant 10 year old boy is what you might call motivated."

"She wasn't but 12 years old herself, but she was precocious. The plans were bounced off her parents and as expected, they welcomed the opportunity to bring 6 rambunctious girls into their home. Sally was one of those girls that got pretty much anything she wanted except that kiss she tried to get from Bobby.

"She didn't get that kiss until Bobby was 16 years old and in the 10th grade and she herself a two-time Senior that should have graduated the previous year with the rest of us.

"She was precocious alright, but not in a book sense. I think that bushel of 'horse apples' that got dumped on her head interfered with her intellectual progress."

"She never finished that second shot at completing 12th grade either, being she got pregnant from 16 year old ... soon to be seventeen year old, 'Horse Apple' Bobby.

"He might have been reluctant as a 10 year old boy, but he was a fast learner. A daddy by the time he was 17, and a convict before he was 21.

"Anyone else notice how whiskey and firelight make some folks ramble on?"

Charlie spoke up, "I just remembered that me and Zed are supposed to go up to the rez tomorrow, so I can introduce him to Ironbear, and I've got to get myself in bed and catch a few winks.

"Come on Wanda, let's see if you and me can climb those stairs without me falling on Marlon Brando."

Off they went leaning against each other whispering things to one another. I could have heard what they were saying if I had tried. I can hear that well, and I can also turn it off, when it's none of my business.

"Anyway Zed, it's back to just you and me, so I'll finish this tale of the slumber party, and let you find your bed too. Is that OK with you, just nod your head?"

I managed to do that without too much discomfort. By that time I would have nodded at a lamppost and begged its pardon.

Chapter 2

"So, we six young girls showed up at Sally's the next Saturday night. We all brought our little bags packed with our pajamas and toothbrushes and various and sundry items.

"One girl even brought her teddy bear. She was the clingy type and it's my guess her bed as a grown woman is covered in stuffed animals and they all have cute little names.

"I also bet you a dollar to a donut that she's got at least one cat, and if she's only got one, you know she's in full acquisition mode to get another.

Nothing wrong with a man or woman having just one dog, but a single woman having just one cat is reason to pause and question if she's in between cats at the moment, or showing early signs of dementia."

"I don't even remember that gal's name, but she was an awful kisser. I do remember that. Colder lips than the school bathroom mirror during the month of January, and we are talking a Wyoming January.

"Yes sir, it was like kissing a corpse. I don't imagine she ever changed and I reckon cats and stuffed animals fill the void."

"That reminded me of something that happened a few years back. I was still a deputy and running my regular patrol route.

"It was a quiet night with little radio traffic and I was cruising along about 80mph, when I saw these oncoming headlights headed my way. Even at a distance, you could see the hazard lights flashing, and that the car was being operated erratically.

"I thought if I turned on my blue lights it would settle the driver down and I could get it safely off the road and find out what was going on. It worked because that oncoming car immediately pulled off to the side and stopped.

"I pressed the pedal to the floor and closed the distance. I saw an old man standing by the driver's door frantically waving his arms."

"I considered whether I was about to confront a mental or drug issue, but as I pulled even with him and got the car in park, nothing about him was setting off alarm bells. He seemed to be what he was ... a desperate old man needing help.

"I got out of the patrol car and before I could ask him what the problem was, he begged me, 'please help me, please oh dear God, please, please help me, I think my wife's dying.'

"I rushed to the other side and found a woman in her 80's, head back, not moving with her eyes wide open. I shined my light into her eyes and saw nothing but an empty void.

"I put my fingers on her carotid artery to feel for a pulse. My God, Zed, that woman was ice cold, and I jerked my fingers back like I had been shocked.

"I looked up to tell the old man that I was sorry she was gone, but he had knelt to the ground and was holding his clasped hands in supplication begging me to save his Lizzie."

"Lord, Zed, I knew that woman was dead and gone, and there weren't nothing left but the wrapper, but I have never seen such an abject look of despair on the face of another human being.

"I started doing chest compressions on her knowing it would do nothing for her, but maybe something for him. Everything I did that night, I did for him, and to comfort his grieving heart. There wasn't a thing I could do for her. She was beyond earthly care.

"I continued the compressions for several minutes and questioned whether I had done enough to satisfy the old man that someone had at least tried to save his Lizzie. I looked down to where he knelt on the ground and I knew I hadn't done enough. Not yet."

"Zed, so help me, I pried Lizzies mouth open and gave her mouth to mouth. I breathed my life into her dead body, and I forced myself to do it again and again.

"I don't know how long Zed, I simply lost track until the old man said, "She's gone ain't she? She ain't never coming back, oh dear God, what am I going to do without her? What am I going to do without my Lizzie? Dear God, take me too, right now, I can't live without her."

"I kind of halfway thought God might just grant that plea, but the old man must have still had a reason to stay. Maybe at that moment he didn't know that his story went on, but God did.

"I left him alone with Lizzie for a moment and went back to the cruiser to call an ambulance to come retrieve the body. I checked in with dispatch and gave them a 10-7 code taking myself off duty. No way I could leave that old man alone in his grief.

"I pondered my previous actions and I was surprised about what I'd done. I am a little leery around the dead. I don't know why, but they give me a sense of unease and I'm usually gloved up and professionally detached when I touch a body. I never would have thought I had it in me to voluntarily put my lips against those of a dead woman.

"You know, sometimes you can breathe hope into the living by breathing into the dead, at least it worked that way that night. Zed, I think that must be the most selfless thing I've done in my life.

"I can feel those lips to this day, if I think on it, but it's not a creepy feeling, not any more at least. It reminds me of the time I thought of someone's needs and did something far away from my comfort zone."

"After the ambulance came and gently removed the remains of Lizzie, I stayed behind with that old man talking.

His name is Dusty Rhodes, and Dusty is his real legal name, not some cowboy nickname. He and Lizzie had been married 64 years, and they were both 82 years old.

"She wouldn't never get any older, but Dusty is still kicking and now approaching 90, and as fine a friend as anyone could ask for."

"He's still driving but needs a walker to get around. He'll be at the wedding and I want you to meet him. He's full of stories about this area and he's been collecting Native American artifacts from this area pretty near his whole life.

"He's got a collection of things that would make a museum curator drool. He's probably worth a few million dollars but you would never know it to look at him.

"His spread probably takes in more than 15,000 acres, which is not unusual in Wyoming, but his land has water and lots of it.

"That makes it especially valuable and just the kind of place developers like to break up into 20 acre ranchettes.

"But Dusty ain't intrigued by money, and his place is called the "Anchorage," and he said he was going to fix it where nothing like that could happen even after he's gone. I don't know what he's done, but he's smart as a whip, maybe even smarter than you."

She paused and shook the bottle of Jameson and tilted it to the light of the fire and grunted some expression of pleasure at seeing some remained, not much, but enough for a swallow, or two.

I took that opportunity to move from my bale to the ground. It was still a bit unsettled down there, but more like the gentle swing of a hammock than the previous rocking and rolling of a storm tossed ship.

Both dogs were snoring and the fire had burned low. I looked straight up at the star-filled sky and I felt like I could reach right up and pluck one like a peach.

I wondered what it would feel like holding a star in your hand, like becoming part of the universe. I didn't think there was a peach in the world to compare to a star, and if I ever found a woman like Wanda for my own, she wouldn't be a peach.

No sir, my woman would be a star, and with that thought I began humming the words ... *Catch a falling star and put in your pocket ... save it for a rainy day.*

I couldn't remember the rest of the song so I just repeated the same line to myself over and over. Like I said, I ain't much of a drinking man and I ain't much of a singing man either, but when it comes to humming, I am world class. If the Philharmonic Orchestra had a humming section, I would be first chair.

For some reason I left behind catching a falling star and started humming a song that had the words ... *walk on, walk on through the rain and the storm and you'll never walk alone...*

That's all I knew but I could hum it from beginning to end, and the more I hummed the better I sounded.

I mean I could feel my humming down in my chest and it don't sound very humble, but I was good, and I mean really good, and I was getting my humming up to a skill level I had never reached before, and it was going so well I launched into Hallelujah, and ran it all the way to the end.

My hummer was certainly well tuned by this time. Merlot and humming really seemed to go well together. I stuck with another old Leonard Cohen song, one of my favorites that I actually knew all the words to, and I began humming...

Suzanne takes you down to her place near the river
You can hear the boats go by, you can spend the night forever
And you know that she's half-crazy but that's why you want to be there
And she feeds you tea and oranges that come all the way from China
And just when you mean to tell her that you have no love to give her
Then he gets you on her wavelength
And she lets the river answer that you've always been her lover
And you want to travel with her, and you want to travel blind
And you know that she will trust you
For you've touched her perfect body with your mind
And Jesus was a sailor when he walked upon the water
And he spent a long time watching from his lonely wooden tower
And when he knew for certain only drowning men could see him
He said all men will be sailors then until the sea shall free them
But he himself was broken, long before the sky would open
Forsaken, almost human, he sank beneath your wisdom like a stone
And you want to travel with him, and you want to travel blind
And you think maybe you'll trust him
For he's touched your perfect body with her mind
Now, Suzanne takes your hand and she leads you to the river
She's wearing rags and feathers from Salvation Army counters
And the sun pours down like honey on our lady of the harbor
And she shows you where to look among the garbage and the flowers
There are heroes in the seaweed, there are children in the morning
They are leaning out for love and they will lean that way forever
While Suzanne holds her mirror
And you want to travel with her, and you want to travel blind
And you know that you can trust her

25

For she's touched your perfect body with her mind

I knew that one by heart because when it says ... Jesus was a sailor and only a drowning man could see Him, and that all men would be sailors until the sea shall free them...
   I knew when I heard it for the first time ... it was written for me.

Debbie continued talking oblivious to my humming. She was in her zone and I was in mine. It didn't matter we didn't hear one another ... we were together, two connected humans giving comfort to one another under a sky filled with promises and mystery.
   One of those stars might fall my way someday and I would catch it, if that was part of my path. It was not for me to know where my journey would take me. My purpose was to do good and accept what unfolded.
   At that moment I saw a shooting star, one of those spectacular ones burning a fiery path to earth, and I momentarily thought it might actually be coming my way.
   Of course, it blazed out and fell to earth somewhere unknown. Foolish to think anyone could catch a falling star, but I took it for an omen from the heavens. I walk my path by faith and use my heart as a compass.
   It had brought me right where I needed to be and I remembered my momma telling me, *keep moving forward even when you don't know where you are going and sometimes the universe will put you right where you belong.*
   I felt like I belonged where I was, laying on the earth of Gauntlet, Wyoming, and with warm thoughts of my mother strolling through my head, I drifted off to sleep using heaven for a blanket.

Chapter 3

The morning chill awakened me right as the sky began to lighten with the pending dawn. That's usually the coldest time of the day, right before the sun relieves the night and takes over the job of lighting this side of earth.

Someone had covered me during the night with a thick heavy blanket, and looking with my sleep filled eyes to the left, I saw Sheriff Debbie lay much like me, but she was so long the blanket didn't cover her feet.

I sat up and shook myself alert and ran my fingers through my hair and yawned. I got to my feet and took my blanket over and covered Debbie's feet and I covered Lucy too since she was laying right there. I felt fairly decent considering I had slept on the ground and drank too much wine and been flashed by Marlon Brando.

The coals were ash covered, but still producing some warmth which was most welcome that chill Sunday morning.

I made a wise decision to visit the comforts of the great indoors and get myself into some kind of order other than disheveled and dusty. I stepped away from both Debbie and the fire and beat my hat against my pants.

Remnants of Wyoming flew free in a sparse dust cloud before falling down to their resting place. I looked over at the fire pit and thought to myself; *dust to dust...ashes to ashes.*

I had plenty of both of that's for sure, and all we really are is dust in the wind anyway. That made me think of the song, "Dust in the Wind" performed by that band named 'Kansas.'

I don't suspect that old Uncle Bob would have given much of a listen to a band named 'Kansas'.

With the tune from Kansas running thru my mind, I started humming it on my way into the cafe. It made my lips vibrate and that made me smile and I broke connection with my hummer. You can certainly smile while humming but not while humming "Dust in the Wind." I can smile and hum all the way through "Ghost Riders in the Sky," and when it gets to this part, I am truly in touch with my inner hummer. I can even feel my chest vibrating.
Yippee yi ooh
Yippee yi yay
Ghost riders in the sky

Funny what a man will do to amuse himself when he's alone. I mostly think, and sometimes I think and hum at the same time. It's a natural progression almost like a mantra. I'm sure some men sing, some whistle, and some are so annoying and insensitive and they do it around others.

I once rode with a man all the way from Mobile, Alabama to the Chesapeake Bay, Virginia ... 891 miles and almost 17 hours on the road.

He was a good friend, might even say my best friend. We were in his GMC step-side truck and we no sooner got underway than he began to whistle.

The man had true talent and he was a gifted whistler, but he was a shrill whistler. He could make bats have mid-air collisions he was so shrill.

We stopped at a truck stop outside Montgomery and while I searched frantically and fruitlessly for some earplugs, he bought what must have been a 5-pound bag of sunflower seeds.

When we got back in the truck, I asked them why the big bag of sunflower seeds. He said he liked to eat them while he drove, and to keep them from blowing back in the truck he just spit them on the floorboard and he'd vacuum them up later.

I thought at least he can't whistle and eat sunflower seeds at the same time. How wrong I was. Like I said, he was a man of uncommon talent and a good friend ... you might say my best friend ever.

By the time we got to Atlanta, and the sunflower hulls began threatening to build up over my shoes, I was beginning to re-evaluate my friendship and question what I ever saw in him.

When we hit the city limits of Charlotte I could no longer see my shoes and I was beginning to suspect my friend of harboring some creepy mental disease.

I recalled back when they would put folks away for excess book reading and imaginary female problems.

No doubt they had a wing for whistlers with soundproof rooms, and some other ones, double soundproofed for shrill whistlers.

I prayed for patience, tolerance and strength. I said, 'Lord, if you can't give me patience, tolerance and strength, please just strike me deaf. I got none of the above.'

I guess I was being taught something by the experience. I'm not quite sure what that was ... pick my friends better? Conduct whistling auditions and reject shrill ones from the prospective friends list? I don't know what I may have learned from that experience other than some friends are only good for a short haul and you can get back from Chesapeake, Virginia all the way to Mobile, Alabama aboard a Delta jet.

We hit the state line of Virginia, and were welcomed by a huge sign that read ... VIRGINIA IS FOR LOVERS…

I was most definitely not feeling love. Sunflower seed hulls were up to my shins and I was wearing shorts. The 5 pound bag of sunflower seeds was empty; not a one was left.

I had eaten a total of eight and I did not spit the hulls on the floor. I stuffed the hulls in my ears to stop the hideous unrelenting sound.

That did not work, and besides that, they were a mite painful. The hurt felt so good, at least it was a different kind of pain, and I kept poking them from time to time, while counting the mile markers go by.

It was an ordeal like trying to regain the surface from a deep dive, and you're running out of air and you don't know if you are going to make it to the surface in time.

I was holding on trying to make it to the finish line, and beginning to wonder if Virginia was a capital punishment state. I knew God promised in the good book that he wouldn't put more on a man than he could bear but I was thinking a misjudgment had been made, or I had misinterpreted. Maybe I was supposed to smite this shrill demon in the cab next to me.
I was planning my move because smiting seemed like it was heaven sent. It is hard to smite someone if you are right-handed from the passenger side, especially when your feet can't get a grip on the floorboard because it's slimy with spittle coated sunflower seeds.

Just as I was about to backhand him and then judo chop him right smack in his whistle box, he pulled into our destination.

I got out and it looked like my legs were coated in ticks. I stomped my feet and two fell off. Only two hulls fell while many dozens remained attached. I thought that was the final straw. No, the final straw was when little birds started pecking at my shins.

That's when I lost it ... I ran screaming into Chesapeake Bay pursued by a flock of little birds. My friend whistled shrilly to stop me but I ignored him.
 Right then I hated him. I never rode in another GMC truck or ever ate another sunflower seed to this day. We parted ways after that. He was miffed that I chose to fly home but I knew I had reached my limits. If his wife ever murders him, I will testify in her defense.

Chapter 4

Lost in my pondering, I realized I was standing there holding the doorknob to the back entrance of the cafe. Just standing there like I woke from a dream.

I shook myself, twisted the knob and made my entrance. I was greeted with lights and the delicious aroma of coffee brewing.

Abraham was on the job and he greeted me, "Hola, Senor Zed, I came by and saw you asleep by the fire and in my country we have a saying, don't step on the tail of the Chihuahua. Here you say, let sleeping dogs lie. It means the same thing, no? Soon mi amigo, we shall have the coffee and we will make the Diablo for everyone and have a nice Sunday breakfast.

"Senor Zed, I have a favor to ask you. I have two younger brothers, fine honorable men I am proud to call my family, that are coming to visit with me and Consuela next Sunday. Their names are Alberto and Alonzo. All of my parent's male children have a name beginning with the letter A.

"I wish them to meet with you, if you will permit such a thing. I have told them how smart you are and also how you are so lucky. They want to ask your advice on a business idea.

"They are not seeking money, only guidance and maybe a little luck. Can such a thing be possible with you? They are coming anyway to see Consuela, and me all the way from Phoenix, before the snows come. They think we are loco for staying in Wyoming for the winter, but I told them you are a genius and to be the godfather of our child, and they wish to meet such a man as you."

"Abraham, it would be a great honor for me to meet your brothers and I will give what honest advice I can share, but I assure you I am not a genius. I am reasonably smart, and I like learning new things, but as far as my intelligence goes, I can only say I am less ignorant than I once was, and I hope one day I can say I am less ignorant than I am now.

"What I have found, Abraham, if you can get three or four people that share a dream and a goal and they work without jealousy or competitiveness, you have the same thing as being a genius, but even better.

"I have known men that I would call a genius. Some were brilliant thinkers and had incredible thoughts ... but that's what they did.

"They thought brilliant things but they did not do brilliant things. Simply having the thoughts alone fulfilled them and they went on to the next clever idea that intrigued them and sparked their imagination. Sometimes a man's intellect is based on the situation and how well his knowledge addresses the need of the moment. Do you understand?"

"I am not sure Zed if I understand this situation of which you speak. Perhaps you can say it in a way that makes it where my head can make sense of it.

"I can learn quick if it is a way that I can make it fit with the things I know, like cooking. Cooking, this is a thing I know very well, but many others, I am stupido."

"No, my friend, you are far from stupid. Let me explain it this way. If two men were lost in the wilderness, and one was a great pianist, a recognized genius in the musical world, and the other was a primitive man that knew how to make fire from rubbing two sticks together and which roots and berries he could gather that were safe to eat; who would be the genius in that situation? Which of these two men would survive?

"Even a simple man, or woman, can be a genius in the right situation. Things that will matter a 100 years from now are the things that should most matter today. How to make fire, grow and find food, and make a shelter.

"I want you and Consuela to help me learn how to speak your language and how to cook. Knowing these things will make me less ignorant than I am today, but I equally desire to learn how to make fire from rubbing two sticks together, to find food from nature, and I would like to learn how to build a home with my hands. If I had a son and wished to teach him how to cook, I would first teach him how to make fire."

"Thank you Zed for making this to where I can understand. You may not call yourself a genius but I do. You know how to teach, and you share love with the people in your life, and you bring goodness with you. A hundred years from now, these things will still matter, no?"

"Yes, my friend, I hope to the good Lord, that 100 years from now, doing good and sharing love will still matter to the human race."

The back door flung open and Sheriff Debbie strolled in looking a mite disheveled. "Where in the name of all that's sacred, is my steaming cup of Diablo this morning and has anyone seen that cat?"

Both Abraham and myself asked at the same time, "What cat?"

"The dang cat that slept in my mouth and left this fur ball behind ... that's what cat I'm asking about."

Abraham and I looked at each other and shared a conspiratorial smile that we managed, barely, to keep from breaking into outright laughter.

It's risky to laugh at any woman first thing in the morning, and when she's 6 foot 4, big as a grizz, and armed, plus having just spent the night lying in the dirt after being flashed by Marlon Brando, its borderline suicidal to laugh at that kind of woman.

Thankfully, the light flashed 'ready' on the huge commercial coffee pot and I sat myself to preparing three cups of life-saving Diablo.

I was still smiling but I kept my head down and tried to think of something painful to distract myself from thinking about cats. Something like hugging a cholla cactus to my bare chest seemed to be doing the trick.

I noticed Abraham was keeping his head turned from Debbie, trying to hide his own lingering smile.

I yelled at him to think about dancing nude with a cholla, and that was more than he could take. He burst into laughter like a broken piñata releasing its hold, and as his laughter spilled forth, mine broke free as well.

Debbie gave us both a smoldering look of disapproval and shook her tousled head.

"Zed, I thought you might be immune from the stupid gene most men seem to carry from birth, but I can see now, it was just dormant and a few cups of wine has released it from hibernation. Bring me my coffee before I have to squirt this mace into my mouth to get some relief."

I took her coffee to her and she grabbed it with both hands and immediately took a substantial swallow. I knew the stuff was blazing hot, but all she did was blow a sigh of relief. She's a peach of a woman ... a big old two-handed fuzzy peach of a woman.

"Zed, do you remember any of what I told you last night?"

I tilted my head to the right. That's my thinking side, and I tried to remember all that she had said before I slid into oblivion dreaming of catching a falling star.

She interrupted my desperate attempt to recall last night and said, "Before I forget, where you whistling last night?"

"Oh HEAVENS NO ... Sheriff, I would rather be keel-hauled than be caught whistling in public." Shucks I'd rather slow dance with a big old fuzzy peach of a cholla cactus. I reached around to scratch my back and discovered a painful spot and I stopped scratching it immediately.

Something must have poked me during the night. I hadn't even noticed till I reached back to rub it.

I regained my train of thought, "Nope, Sheriff, you will never catch me whistling. I have a strong aversion to whistling like some folks do to snakes. I had a traumatic experience due to severe prolonged whistling exposure. You might say I have Post Traumatic Whistle Disorder, or PTWD, and I'd rather do naked yoga wearing spurs than listen to whistling."

"God forbid Zed, you look like Zed, but you are starting to sound like Charlie. I swear, if you ever get Marlon Brando tattooed on your behind, I'll have to take back what I'm about to tell you. That's the reason I asked you if you remembered what I said last night.

"I was going to ask you if you heard anything that might have made you uncomfortable, but I know the answer to that already. Foolish of me to even think it, much less ask.

"Zed, I want to make you a full-time deputy that don't work full-time. I know you wouldn't expect any pay, and I couldn't get the county to approve you working part-time for a salary anyway.

"I only want to use your knowledge on something important, like when I need an objective mind to take a look and help me think it out, and I need someone lucky like you.

"You know, when you and I rescued that little girl from that tomb in the ground, God could have allowed either one of us to push that boulder aside.

"I think he wanted me and you to work together and not just that once. I think he wants us for a team. Let me tell you the rest ... I was awake this morning when you covered my feet with a blanket and you made sure Lucy got covered too.

"My daddy used to cover me like that every night as he tucked me in. When you covered me with that blanket, I had the strongest vision of my daddy standing right there looking down, and he was smiling.

"Zed, I thought I could reach out and touch him, and he was glowing too, Zed. He was glowing bright, all warm and golden, and I felt such a sense of comfort and love wash over me.

"I heard a sound and I looked over at you and I could hear you humming 'Ghost Riders in the Sky,' and Zed, as God is my witness, you were glowing too.

"I could feel your humming way down deep in my chest, like I was humming too. I looked back at my Daddy, and my Momma was there now. They were smiling at me holding hands."

Debbie began to cry and big tears rolled down her cheeks, and she couldn't go on. I went to her and embraced her as tight as I could. She was wracked with emotion and shook from the feelings coursing through her body and I felt her tears running down my neck.

I held her and she held me, for a while. I don't know how long, but until she could speak again, and she spoke, "Zed when you got to the part where you were humming ... ghost riders in the sky ... they smiled at me one more time and while still holding hands they floated away. I could see them smiling at me until they faded out of sight."

"Zed, I don't believe in the supernatural, but what I saw was real, and you know Zed, I can still feel you humming down in my chest. Now, if that isn't a bonafide flash, I never expect to have one."

We released our hold on each other and stepped back. My eyes were wet too. What a powerful experience to share with another human. She and I were already good friends but right that moment we bonded, and it was a spiritual bond.

I had no doubt she had experienced exactly what she said she did, and I think her Daddy approved of me, because I thought God made Debbie perfect too, right down to each and every hair on her head. Her path and mine had joined.

I glanced over at Abraham and he was kneeling on the floor crossing himself and saying, "Madre de Dios, I have seen a miracle. You two were glowing like the sun holding each other and God was here in this room...I felt him touch my heart," and then he began to cry too.

Debbie and I jointly lifted him to his feet and we hugged each other in a tight embrace.

Charlie came down the stairs and looked at the three of us hugging with tears running down our faces without any shame or attempt to hide them, and he looked at us in stunned amazement.

"I know I missed something mighty powerful here but I don't know what it might be. Feels like I came in at the end of a good movie like, *'It's A Wonderful Life,'* you know that one that Jimmy Stewart was in. Feels like that's what I might have missed ... something magical or miraculous."

"Si, Senor Charlie it was a miracle here in the kitchen. They were shining like the sun holding onto each other. I have seen this thing with my own eyes. Madre de Dios!" and he crossed himself again.

"I surely would have liked being here when that happened, but I don't doubt what you say. I never thought I would see tears come from the Sheriff's eyes, not in this lifetime.

"I don't second guess the good Lord, no sir, if he had wanted me to be here, he would have had me here front and center, but I think Debbie just became a member of our growing family."

Charlie walked up to Debbie and opened his arms and she walked into the love that was offered and we were all connected in a golden web spun by a master weaver. What do you do or say after a moment like that? We all seemed stunned by what had transpired and our thoughts turned inward.

I cradled my cup of coffee, and the warmth was welcome, like I was holding a fallen star safely from falling any further. It meant something but I had no idea ... not then.

Later down my path maybe it would be revealed to me. All of this, everything that had taken place, had some meaning of great importance to us all. I was 100 percent sure of that.

Chapter 5

Charlie brought me back to the present when he began talking about the day ahead. "You and I better get us some grub going so we can get started up to see Ironbear. He's anxious to see you."

"How does Ironbear even know about me? You and I have not been apart since I met you, except when you went to the park and put that emerald ring on Wanda's hand."

"Zed, I told you that old man knows things and sees things others don't. He sent word to me to bring him the white man marked by the end of white man's letters.

"That's gotta be you ... Z, for Zed, the last letter in the alphabet. He ain't ever asked me to bring no other white man to see him. It's a strange thing for sure, but I reckon we'll figure it out along the trail."

Abraham had collected himself somewhat and asked, "So, after such a start on this miracle Sunday, what shall I prepare for us to eat to celebrate this day to be remembered?"

"Abraham, I remember a southern delicacy we used to eat in Alabama, quite often as a breakfast meal. It's called 'biscuits and gravy.'

"Momma T would make these big, fluffy biscuits in a huge skillet and she called them cat-head biscuits. I asked her why, and she said because each one was the size of a cat's head. Hers was huge and more like a bobcat's head.

"The blackened old skillet she used was enormous and she had to use both hands to lift it. Apparently huge skillets, and lots of them, are part of Cajun cooking. Abraham, do you know how to make biscuits?"

"No, my friend, I have heard of them, but never have I seen them made. If once I could have seen it done, it would be mine to know today. I remember things about cooking like my brain, she is a camera, no?"

"You are saying you have a photographic memory for cooking?"

"Exactamente! Zed. Show me once and I know it forever without a recipe. What I see, I can repeat."

"That's perfect because I am going to show you how to make Momma T's cat-head biscuits and then it will be yours to know.

"That's one reason I felt immediately comfortable the first time I stepped foot into this kitchen. There's enough blackened iron frying pans hanging here to outfit three Cajun kitchens. We are going to need the two biggest ones we've got."

"AYEEE, I can feel my inner Cajun coming out."

"But before I get my head into this cooking, I want to answer Debbie's question. I am honored to accept the position of a part-time deputy, and I hope I can in some way be of value to you in that position."

"WHOA, hold your dang horses, you're telling me we are going to have two genuine lawmen in the family? Lordy, lordy, old Uncle Bob ain't just rolling over in his grave. No sir, he's bouncing side to side like a runaway pinball.

'He's making leaves quiver in the trees above him and toppling tombstones like dominoes in a row. If anyone of you rascals ever hook up with someone from Kansas, we'll have to do an exorcism on Uncle Bob's gravesite."

Charlie shook his head and mumbled, "Two law men in the family, lordy, lordy."

"Charlie, you keep that big old peach of a woman company, while I show Abraham how to whip up a southern breakfast so good it will make you want to slap your momma from the table ... AYEEE!"

"Oh no, Senor Zed, I do not want to slap my sainted mother from the table because then she would kill me."

With a huge smile, he continued, "Maybe this thing, my brain should not take a picture. Some things it is better to not know, because the forgetting of these things is like trying not to think of something, like not thinking of a Chihuahua."

"Once I say it, you think Chihuahua too. It can't be helped. It is the same with taking a picture of a bad thing. A simple poke can make a bad thing pop up like a Mexican jumping bean.

"I say dog, and you think Chihuahua. You say cantaloupe, and I think of Raoul cutting of the tip of his finger slicing melons ... a bad thing. You say AYEEE and it makes me think AYE YAI YAI ... good thing."

All of that delivered with a beaming smile. He had gone through some kind of change too. He was feeling more confident expressing himself, and as he was doing so, he was revealing himself to be a more interesting individual than I had realized. It's amazing the side of people that may only be revealed when they feel safe and accepted.

Abraham was showing himself to be a very bright and entertaining young man. I thought of what he had said in English, and how well I understood it so clearly, and I imagined me trying to say the equivalent in Spanish.

One should never make fun of a person that speaks English imperfectly or with an accent, unless you can say the same words in their language perfectly without an accent.

Most places I've been in this world, the local people seem pleased you try to make an effort to speak a word or two of their language. They smile and try to help with your pronunciation.

I can probably say 'hello' and 'thank you' in a dozen languages but none of them perfectly and none of them without an American accent, but no one ever made fun of me. Some of those cultures might even consider such an act shameful. Some cultures are more cultured than others.

That's one thing you learn from putting your feet on foreign soil. You can get quite an education traveling, especially if you're polite and willing to learn.

But if you are thinking Paris ought to be like Wichita, and you're disappointed because Notre Dame and the Eiffel Tower are so far apart, and not everything is all close together like 6 Flags in Atlanta. If that's your attitude, you might as well keep your happy butt in Wichita, Kansas, the weenie capital of the world, at least according to my Dad.

"C'mon Abraham, we are making cat-head biscuits and while we do, I'll tell you all about S.O.S. and how it differs from what we are making which we'll refer to from now on, as S.O.B."
Abraham grinned at me, "You make a play on words, no?"
"Not at all Abraham, one is 'Stuff On a Shingle,' and we are making 'Stuff On a Biscuit.' Same stuff ... just on a biscuit."
"Abraham, go ahead and turn the oven up to 450 degrees and let it get good and hot. I'll put a bowl of Charlie's lard, a stick of real butter and a jug of milk in the freezer to chill down."

"That's one of the secrets, according to Momma T, for making the best biscuits. You start with chilled dough and you don't overwork that dough either. I asked her why she chilled it, if she was just going to stick it in a hot oven.

"She said, when it's chilled, it cooks on top first, keeping the insides fluffy, and it made them rise instead of spread out, giving you tall fluffy cathead biscuits. The last secret was to cook them in a well-seasoned, deep lipped, iron skillet so they can rise high."

Abraham and I, began preparing the items we needed, while I sat the deep skillet over an eye to melt the teaspoon or so of lard I scooped inside. Abraham watched it all with intensity.

We continued on with the cooking process while Debbie brought Charlie up-to-date on my new deputy sheriff-at large status. Abraham decided we would go all out on this breakfast and he begin frying some potatoes and onions and asking what else would go well with this dish.

I told him we often had cantaloupe or strawberries for color and contrast and taste. All we he had available were peaches.

Appropriately, they were big fuzzy peaches that filled two hands, and we decided that would be good enough. You have to make do quite often in life with what's on hand.

Everything was coming together and we hit a space we could relax for a bit. We poured ourselves another cup of Diablo and fixed up Debbie and Charlie too.

Charlie announced his intent to fill his belly plumb full to bursting, because he couldn't remember when he ate last.

That brought a retort from Wanda who was just coming down the stairs, "You better put a tight rein on that appetite of yours, or you'll outgrow the bed in the Double L before we're even hitched and you'll find yourself sleeping outside in a bedroll.

"Another thing, if you boys are planning on driving my Jeep to see Ironbear, you might want to lay off the green chilies this morning. You catch my drift, pardner?"

"I most surely do Wanda, I most surely do, but it seems almost sinful to eat fried taters without green chilies."

"If it keeps you from tooting on my sheepskin seat covers, I'm sure the good Lord will forgive you for not smothering your potatoes in high octane fuel this one time."

Debbie cleared her throat, I have two more things to give Zed," and she pulled out a deputy sheriff's badge inside a leather folder and a Wyoming driver's license made out to Zed Bowden, and handed them to me.

"Debbie, how in the world did you get a Wyoming driver's license in my name and where did you get a picture of me?"

"Zed, here's your first lesson as a lawman. If you were on a witness stand and sworn to tell the truth, and someone asked you how did the Sheriff get your driver's license, what would you tell them?"

"Debbie, I would have to say, I don't know."

"Exactly so, Deputy Bowden, and that's what you would have to say 6 months from now, or 6 years from now, because I ain't going to tell you."

All this said with a serious look on her face, and she went on, "As for the photo, that was easy. Those photographers took hundreds of pictures of us the night of little Katy's rescue.

"I just picked out the one that looked like you might be halfway normal. Sometimes you've just gotta make do with what you've got. Finding a picture of you looking normal was not an easy job, no sir, not easy at all," and then she grinned.

I grinned back at her and said, "I'm mighty obliged Sheriff," and tipped my hat.

"I'll need to get you pistol qualified and teach you a little hand to hand combat, just in case. You never know when it might be needed and it might be fun, and I promise I won't hurt you none."

I stepped up to her and extended my hand, as she reached to shake mine, I put her in a solid wrist lock and extended her elbow and gave a slight rotation. "Guess you know I could take you to the ground now Debbie. You would have to go or lose the elbow. That would be an unkind thing to do to anyone with a broken ankle, especially when she's your new boss."

I smiled and released her and said, "I've been studying martial arts since I was 17 years old, and you won't have to teach me much. I started with a Vietnamese shipmate of mine named Minh, way back in Bayou La Batre, Alabama. He was as good a martial artist of anyone I've ever encountered.

"We were in a bowling alley onetime in Mobile, having a nice weekend break, and I thought I would slip up behind and grab him for a joke. The next thing I knew I was lying flat on my back seeing stars. I looked up dazed to see Minh standing above me, looking embarrassed and extending a hand to help me up.

"He said instinct took over and he reacted to what he thought was a threat. He apologized profusely for what he'd done. Right then and there, I asked him to teach me and he agreed.

"I learned, and I learned well because Minh was an excellent teacher. The first thing I learned is never to judge a man by his size. Minh was barely five feet tall and he was always smiling, but he was a very dangerous man. Probably the most dangerous man I've ever known, and also one of the kindest."

"That's a most impressive demonstration you just gave me Zed, what was the name of the discipline Minh taught?"

"I asked him several times and he simply called it, 'Live Or Die,' and it was brutal and effective. He taught me for three years until he opened a Vietnamese restaurant over in Biloxi.

"I continued to practice on my own after that, and after I took to sea full-time, almost always there was a crewmate from China, Thailand, Japan or Korea aboard ship.

"Many knew a little of martial arts, and some knew a great deal. I practiced with many different people studying judo, Jiu jitsu, karate, aikido, and kickboxing.

"I have years and years of picking up a little of this and a little of that. I am not an expert in any of them, but what I know, I know well, and it kicks in like an automatic response when necessary.

"I don't even think about it. My shipmates used to awaken me by poking me with a broom. Because I tend to come awake like a Gaboon Viper, ready to strike. Just call me the 'Wyoming Kid,' I grinned and tipped my hat."

"I guess now you are going to tell me you're an expert with a pistol too?"

"I wouldn't go that far Sheriff, because as you well know, to be an expert with a pistol requires constant practice, and I haven't had much experience lately, but I suspect it will come back pretty fast."

Debbie smiled and shook her head, "Zed, the more I know you, the better I like you."

"Well Debbie, I can sincerely say the same thing about you and the rest of the crew here as well."

"Senor Zed, I think the biscuits may be ready. They are golden on top and they smell very nice."

"That's just the way we want them, so let's get to eating, but shouldn't we wait for Consuela?"

"No Zed, she might eat pickles, or nothing, but she was in the tub with bubbles up to her chin and singing like an angel when I came down. I covered you and Sheriff Debbie with blankets from our van, but I did not step on your tails or poke you with a broom.

"I let the sleeping Chihuahuas lie, especially the one big as a bear," all this delivered with a smile as he retrieved the big skillet of biscuits from the oven.

"Ay caramba, Zed, look the biscuit is now just one grande biscuit, bigger than a tiger's head. "What have I done wrong Zed?"

"Relax Abraham, that's exactly how they are supposed to look. See the little lines of separation, that's where the biscuits became friends with their neighbors but they are not married to each other.

"They are like a river with muddy water flowing into the ocean and keeping its color and identity separate from the saltwater."

I grabbed a hot pad and flipped the biscuits over a large cookie sheet and they came out as one big clump of steaming cathead biscuits, golden brown and filling the air with a mouthwatering smell. I took a spatula and separated them one by one, and put two to a plate.

"I have it now, my friend Zed, and you can all go sit at the rock table and Abraham will bring it to you."

"Not today Abraham, we cooked it together and we'll serve it together, so if everyone will skedaddle out of the kitchen, breakfast is served."

They left us like a galloping stampede, and we fixed the plates with biscuits and gravy, fried 'taters and onions, and sliced peaches.

It looked colorful and good enough for a magazine cover. Soon enough, we were all seated and eating like it was a contest.

Wanda spoke first, "Zed these are outstanding and it makes for a really hearty and satisfying breakfast. You reckon you can make these from time to time? I expect they'll be a big hit with our cowboys and roustabouts, and shucks, anyone would like this. It's delicious and satisfying, and two of them is more than I can eat."

I looked over at Abraham, and kind of raised my eyebrows in a silent question, and he nodded back at me. "I would be glad to make them from time to time, but Abraham can make them now just as well as me, *Es verdad mi amigo?*"

"Yes Zed, I have it pictured in my head, and I'm confident I can make them exactly like this every time."

Debbie had an opinion too, "They are truly outstanding and I know a thing or two about biscuits, but I disagree with Wanda, I can eat two just fine, and four sounds like more my speed."

Abraham indicated he was going to go get more for Debbie, but she spoke up, "You just sit right there Abe, I know my way to the kitchen and I think I'll put some of that sausage gravy on my fried taters this time, since green chilies is off the menu today."

"Debbie, I didn't put green chilies off limits to you; just these two yahoos, about to go off in my Jeep with its sheepskin seat covers. I might could trust Zed, but Charlie and green chilies? It would be downright animal cruelty to expose those poor sheep to that kind of torment that Charlie can dish out."

I asked Wanda, "Aren't those sheepskin covers kind of hot in Wyoming this time of year?"

"You would think so Zed, because wool is the best for keeping you warm when it's cold, but it's also a natural body temperature controller. The hairs are hollow and when in contact with human skin they regulate a steady body temperature.

"In hot conditions, like we have here in the desert, sheepskin absorbs human sweat instantly, and emits it into the air seven times faster than any old synthetic fabric would do and cools you down quicker too."

"Plus, they won't burn the hide off your body when you get in after it's been sitting in the Wyoming sun all day. Matter of fact, I've ordered a set for the Double L. They should come in mighty handy down in Arizona and other places we go where is stays hot all year."

Charlie bowed his head and shook it mournfully side to side, "Lordy, lordy, two lawmen in the family, I'm banned from eating green chilies, and dadblamed sheepskin covers in the Double L. My life is flashing before my eyes and I shudder to think, what's next?"

"Pedicures and eyebrow waxing?"

Wanda smiled, "I think a pedicure is just what a man that's lived his life in boots and desert dirt needs to make himself a presentable groom, but I can pluck those bushy eyebrows just fine, like I've been doing for the last 30 years."

"C'mon Zed, let's vamoose before this woman gets one of the Hollywood plastic surgeons flown in to prettify my scarred up rear bumper group."

"You two go on and skedaddle, I don't have time to flap my gums with you two today. I've got my wedding plans to put together and I think every lady in the county has volunteered to help, so I don't need any male input messing up my well-oiled matrimonial machine."

Chapter 6

Charlie and I bid them all goodbye and headed for the door with Charlie mumbling under his breath. I headed for the passenger door and Charlie said, "Hold on Deputy Zoo da Zed, you're legally licensed now, and you can drive this buggy while I sit in the passenger side and focus my addled brain on not farting on these precious sheep."

"Hell's bells boy, it's like getting butt-hugged by an Albino Sasquatch, and it's hard not to toot if you're being butt-hugged by a Sasquatch, don't make no difference what color it is."

I grinned and buckled the seat belt, and cranked her up. I put the Jeep in drive and headed north out of Gauntlet toward to the Wind River Indian Reservation and my first meeting with Ironbear. The Jeep rode real nice; much smoother than Charlie's old Ford.

Charlie began telling me about the reservation, "The Wind River is in a way a monument to the stupidity and ignorance of the white man and the shameful way they have treated the red man.

"To most whites back in those days, an Indian was an Indian, didn't make no never mind about what tribe they were from or what Indian nation they identified with.

"Acting out of sheer ignorance, or they just didn't give a hoot, they stuck the Arapahos and Shoshone on the same durn reservation. Those two are mortal enemies and there ain't much friendship between the two of them to this day.

"No siree, they get along like cats and dogs for the most part, but just like you can find a dog like Dimmit that got along plumb natural with Mavis, you'll sometimes find a Shoshone that gets along with an Arapahoe. Ironbear gets along with everybody. He is a man greatly respected on the rez.

"The Arapahoe and the Shoshone have different languages and customs. They even have different governments, and even different casinos. Most are poor from either tribe, but there are some well to do from both tribes.

"Ironbear is a man that has done well. You'll see some of the prettiest purebred Hereford cattle you'll ever lay eyes on, and the same goes for horses, especially some magnificent Pintos.

"There's about twice as many Arapahos as there are Shoshone, and somewheres around 30,000 of them altogether. The whole reservation is millions and millions of acres with folks scattered, but most living in communities.

"Now, Ironbear is a Shoshone, and a mighty proud one too; but he's a medicine man, and I guess he's got some kind of medicine man code where he's got to treat anybody if they're hurt or ailing, even if they are an Arapahoe.

"The Arapahos speak Ironbear's name with respect and more than a little fear. He's quite an impressive man and sometimes a little spooky.

"You'll see what old Charlie's talking about soon enough. Take the next left up ahead on to that gravel road cause we are getting close. I'm sure Ironbear is putting the coffee pot on the stove right now, 'cause he knows we are coming and just about when we are going to be pulling up to his diggings. He does it every time I'm here. He'll say, come in the coffee's just finished."

Now, Charlie's version of close might be the right word for Wyoming, but ten twisting miles gaining elevation with every mile is not my definition of close. Finally, Charlie directed me to turn in between these two tall squared timbers in the ground that were joined at the top by a hand-hewn crossbeam. Hanging from the cross member was the silhouette of a grizzly bear cut from a heavy metal sheet. I liked it. It was impressive and ruggedly artistic, one of those kind of things you would remember later. And after one more sharp curve to the left, we were there.

Not at all what I expected, not after seeing some of the dilapidated homes we passed as we made our way here. I recognized the structure immediately.

It was a Swiss log chalet, quite small, with brightly blooming flower boxes under every window. It had protected wings off to either side like a porch or a deck with rafters overhead but no roofing. Instead, they were shaded by a profusion of green vines that intertwined, much like a grape arbor.

There were birds and squirrels everywhere, scampering around like it was a Disney animated movie. They darted about, oblivious to our presence, chirping and singing like they were in the Garden of Eden. I was watching this panorama unfold when the door opened and a tall dignified man with shoulder length grey hair gracefully descended the steps and came our way.

He was wearing faded jeans and a denim shirt with patches on the elbows. Around his neck was a leather thong that had a small leather pouch dangling against his chest. He was both barefoot and hatless as he walked up to Charlie and embraced him.

Patting him enthusiastically on the back, he said, "Welcome my old friend, it has been too long and you arrived just as the coffee finished perking."

Ironbear stepped away from Charlie and approached me. He put his hands on my shoulder and looked deep into my eyes. It felt like he was gently probing my soul. It was not intrusive or unsettling in any way, more like feeling someone gently brushing your hair.

I looked back into his eyes the same way, and I could sense a magnetic like connection, and a mind backed by a keen intelligence. The first words he spoke to me were, "You are in pain, please turn around."

I was clueless about what he was saying, but I turned around. He took his index finger and drew a large circle on my back and said, "Within this circle is the source of your pain and as I make the circle ever smaller, you will feel the pain that will be yours to bear in coming days. He continued drawing and as the circle became smaller I became aware of a growing pain that I had first become aware of early that morning, shortly after I arose from my night of sleeping on the ground. The smaller he drew the circle, the more intense the pain became, and just as I was on the verge of voicing my pain, he stopped.

He said, "You have been bitten by the black spider with the mark of red. This pain you feel now will become stronger. It will rarely kill a grown man but it can cause you to become quite ill. It must be treated and this is something I can do, or you can go to the white man's doctor in Lander, and they will give you chemicals. They fight venom with poison, and that is not my way."

His voice was rich and vibrant and so soothing that he automatically instilled confidence in me that he knew what he was doing.

I replied, "Charlie has spoken of you with great respect and I respect Charlie as if we were my natural father. A son should honor his father, and extend respect to those his father has found worthy. I would be honored for you to treat me."

"Come then my friends, let us go in the house and have coffee while I remove this evil thing from your body."

The inside of the house was just as pleasing as the exterior and the massive logs gave the small structure a look of such a solid nature that I could easily visualize this as the ultimate shelter from the storms of life that nature and man might throw your way.

I had the strongest sensation of coming home to a house I had often dreamed of but had never found in all my travels around the world. This house welcomed me like a friend.

In the center of the main room was a stone fire circle with a huge copper vent hanging overhead that served as a chimney to vent the smoke through the roof. Around the fire circle that could easily accommodate five foot logs were thick buffalo robes that provide seating right at eye level with the flames.

Only a small fire was burning now, but I suspected it got quite cold at night at this elevation. It was a perfect mixture of the old and new, and a place where serious people could discuss serious things. It was a thing of beauty and it evoked a spiritual feeling in me.

"Not exactly a tipi is it Zed, but it has the sacred circle of my people at the center, and trust me, it is much warmer than a tipi when the Wyoming winter seeks to freeze a man's eyelids together. Please remove your shirt while I get my bag," and he spoke out, "Come Snowbird, I need you."

A voice spoke down from the loft, "I am coming grandfather." A young girl began descending the ladder from the loft. She came down backward and I could tell she was lithe and trim, but when she turned around I was stunned, not only by her remarkable beauty but how much she reminded me of my dear mother.

She had to be no more than 17 or 18 years of age, and her beauty was breathtaking. I felt an immediate desire to protect her from the cruelties of the world where many people would use her for her beauty and then toss her aside. She approached us with the same confidence and bearing that Ironbear wore like a mantle.

This one would not need much protecting, not from what I could see. She not only looked like my mother, she exuded that same self-sure demeanor that she could weather anything that came her way. She might bend but she wouldn't break, and woe unto the man that didn't see the steel beneath the beauty.

She introduced herself, "I am called Snowbird by my grandfather and I am pleased you have come to our house. The bite of the black spider with the red mark is painful but my grandfather will heal you."

Ironbear came back into the room bearing a well-used leather postal bag, just like they used to carry the mail when they walked house to house. He sat the bag down beside me and asked Snowbird to fetch a coal from the fire pit with the tongs.

He removed a small leather wrapped item from the bag, and unwrapped it with reverence. It contained a strange and unfamiliar looking object that I could not identify.

Ironbear saw my look and he explained, "This is a madstone taken from the belly of an albino deer. It has been in my family for hundreds of years and it is very powerful. It cannot be sold, but it can be passed down from healer to healer, one generation after the next. After I am gone, it will bequeathed to Snowbird, because she was also born with the healing power within her.

"Healing is a gift bestowed only by the Great Spirit. This stone will draw the poison from your body, but first we must bring the hot coal close to the bite.

"The venom seeks your heart and the heat will confuse it and bring it back to the source of the bite. Then I will put the madstone on your body, it will stick to you until it has pulled the evil from your veins. I will bring the coal close now and you should remain still."

Grateful for the warning, I steeled myself against the approach of the coal. I felt the heat and it was so intense and painful I thought Ironbear had actually touched it to my skin. But he went on to explain, "The pain you are feeling is the spider's venom being pulled back to the place of the bite."

The pain became really intense and I thought I would have to move, but Ironbear tossed the coal into the fire pit and slapped the madstone over the bite.

Immediately, I felt an intense vibration from the stone and I looked back at Ironbear to question if this was normal, but he also had a surprised look on his face, almost like he was stunned.

At last, he spoke, "My hand is also stuck to the stone, and the stone is stuck to your back, and until it releases its hold, you and I are sharing the same spirit.

"I have heard of this from my grandfather when I was just a boy, but never have I seen this thing happen with my own eyes," and he began to chant and Snowbird joined in.

The words were much like humming and simple to follow and I joined in...
WO--HA--LI
HEY--YA--HO
HEY--YA--HO

We chanted in unison with Charlie nodding his head to the beat, until finally the vibration stopped, and the madstone released from my body and Ironbear's hands at the same time, and fell lifeless onto the buffalo rug.

"Wow!" said Snowbird, "That was some powerful medicine." "What does this mean grandfather?"

"I do not know my child, but, it is a thing of mystery that must be searched and explored for an answer. Quick, bring me a smudge so we can cleanse our house, our guests, and the madstone."

Snowbird took a bundle of sage and stuck the end against a coal and soon had the smoke curling from the tip. She first cleansed herself, and then handed the smudge to her grandfather.

He passed the smoke around him like she did, and then handed it to me and I mimicked their actions before passing it onto Charlie, who followed the same procedure, before returning the smoking smudge to Ironbear.

He then smudged the mad stone on both sides, and then wrapped it back inside that square of buckskin, securing it with a rawhide thong before returning it to his medicine bag. "Now, my friends, we shall have coffee and talk of this thing we have experienced."

Cups were poured and passed from hand to hand as we all took seats around the fire. The coffee was good and strong and tasted of living water that had never flowed through a pipe.

Ironbear began to speak, "What has just happened is of great importance and signifies something of great meaning.

"Like many messages from the Great Spirit, or God Almighty if you prefer, it is up to the recipient to divine the mystery of the message. Never have my hands been stuck to the madstone during a healing and never have I seen it shake with such power, not even with my grandfather before me, and he was a medicine man of great reputation throughout the people of the Shoshone Nation.

"Charlie, you must leave Zed with me for three days, and he must undergo the purification right and spirit journey without delay. You have known me many seasons now Charlie, and you know I would not ask this thing if it were not extremely important. God has knocked on our door and we must open without hesitation."

"I understand my friend and I agree it is urgent, but Zed must answer for himself."

I decided without giving it much thought that I would stay, because everything about this intrigued me, and the day had been an unending revealing of mysteries, back to back.

"Of course, I will stay, and I am honored to be asked. I too, wish to know more of what this day means and why this house feels more like a home than in any house I have been in before."

"I must tell you, your granddaughter looks so very much like my mother I can almost believe it is her standing before me. Charlie, please apologize to Wanda for me, but I must stay and see where this leads."

"Don't you worry none about Wanda. She don't need our help planning this wedding shindig. She can do that as easy as Dimmit swallowing a cheeseburger. All she needs us to do is show up reasonably dressed, with our hair combed, and be on time."

"I'll explain it all to her when I get back to the cafe. Dimmit might be the one a tad put out 'cause I've seen how he's latched on to you. You know, that smart old dog knew you was family right from the get go."

Chapter 7

With my future sketched out for the next three days, I relaxed in the warm glow of the building friendship between Ironbear and myself. There were a million questions I wanted to ask him, but when you are in the presence of a truly wise man, the ears are more important than the tongue.

I asked his permission to turn on the tape recorder in my pocket, so I could study his words later. He extended his flattened hand towards me with the palm up, moving it from east to west, and nodded his head in agreement.

"Zed, I see in your eyes you have many questions to ask of me. Some I will answer now, and some you will learn yourself over the coming days. Knowledge is like the flow of a river and it should not be rushed. Too much, too fast floods the mind and little is retained

"First, I will tell you how I became known as Ironbear. My boyhood name was 'Kwatoko,' which means 'bird with a big beak,' and I bore this name into early manhood. In our culture it is common to have different names as we walk on the wheel of life."

"For seventeen years, I was known only as Kwatoko. One day I was crossing that mountain," Ironbear paused and pointed at a peak rising a short distance from his cabin.

"And as I made my way, a fierce storm caught me near the crest. I had run far ahead of my family who were traveling with me. The journey to the trading post was only a journey by foot of less than 10 miles, but more than 50 miles by bad road. We often would go there and back in one day.

"I lived to run in my younger days, and I could run for hours without fatigue. I thought I could outrun the storm but the black clouds were faster than my feet. I saw the flashes of lightning coming down to the ground followed almost instantly by thunder so loud it shook the earth and deafened me. As I ran, I saw a huge bear running full speed towards me. He seemed to be confused by the approaching storm, or maybe it was our fate to meet that day.

"Just as it seemed we would collide with each other, a tremendous flash of light enveloped us both. I awoke with the cries and wails of my family ringing in my ears.

"The great bear was dead with his nose touching my forehead, my family thought I was dead too. My moccasins had been blown off my feet, my shirt was in tatters and my hair was smoking. My mother gently put mud on my feet because they were badly burned."

He interrupted the tale, stood up, and unbuttoned his shirt and then took it off letting it fall to the floor. He turned to show me his back and it looked like the 'Tree of Life' had been tattooed on his back. I was familiar with this phenomena, known as a Lichtenberg figure, but have never seen it on a human, except in photos. It was more impressive than any tattoo I have ever seen. It covered his entire back

Ironbear continued his tale as he put his shirt back on. "I was unable to walk, so my family made a travois and drug me by hand back down the mountain to my grandfather's lodge. He treated me for days, and his knowledge and skill were so great that I not only lived, but also regained my ability to run like the wind.

"As I recuperated and regained my strength, one day my grandfather approached me and said, 'your name Kwatoko, is no longer yours, you have been branded by the Great Spirit with your new name.

As the bear's spirit left his body, it merged with yours, and the lightning bolt found you like you were made from the white man's iron. You will now be known as Ironbear.' And I have born that name now for sixty winters with pride and purpose.

"My granddaughter, Snowbird, was named by me. She came to lodge with me when she was just 13 years old. Her parents died in in a car wreck, and the drivers and passengers of both cars were all drunk and no one survived the crash.

Snowbird came to me as a child named Kima, which means butterfly. It did not suit her, because the butterfly leaves before winter and does not return until the wild flowers of spring paint the meadows with their bright colors.

"She did not run to the town like many of our young people do when the deep snows of winter come to this place. She has stayed here loyal by my side learning what I know, because she was also born to be a healer.

"The number 12 is lucky for my people, and the red Cardinal is associated with that number. Cardinals are seen all 12 months of the year even in the deepest snow and we call them Snowbirds.

"They are birds of enduring loyalty staying true to their mates for life. Many Native tribes believe that the red cardinal is a symbol of good luck and that is what my Snowbird has been to me.

"She is my good luck and she is my sunshine in the shadows, and her voice is always cheerful with song, even when the winds howl and the snow piles high. She is a most intelligent woman and I believe she is richly blessed by the spirits of our ancestors."

"I have learned that good fortune follows in your footsteps as well Zed, and that is a strong sign of being well favored by the spirits and of you living a life of truth and honor.

My friends, now we will dine on some excellent buffalo stew and cornbread prepared by Snowbird, and for my new friend Zed, it will be his last food and drink for three sleeps."

"He and I will soon leave for a sacred place in the mountains where he will be tested and examined by the spirits to find the purity of his soul. This is normally performed on young boys as they approach manhood, and they spend weeks and months in preparation, but in Zed's case, we have to follow the guidance from above and go now. We have only a short window of opportunity to be best connected to the giver of visions.

"The spirits are telling me to hasten because tonight is the night approaching the coming of the yeba-mea ... the full moon that signifies the approach of Fall, and a most propitious time for a Vision Quest. Come my friends and let us eat, for Zed and I have much to do and miles to walk on a steep trail."

We got up and fetched bowls and spoons. Snowbird placed a substantial slab of cornbread at the bottom of each deep bowl, and she then dipped the rich and savory stew on top of the bread. She used an exquisite wooden ladle that looked like it was hand carved. It was decorated in multi-colored Native American symbols.

I spoke to her, "That ladle is a work of art, where did you buy something that beautiful? It belongs in a museum."

She smiled back, replying, "I made it myself. It is carved from birch. It is what I do when the winter snows keep us bound to the house."

"Snowbird, you have great skill and if you will allow me, I would like to buy it from you?" Her eyes flashed, "Mr. Zed, you cannot buy this from me. No man can. It is made from my heart and spirit, and I carved it with love to show my respect to the tree for her gift, and the symbols are sacred to me.

"No Mr. Zed, this you cannot buy, but I give it to you, from my heart to yours. I saw the thing with the madstone and I knew then, I would have to give you something from my heart, to honor being allowed to see such a thing, but also for the look of love I saw in your eyes when you said I reminded you of your mother."

"My heart leapt when you said that and I saw a man I respect. A man not afraid to show his feelings and even now, I see your eyes beginning to moisten. When you return from your vision quest, the spoon will be cleaned and wrapped in a skin I tanned myself.

"I will pray for you without ceasing while you are on your vision quest, and I will pray your mother comes to give you strength." She leaned across the table and kissed me on the cheek, prompting Ironbear to say, "Granddaughter, are you are now in the habit of kissing men?"

"Only you grandfather, and now Zed. You are the only two men I kissed in my life, my own father did not want me to be close to him, and even my mother was cold to me, and often too drunk to know I was alive. So, I shall practice on you two old men until a young handsome man travels 10 miles over the mountain just to see my face.

"I will kiss him too, if he is not too ugly, at least not any uglier than you two. Maybe I will kiss him more than once, if he is not uglier than the men I have already kissed."

That broke us all up. The girl had spirit and wit, and obviously, a lot of determination to overcome her dismal start in life.

"I am moved by your gift to me, and I accept it with deep gratitude. I shall always treasure it, and when I look at it, I will think of you, and then I will think of my mother. I will have a gift for you when I return. I don't know what it will be, because it will be up to my vision, if I have one, to decide that."

Ironbear beckoned us to bring our bowls to the fire circle and as we all took our places, Ironbear sat down his bowl, and raised his hands to the sky, and began to pray.

"Great Spirit and forces unseen, this day we pray and ask You for guidance, humbly we ask You to help us as we journey to the sacred place seeking Zed's vision.

"We ask to be seen as images of love and peace. Let us be seen in the beauty of the color of the rainbow. We respect our Mother the earth, and we show our love by how we walk gently in her presence.

"Guide us now Great Spirit, and I ask your protection over my granddaughter until I return."

Ironbear lowered his hands and we began to eat. The stew was amazing. I was sure I could eat two bowls easily, especially knowing I was about to hit a 3-day dry spell, but I could barely finish this one. It was that rich, and immensely satisfying. I congratulated *Snowbird* for the quality of the meal.

"You are welcome Mr. Zed, maybe you will see a pretty young man, and you tell him he can get the best buffalo stew and cornbread in Wyoming ten miles on the other side of the mountain, and maybe a kiss too, if he's not too ugly."

I really was starting to like this young girl. She was charming, quick-witted and seemingly unaware of how beautiful she was. That's the greatest beauty of all, where they so totally forget it that, you can too. I really appreciate people that show you the beauty of their soul and don't depend on their external looks as a substitute for developing a pleasing personality.

"Come now Zed, we must begin our journey."
"Wait just a minute and I'll go to the Jeep and get my hat."

"You won't need a hat Zed, and it would be something awkward for me to carry."

"OK Ironbear, you grab your hat and I'm ready when you are."

"I will go bare like you, as I am currently hatless thanks to the wind. It is probably riding the head of some bald white man in Montana, by now."

I excused myself and went out to the Jeep and retrieved my almost new straw cowboy hat. It had begun to feel natural, but now it had another purpose. I returned to the house and walked in with the confidence as if I had been coming here for years.

I came and stood in front of Ironbear and said, "I would count it as an honor if you would accept this hat as a gift of our friendship. I will buy another just like it for myself, and another just alike for Charlie, so that when others see us together they will know we walk the same path and are friends of the spirit."

"You speak fair and pleasing words, and I accept this gift with humble thanks. Now, let us bid the others goodbye because we must depart." He grabbed a woven basket by the door that had sturdy leather straps, slung it on his back and put his new hat firmly on his head.

"Farewell granddaughter and goodbye to you Charlie. We will see you in three sleeps."

I tried to hand Charlie some money so he could buy our hats when he drove back through Lander, on his way to Wanda's.

He pushed it away … "Guess I can afford a couple of hats now that I am a man of means before I surrender by spendthrift ways to Wanda's frugal oversight. Might be one of my last free acts of bachelorhood, son. Go now with Ironbear, and listen to what he says. He will guide you true. He's a fine man and a trusted friend. They don't come no better than him."

With that, we turned our backs and I followed Ironbear into the forest.

Chapter 8

The trail took us through sparse trees, rocky outcrops and some dense scrub oak, heavy with walnut sized acorns hanging from the branches. My senses were alive and I felt absolutely energized. Perhaps it was some residual effect from my exposure to the spider venom and the totally unexpected reaction when the madstone was placed on my back, but my perception of color and my sense of smell were remarkably enhanced.

Ironbear raised his hand and I stopped. A forlorn solitary spike elk crossed our path and moved on, never having sensed our presence. Ironbear turned to me and whispered, "It is the time of their rut, and the herd bull run the young males away to keep the cows to himself. The young ones like him are lost and confused. Perhaps one day he will be a herd bull himself, but for now he must walk alone, like you soon will."

He turned and I followed as we continued our journey. The wind rustled the tops of the trees and the sunlight streaming down through the rustling leaves cast dappled shadows around our feet. I felt as if I was dancing with Mother Earth.

We walked in silence for many hours, and every step seemed like I would remember it forever. I was alone with the thoughts running through my head, anticipating what lay ahead and hoping I would be worthy of this quest. Ironbear stopped at the edge of a precipitous drop off where the trail seemingly ended.

It must have been at least 500 feet down to the jagged canyon floor. I looked around and questioned if this was the spot. It was not what I expected. The view downward was certainly dramatic but the stopping place didn't feel spiritual or mystical to me at all. I kept silent awaiting Ironbear's explanation and he soon spoke.

"Zed, young Shoshone boys have a year to pray and purify themselves before pursuing their vision quest. I feel you have spent much of your life already preparing for this day and the spirits are urging me to bring you to the sacred place. Now, you must show courage and determination for the trail continues along the face of the cliff."

He paused, and directed my attention to a narrow ledge, maybe 6 inches wide, that followed the face of the cliff until it vanished from sight around a bend.

"You must walk in this fashion," and he demonstrated by raising his arms wide above his head with his palms flat and he turned his feet outward with the heels pointing towards each other. He took his right foot and slid it along the ground and then brought his left foot towards the right in a gliding motion, never losing contact with the ground.

"You must keep your palms flat against the cliff and never break contact with the rock. Keep your face and chest in touch with the cliff the whole way. Do you understand what I have just told you?"

"Yes, I understand what I must do."

"Good, now show me how you will do it."

I did the same gliding routine demonstrating that I knew what I must do to follow the trail wherever it might lead. Ironbear removed his hat and sat it on the ground and broke a thick twig and laid it across the brim and another across the back.

"There," he said, "I have made it known to my animal friends the hat is not to be disturbed in my absence. I give them respect and they return it to me." He removed the woven pack from his back and removed a leather pouch similar to the one hanging from his neck, only larger.

"Zed, now remove the contents of your pockets. You must carry nothing with you from your world on this journey. I took out my wallet, my keys to the cafe, and the blue plastic case wrapped in a red rubber band. The same one that previously contained the $200 I had given to Charlie on the day we met.

Ironbear placed all these items into the larger leather pouch and cinched it closed and placed the thong around his neck. Next, he pulled a leather loincloth from the pack and instructed me to remove all my clothing.

"Everything? I asked?"

"Everything, you will wear only the loincloth to the sacred place."

I undressed and folded my clothes and laid my boots and socks on top and then put on the loincloth. Ironbear picked up my clothing and placed it inside his woven basket. He took a piece of stout cord and tied one end to a tree and the other end to the pack straps and then eased the pack over the drop off until the line drew taut. He explained his actions saying, "My animal friends are not so respectful of the property of a stranger.

"I will say my prayers now silently to the Great Spirit and you pray also to your God, for I am convinced there is but one God for all men. We prayed, and I prayed that I would be worthy, and I also gave thanks for the privilege and honor to be here and undergo this experience.

Ironbear lowered his hands and said, "Now we begin, and as my Buddhist friend would say, 'Become one with the rock." He led the way with his head turned to the right, both palms flat against the cliff surface and toes pointed in opposite directions, he slid his right leg forward and began a slow measured glide down the path.

About six feet away he stopped. "Zed, we will maintain this distance between us. Closer would be foolish because if one of us should slip and the other reach out to save him we would both fall. My face will be turned away from you and I will not be able to measure your progress. I want you to count each time you move your right foot further. I will be able to tell where you are and if you stop counting, I will know you have stopped."

He did not wait for my answer and took another step to his right. I placed my palms flat against the rock wall, chest touching as close as I could get it, and with a reminder to myself ... become one with the rock ... BECOME ONE WITH THE ROCK ... I took my first gliding step and said, "One."

By step number ten, the wall seemed glued to my chest and no longer felt cold and alien. Sweat ran into my eyes and down my spine. When I got to my thirty-eighth step, Ironbear's calm voice stopped me.

"You have passed the first test of bravery to come this far. There is no shame in going back, but you will have to go backward with your face turned the wrong way, until you can come to a dip where you can turn your head around. To come further, you must pass another test requiring courage and focus.

"On the ledge in front of me is a rock protrusion like a knob at stomach height. To pass this knob, you must compress your stomach until you think it will touch your spine, and expel all breath from your body. You must not breathe again until you are on the other side of the bump. I shall go now," and he moved on.

I couldn't see the bump until Ironbear made it to the other side, but I could see it now. I gave thanks for my years of running around slippery decks in storm tossed seas. "Become one with the rock became my mantra ... Become One With The Rock."

I slid my way until my belly made contact with the protrusion. I expelled all the air from my lungs, as much as I possibly could, and tried to pull my navel all the way back to my spine, and slid my leg right, and in one more stride, it was all behind me and I drew a cautious breath. The shrill cry of a hawk overhead cheered my victory.

I heard words I was grateful for, "Just three more steps Zed, and you will be where you can stand beside me on solid ground."

I didn't rush or delay, but I breathed a sigh of relief when Ironbear's hand grabbed mine and he pulled me to his side in a natural alcove big as a large dining table.

I could see the narrow ledge continued precariously on from there, around yet another bend, and I steeled my mind to continue this harrowing journey. I asked, "What do you do with young men too plump to get past the rock protrusion?"

"There are different sacred places depending on the ability of the man on the quest. This is the one most demanding and few men are brought to this place."

"Does the way continue around that bend?"

"No," he said, and pointed behind me, "The way is up from here. It is not far."

I looked at the rock face, and saw handholds and footsteps had been chiseled in place and as I looked upwards, I could see they went all the way to the top. Ironbear began climbing and when he was halfway up I followed.

It was considerably easier going than the narrow ledge and only about fifty feet to the top. When I reached the crest, Ironbear was waiting.

I found myself on a flat rocky shelf open on all sides with a ten foot circle in the center marked out with painted stones of different colors. My guide removed the larger pouch from around his neck and extracted four small jars, which he placed at his feet.

He then addressed me, "We are descendants of the Newe, which means The People. You are in one of our most sacred places of the Shoshones, and never before has a white man been brought here.

Such a thing would not be possible except I had a dream that a white man would come to me, and inside his chest would beat the heart of a red man. He would be bearing a name ending with the last of the white man's letters and I was to bring him here before the fullness of the fall moon.

"I have dreamed this same dream every night for seven sleeps. It is a mystery to me what this dream means. Here you will seek your vision, and I will depart from you and go to a place and pray for you.

"I will pray for you three days and three nights, just like Snowbird will be doing back at the house. You must stay within the circle outlined by the painted stones without food, water, or sleep for three passages of the sun.

"You must clear your mind from what you know, and allow things beyond your experience to come to you ... if they choose. I have confidence we are in accord with the spirits and I have fulfilled my sacred obligation by bringing you here.

"Now, it will be up to you to seek your vision. Stand before me and I will prepare you for your journey."

I stood up and he picked up one of the jars from the ground and removed the lid. The contents appeared to be a black greasy paint. Using his finger, he drew a circle on my chest and then drew a line from top to bottom halving the circle.

Next he drew a line from left to right dividing the circle into four quarters. Taking the jars one by one, he colored the sections, one each ... yellow, white, red and green. He replaced the jars in the pouch and slung it around his neck.

"This is the Medicine Wheel of the Shoshone encompassing the Four Directions ... North - South - East - West. It also represents the stages of life ... Birth - Youth - Adult - Death, the four seasons ... Spring - Summer - Fall - Winter, and the four connections to the heart ... Spiritual - Emotional - Intellectual - Physical. It is a sacred symbol of the Shoshone.

"Each new day as the sun rises from its sleep, you will face east, and as the sun makes its journey across the sky, you will turn to follow its passage and the same when the moon rides the skies across the starry plains.

"You may leave the circle only to relieve yourself. I leave you now, and will return after the passage of three sleeps, but neither you nor I will sleep. I shall pray, and you will seek your vision. Farewell my friend, Zed."

Within seconds, I found myself alone. I went to stand in the center of the painted stone circle, and slowly turned completely around taking in the view. It was magnificent. I had the view of a bird high aloft riding the air currents looking down at the world below. I could see for miles in every direction and the air smelled of the surrounding forests.

It was exhilarating and it was easily the most spiritual place I have ever been. The emotion it evoked was beyond words; it could only be felt by the soul and translated by the heart. I said a prayer…

"God, I feel as though you have been leading me to this place all along. I am humbled and amazed by my life since my journey brought me to this place. You have given me friends that gladden my soul and feed my spirit. I have found a purpose greater than I have ever known. I have found a family and I sense I may have come to a place where I am supposed to anchor and make a home."

"I will trust in the journey and walk with You in faith, just as I did on the cliff below. I ask that You give me strength and the spiritual eyes to learn why I have been brought to this high place. I know men call You by many names ... God, Jehovah, Lord, and now, Great Spirit. I acknowledge you as my Creator, and my purpose is to serve You … Amen."

I turned to face the sun now beginning to set in the west. I squatted down on my heels like I had learned from my Asian friends. It seemed a strange position to me at first, but I soon learned it could be maintained for hours and was much better for your health and spine.

It made me think of ancient man and how he had adapted positions of relaxation like the Aborigines of Australia, and the Masai warriors of Africa … standing on one leg with the foot of the other leg resting on the knee, like a stork.

I might even try that stance myself before this quest was over. I tried to clear my head of thoughts of the world that awaited me on my return, and the more I tried to clear my head, the more they insisted on trying to capture my focus. My mind whirled from one thought to another, like a newsreel flashing the highlights of my life.

I thought of the Red Desert which made me think of Charlie and Dimmit, and then to the Liars Lounge, one-armed Uncle Bob, his diggings, pothole beans, bathing in the water trough and on and on, my thoughts raced.

My life had become a whirlwind of amazing encounters and I finally stopped resisting and let my recent life play out, right up to my having met Ironbear and Snowbird. Snowbird, who bore such a startling resemblance to my mother, and her personality also matching hers I wondered if she was really going to pray for me three days and three nights, fasting and not sleeping?

I was immediately ashamed of my thought. Of course she was, just exactly as she said she would, and so would Ironbear. They deserved more respect than that, even if it was but a fleeting thought passing through my brain. You have to be on guard for those thoughts of your lesser self creeping into your mind, because they like to create doubt and indecision.

I thought of the tens of thousands of miles I had traveled, endlessly around the globe, and the things I came to know from lessons taught along my journey. Some of the teachings had been harsh, and those are the ones that taught me best of all. Now, here I sat squatting naked, except for a loincloth, alone on a flat rocky promontory.

Chapter 9

I felt enormously fulfilled and at peace. It seemed like my whole life had been a preparation, or dress rehearsal for this very moment. I remembered my mother's words often said to me, *"Son, if you keep moving, even if you don't know where you are going, sometimes the Universe will bring you right where you are supposed to be."*

I had seen that play out through my entire lifetime. Ever since my arrival in Wyoming and meeting Charlie, it seemed I was finding nothing but good everywhere I turned and I was finding myself continuously right where I needed to be at just the right moment.

The mental flashes had started coming with great rapidity since I arrived in the Red Desert, and so far, by following my instinct and listening to my heart and soul, it had brought nothing but good to others and to myself.

I raised my eyes to the western horizon, and saw the last vestiges of this day's sun, compressing into a thin reddish-orange line, gradually fading, until it blinked out. Somewhere in the forest down below, a bull elk let loose a bugle, challenging all comers to a duel to see which of them would rule supreme and claim the title of being the reigning herd bull.

Far off in the distance another bull responded and no sooner had his bugle ended, than two others much closer joined the conversation. Of the last two bulls, one sounded immature and inexperienced. His bugle did not contain the menace and power suggested behind the first one. The suspected young one attempted another bugle and the first challenger cut him off with a roaring rebuke.

These were the first elk bugles I had heard in my life, but the meaning and tone was unmistakable, even to a novice. Apparently, the youngster got the message because he made not another sound. The other mature bull was not deterred or intimidated in the least. He issued another roaring challenge. The reply he received was deeper, harsher, and filled with unsuppressed rage.

The dominant sounding bull was on the move and was rapidly closing the distance to this trespasser. They continued advancing and bugling until they both suddenly went silent.

Within minutes, the silence was disturbed by the sound of antlers clashing, and the sound of battle reverberated from the canyon below. The fight didn't last long … maybe 3-4 minutes, and then the forest was still. The sudden silence caught me off guard.

My senses had been captivated by the sound of the struggle and my mind was occupied trying to visualize what the conflict looked like and then … it was over … like flipping a switch.

I listened waiting for sound of the fight to continue, but there was nothing until I heard the victor bugle his harsh, angry challenge to the world. The challenger answered him but he was steadily moving further away, a lesson learned, and not eager to have a re-match.

I turned back to the east to be faced with an enormous moon shining in my face almost at my eye level. It was not yet completely full, but within two more nights, it would be at its peak. I could not imagine it being any more a magnificent sight than what now mesmerized my eyes.

Years and years at sea had privileged me with many awesome moonrises but none ever seemed this close. It looked as if I could reach out and touch it, and maybe it would grab me as it passed over and take me with it.

You can look deep into the moon for hours and search it for answers. Mankind has been doing that since the dawn of time.

I probed it with both my eyes and mind, searching for clues, or some insight into this quest, but the moon revealed nothing. It continued a slow tract across the night sky bathing me in a pale yellow light, but remained a silent companion.

I lost track of how long I was entranced by the Shoshone 'Yeba-mea" moon. I could recall no conscious thought since I had turned to face the moon. I guess I was suffering a serious case of being moonstruck. The stars hung in the sky like ornaments and they glittered with a brilliance that made them seem to be alive.

I thought again of my mother, and I wondered if she could look down from the heavens and see me. That thought comforted me and it was easy to imagine her presence being in this sacred place.

I was cold, but it was a manageable cold, and I knew it would be even colder right before dawn. I was neither hungry nor thirsty. I was simply expectant, as if awaiting important news from afar.

I detected a small change in the wind as it shifted, coming more from a northerly point than the west wind, which had prevailed, since my arrival. That could mean a weather change on the way. Nothing I could do about it but wait and see.

An owl hooted somewhere nearby, and I wished I knew what kind of owl it was, and all about its habits. I determined I would learn and become familiar with more of Wyoming's wildlife. Maybe Ironbear would teach me and that was an intriguing thought.
What better man to learn from than a Shoshone medicine man who had lived here his whole life?

My thoughts drifted to the animal world. I reflected on the many species I already knew something about, but the ones that really intrigued me the most were the ones sharing the star filled Wyoming night with me.

The first night seemed endless but I was not bored. It was much like sailing solo far from land with no one but yourself to depend on. You stay alert because there's no other choice. This night, even though it seemed endless, began giving the barest hint of light in the eastern sky.

It was cold, really cold, and I welcomed the anticipated warmth from the coming sun. I had been involuntarily shivering for more than an hour and my teeth were almost on the verge of chattering.

I still was not hungry but thirst was beginning to manifest itself. With two nights left to go, I knew my thirst would become much more of a problem than the discomfort I was feeling at the moment. I could handle not eating for three days, but three days without water was going to be grueling.

The sky lightened more and soon it looked as if it was on fire. A clear sign that the high pressure system of good weather I had previously enjoyed had passed on east and a low pressure system was ushering in a weather change.

The old sailor's saying, "Red sky in morning, sailor take warning" was a weather predictor that had been used by sailors from times as far back as Jesus. Somewhere in the Bible, maybe in the book of Matthew, are the words spoken by Jesus, 'And *in the morning, It will be stormy today, for the sky is red and threatening.'* Some folks don't believe in Jesus, and some don't believe a red sky in the morning means a storms coming. I believe in both.

Coyotes began heralding the arrival of the sun and their cries seemed excited, almost anxious. I was surprised at the sheer number that I could hear. The moon phase, and possibly the impending storm, seemed to have them worked up to a fever pitch this morning. There must have been dozens of them howling back and forth.

I added coyotes, or as Charlie would say …
ki-otes … to the list of animals I wished to learn more about. I had so much to learn about this new land and I was eager to further my education. The sun eventually crested and I looked directly into it.

I have been gazing at the rising sun for years, and have built up a tolerance from mere seconds when I first started, to where I could look now for up to ten minutes before I had to avert my gaze.

Sun Gazing is revered and worshipped by many ancient cultures around the world. Many people of other cultures think the sun feeds the soul through the eyes. Some scientists agree that it has an impact on our brain, and have validated it in studies. There is a pea-sized gland in our brain shaped like a pinecone, and it is called the pineal gland, sometimes referred to as the 'third-eye'.

All animals with a skeleton have one located in the middle of the brain centered right behind the eyes. This tiny gland produces melatonin, a substance from serotonin that regulates sleep and seasonal cycles in all animals, including humans.

It lets bears know when it's time to hibernate, geese know when to fly south, and elk when to fight it out for the right to breed. It's a theory, and one I believe to be true, that modern man exposed to pollution, chemicals in our food, along with lifestyles that isolate us from nature, have allowed this 'third eye' to become cloudy and out of sync with nature.

I suddenly felt a compulsion to raise my outstretched arms to the sun, not in worship, but in honor of its Creator. The warmth greeted me and it felt like a hug from a dear friend. It was healing in a most welcome way, for my shivering stopped almost immediately, and at least for the moment, I forgot about my thirst.

I let the warmth seek deep into me, and my mind went into neutral. I don't know how long I was detached from my surroundings, quite some time apparently, as the sun was overhead and a large bird of prey was circling overhead and making fierce cries too loud to ignore.

I looked upward, but even shading my eyes against the sun, I could not make out what it was, other than it was large and majestic. Maybe a Golden Eagle, or a Bald Eagle, the brightness of the sun made it impossible to tell. I looked down and I could see the shadow of the bird as it circled high overhead.

I followed the shadow along on its circuit and it began to encircle the perimeter of the circle that I was in marked by the painted stones. Round and round, the shadow flowed dancing around the circle of rocks. The bird again began uttering its fierce call and this time I counted them …

Twelve times the bird shrieked out its harsh call to me below. I recalled Ironbear telling me that 12 was a sacred number to the Shoshone, and I am sure the 12 calls of the bird meant something.

Maybe Ironbear could explain it to me. I heard the distant rumbling of a storm from behind me and as I looked toward the horizon, I saw the skies were black with immense thunderheads towering far into the sky. I could see bolts of lightning flashing horizontal for a great distance and jaggedly threading in and out of the clouds.

It was magnificent and sobering at the same time. Here I am, high and exposed on the tallest thing around, with no sails to trim, no hatches to batten down, and worst of all, no place to seek shelter. Nothing to do but put the bow in the wind and ride it out. I finally sat down on the ground.

No sense in being any higher than absolutely necessary. I faced the storm and waited what I knew was coming and I didn't have long to wait. The wind gained strength and buffeted my body and blew my hair back from my face. The coming storm was intensifying and the sounds of the thunder clashed and rolled over one another until it sounded like an approaching artillery barrage.

Small drops of rain began to hit my bare skin and I was soon drenched and once again shivering from cold. It quickly became worse as the fury of the storm descended on me. Massive drops of rain fell hard enough to sting and every bare part of my body was pummeled unmercifully.

Bolts of lightning began striking the canyon floor below and I heard a tree explode from a direct hit. I closed my eyes against the rain and expected to be hit by lightning at any moment. I thought of tilting my head skyward and opening my dry mouth to the storm. At least I wouldn't die thirsty, but I immediately discarded the thought as unworthy.

I had committed to three days and nights without food and water. Opening my mouth to the rain would be a violation of trust and no one would be harmed by it more than me. No one would know, but it would not be a memory I would recall with pride.

I would know I had failed myself, and by doing so, I would always have a memory of being less than I should have been. Like most folks, I had enough of those memories already. I kept my eyes closed, head bowed, and lips tightly compressed as rain flowed down my face so tantalizingly close. All I had to do was to open my mouth.

I kept my mouth and eyes tightly shut until a tremendous flash of light penetrated my closed eyelids and my ears and body were assaulted by the sound of thunder so incredibly loud it felt like I was in the belly of the beast.

I opened my eyes, and as I watched in disbelief and awe, blue fire danced around the circle of rocks and while it danced the rain briefly stopped until once again commencing its punishing assault on my skin. I closed my eyes and bowed my head only to be smashed by another thunderous hammer of sound and a light so incredibly bright it penetrated my skull.

I saw colors in my head … Red … White … Yellow … Green, the sacred colors of the Shoshone medicine wheel. I opened my eyes and again was encircled in a ring of fire but the fire was the same four colors of the rocks and the flames leapt high all around me, until I was enveloped in a rainbow of colors, like I had been swallowed by a rainbow. I felt my body vibrating like a tuning fork and I began chanting over and over…

WO--HA--LI

HEY--YA--HO

HEY--YA--HO

WO--HA--LI

HEY--YA--HO

HEY--YA--HO

I have never been more afraid, nor have I ever felt more alive.

I was getting my vision and it was more than I could possibly have anticipated in my wildest dreams. The colored flames turned to tiny horses the size of small dogs circling the stones. Some of the horses were black and some were white.

First, a black one and then a white one. On the withers of all the white ones were red handprints, and on the withers of the black ones a white handprint.

Only the white ones had riders, and they all appeared to be Shoshone warriors dressed in loincloths like me; their long raven hair was flowing behind them as they thundered around the circle. The tiny warriors began chanting with me…
WO--HA--LI
HEY--YA--HO
HEY--YA--HO

After each chant, the riders changed from the backs of the white horses to the backs of the blacks, and the white horses galloped on unmounted. Twelve times they chanted with me and twelve times they changed the color of their mounts, and after the twelfth chant they turned to smoke and vanished as if they never existed.

I had no idea what any of this meant. It was so beyond the realm of my experience, having never had anything approaching supernatural happen to me that I couldn't begin to comprehend anything that would explain this phenomena.

I hoped Ironbear would be able to interpret this for me. I had no doubt I could describe it to him as if I was still looking at it. It had burned an unforgettable image on my mind.

The storm had somewhat abated but it was far from over. More lightning and rumbling were approaching from the west and I was soon again intensely cold. The wind, which had slackened, gathered speed for another assault on my body and mind.

The fury of the storm descended on me and it was even more ferocious than the first storm that had sorely tested me.

This storm seemed bound and determined to blow me off this flat rock where I was perched like a lightning rod. It felt as if it was focusing all its energy to hurl me into the darkened jagged rocks far below. I estimated the wind was near hurricane force.

I recalled the story of Wyoming winds so fierce they blew locomotives from the rails. My 185 pounds wouldn't have much of a chance up here with nothing at all to break the force of the wind, or without anything to hold on to.

I laid down with my head facing the storm with my arms and legs spread-eagle to the wind and tried to hold on. The wind howled and tore at my flesh like it had a personal and intense dislike for my existence and especially my presence on this rock.

I felt the wind move me several inches, and I began to pray … Oh Lord, help me become one with the rock, please help me become one with the rock … and the rock changed and softened to a thick mud like substance until it encased my arms and legs and then it changed back to rock.

I was anchored and unmovable unless my arms and legs were ripped from my body. The wind screamed like a banshee and hurled itself at me with a force that would surely had blown me to my death if I had not been so solidly anchored by the stone.

The rock embraced me and protected me from the rage of the tempest. It made me recall the words about building your house on the sound foundation of a rock. I always took that to mean put your faith in Jesus.

Here I asked the Lord to help me become one with the rock and He had done so. Of course no one would ever believe this if I told them with the possible exception of Ironbear and Charlie. Those two would believe me, of that I had no doubt.

The wind screamed a final bitter howl of defeat and left me to go torment some other poor soul. I felt relief but also some concern because my arms and legs were still imprisoned in an unyielding grip of stone. I calmed my own fears because if He put me here He could get me out.

 I once more was stricken with a bone chilling cold and since prayer had worked so well for me, I again beseeched the heavens … "Dear Lord, show me mercy and bring me something to protect me from this icy torment." I prayed with my eyes closed and gave thanks for being saved from the ferocity of the storm and for being shown these stunning and astonishing visions.

I opened my eyes and gasped in surprise. In front of me, close enough to touch, if only I could have freed my hands, sat an enormous grizzly bear with his fur emitting tendrils of smoke. He gazed at me with a genuine look of interest with no hint of malice on his face.

His mouth opened and he spoke to me, "Little Brother, I welcome you to this sacred place. The rock you have become part of has been here for millions of years absorbing the warmth and heat from the sun."

"It has embraced you, and you can share its stored warmth. Open your mind and let it flow into you. It has more warmth within than can be found in the hearts of selfish men."

I did as the great bear directed me and immediately I felt as if I was sinking into the luxury of a hot bath. I asked the bear, "What does this mean, and how do I address you?"

"You may call me Brother, for your spirit and mine have been joined by the Great Spirit, and we will walk the path of life together. Some of the meaning I can tell you and some you will have learn from others, because life will provide you with many teachers, but much you will learn on your own by staying true to your path."

"You mean by following my path and fulfilling my purpose to do good?"

"Yes, you have shown that you take the blessings that come your way and you use them to enrich the lives of others. You have a greater purpose than you can imagine and if you stay true to your path Little Brother, you will be showered with opportunities to do even more good."

"Brother Bear, are you a spirit, or a vision?"

"What I am is what people see when they look deep within themselves. We are all spirits, and some few worthy humans are given visions, but only those that walk in the light and who have set their egos aside.

"What I am to you my Little Brother is a window to your soul. The rock will release you when I depart. You can still share its warmth through the night but tomorrow will come your greatest test, for you must confront it alone without help from nature.

"You will be punished by terrible thirst and tormented by evil spirits called Nimerigars. The Nimerigars are an ancient race of little people and they are bitter enemies of the Shoshone.

"They will attack you and everything your path stands for. They are hostile to anything good and worthy in mankind. The Nimerigars are cruel little demons driven by jealous rage and have an unrelenting hatred of the human race.

"They will attempt to attack your mind with doubts and clever lies. Their sole purpose is to cause you to question your faith and to wander from your path.

"The only help you will have during this trial must come from deep within you. You must learn to summon your own help, and seek the souls that will journey with you and light your path.

"These souls will become part of your bear clan and you will walk your path together. All of you will wear the mark of the bear on your skin. I leave you now, because you have more to see this night that will guide your spirit."

The Great bear said, "Farewell, my Little Brother, be brave and keep the faith … stay true to your path" and then he disappeared. The great bear quickly faded into nothingness, until all that remained was a wisp of smoke that was taken by the wind.

As he vanished, the rock released its hold on me. "Whoa," I thought to myself, "a talking grizzly bear for a spirit brother?"

By this time, nothing would have fazed me. I wouldn't be at all surprised to see a fox show up and play, 'Yankee Doodle Dandy,' on a fiddle. I was being inundated with visions far beyond anything I've dreamed or read about.

So much to reflect on and I was filled with questions and so very few answers.

The storm finally blew itself off to the east and the night sky sparkled with brilliance and clarity as if it had been polished clean by the violence of the winds. "Could this night get any stranger?" I wondered.

I didn't have long to wait for an answer to that. Aspen trees began sprouting out of the rock until they were fully formed, and this kept happening until the stone shelf outside of my painted stone circle was populated with a grove of mature Aspen trees resplendent in their golden autumn foliage.

The leaves on the trees began to whisper to one another. I looked at each shimmering surface and I could clearly see the faces of all mankind ... men and women of all colors and all ethnicities, the entire diversity of the human race were represented in the faces on the leaves.

The leaves began to fall from the limbs individually and in groups. The space outside the circle became a swirling mass of golden enchantment that danced and mesmerized my eyes. They spun so fast that they lost all trace of individual identity and became a homogenous mass.

Then they began drifting down and spiraled to rest within the circle of stones. They piled high around me and each leaf turned its face toward me and smiled ... each and every one gave me an angelic smile and I smiled back at them in gratitude.

Then they departed as an updraft of wind sucked them into the night sky. I could see them twirling upwards, illuminated by the moon, and I watched them in awe until they went completely out of sight.

I pondered the meaning of this latest vision for a long time. The faces of all types of people living on this planet pictured on the leaves on the same kind of tree?

Then all of them falling gracefully, and amazingly coming to rest within the circle of stones. Not one single leaf excluded, with none of them falling outside the sacred circle of stones. All of them turning their faces in unison towards me and smiling at me? I thought I knew what this might mean and that's mostly what I thought about throughout the long night.

The moon illuminated me as it traversed its orbit and it began sinking lower and lower until it sunk below the distant horizon. That was my signal to turn and face the east to welcome the arrival of the sun. It took very little time to make its appearance and this time there were no clouds to herald another storm, but the sun seemed abnormally pale, and it offered me no warmth.

The stone beneath me also released its heat as if I had suddenly become untouchable and unworthy. I tried to look into the sun, but even though it was cold and pale, I found myself quickly looking away. The sun, my old and faithful friend, felt alien and strange to me and it pained my eyes to look at it.

There was no comfort or welcome to be found there. I felt utterly and more completely alone than I've ever felt in my life. I could no longer feel the power of love, either from without or within. I was marooned and abandoned and my heart felt like it had turned to stone. I was unloved and could no longer give it to another. I fell into a deep and dark suffocating pool of despair.

I began to shiver violently and although I was not being baked by the sun, my thirst became so intense that my tongue felt swollen and permanently glued to the roof of my mouth. I had to get up to relieve myself and as soon as I stepped outside the protective stone circle, the temperature seemed to plummet twenty degrees. I didn't let any grass grow under my feet and I finished quickly, returning to the sanctuary of the sacred circle.

Once back inside, it couldn't be described as warm, not by any stretch of the imagination. It was still miserably cold, but not as miserably cold as I had been when I was briefly outside the circle. I passed the day in mental and physical torment unable to focus on anything but my unbearable thirst and the unrelenting agony racking my body. I wept and wept as I never had before, not even with the death of my mother.

Each passing second was agonizingly, excruciatingly slow … like the drip of a single tear from a grieving heart … much like the ones still falling from my eyes. I thought of Christ on a cross.

I had not been persecuted and judged like Him, but I understood the greatest pain He endured was what I now felt … feeling abandoned from the love of God. I raised my face and hands to the heavens and screamed, "My God...why have you forsaken me?"

I waited and I waited for an answer … another vision, some miracle, that would restore me to His favor. Nothing came from my plea to be rescued, and I then prayed to an unhearing God to stop my heart. Death was preferable to this feeling of absolute and total despair.

I heard a sound and I opened my eyes to find the painted circle completely surrounded by a band of hideous and savage little men. They screamed vile curses at me and bared their sharpened teeth. Their teeth were shaped like those of the Great White shark, made for rending flesh and shearing bone.

They were all armed with short red bows and tiny arrows tipped with some foul smelling substance that nauseated me even from a distance with its vile stench. I knew these were the Nimerigars, and that they could smell both my fear and my sense of abandonment. They taunted me, daring me to step outside the circle and fight them.

One of them screamed that soon my soul would join with the others hanging on the trophy pole outside their lodge.

Their voices screeched into my ears sounding exactly like hundreds of fingernails scratching down a blackboard that had no end. I could not imagine the deepest dungeons of hell sounding any worse than this.

I grew angry … angry at the Nimerigars, and also angry at God. "What have I done to deserve this cruel punishment?" I rose to my feet and raised a clenched fist to the sky and shouted, "Why me, what great sin have I committed to be cast adrift at the mercy of demons?"

I raised both fists to the sky and the demons began launching their tiny arrows aiming towards the painted circle on my chest. It was like being attacked by a vicious swarm of hornets.

The arrows barely had the power to penetrate my flesh but the vile substance smeared on the points burned worse than the sting of a Portuguese Man of War. I ripped them from my flesh but still they came like a wall of death, until it overcame me and I sank to my knees prepared to lose my soul.

I closed my eyes and awaited my fate. My pain was so agonizing and widespread that it took me awhile to realize the arrows had stopped striking my body. I opened my eyes and found that the day had turned to night and standing before me was an albino buck deer.

I didn't know if it was true night or part of the vision. My mind seemed to be completely detached from reality, I watched the buck step nimbly over the painted stones and he came to stand by my side. I waited for him to speak but he just turned broadside to me and his abdomen began to glow until a bright shape began to appear pulsating like a drum. I realized I was looking at the madstone within the belly of the deer.

My arrows began releasing from my flesh and they were drawn with tremendous force deep into the madstone. Immense clouds of arrows sunk into his belly until none were left in me. Also my pain and the vile stench from the poison were gone.

I looked at the buck and he looked calmly back at me with his pink-rimmed eyes. He showed no pain or any awareness that arrows had punctured him by the hundreds. He blinked, maybe in farewell, and vanished.

I bent my head to give thanks for my deliverance and to ask forgiveness for my lack of faith. I prayed a very long time, sometimes without words. I bared my soul to God. How long I stayed on my knees, I don't know. I had no concept of any passing time but as I opened my eye, I saw the full fall moon signaling its beginning surrender to the sun.

People began to appear, but this time within the circle and they all faced inward towards me. Some I recognized immediately ... Charlie and Wanda. Debbie was there with Dimmit and Lucy and they stood beside Abraham and Consuela.

There were Ironbear and his granddaughter, Snowbird, both looking at me with pride and approval, and around Snowbird's neck was the oddest thing ... it was a stethoscope draped from shoulder to shoulder.

Standing next to them were many other faces I did not know. One elderly man that was standing proudly behind a walker I took to be Dusty Rhodes, the elderly man that Debbie had spoken about. The other faces were strangers, but the faces were like the ones on the Aspen leaves that came to lay within my circle.

People of every kind on earth, and I knew what this vision meant. These were the people that would help me on my journey, or ones I would meet on my path. All of them would be teachers and some of them would also be students.

My purpose had broadened from not just doing good, but actively teaching good to others. For this vision I needed no interpreter. I smiled at my circle and they smiled in return.

They each extended a hand holding a smoldering smudge and the smoke condensed in on me until I was immersed in a thick cloud of fragrant sage and sweetgrass. When I could see again, they were gone. The last face I saw was Snowbird and her face seemed to be changing and then she too disappeared in the smoke. I knew I would see them all again.

I turned and sat cross-legged to greet the coming dawn immensely grateful for all that happened and equally grateful it was drawing to an end. I had so much to explore and understand, and I was anxious to talk about all of this with Ironbear. I began chanting...
WO--HA--LI
HEY--YA--HO
HEY--YA--HO

I did this repeatedly while gazing deep into the rising sun. This sun welcomed me as a friend this time, and allowed its energy to flow into me. I continued to chant...
WO--HA--LI
HEY--YA--HO
HEY--YA--HO
WO--HA--LI
HEY--YA--HO

HEY--YA--HO

I realized I was no longer chanting alone and I turned to find Ironbear facing me and joining me in song. He too raised his arms to acknowledge the rising sun. We continued our chant in perfect harmony, as if we were listening to the beat of the same drum. We both stopped at the same time and he rushed to me and embraced me in a bear hug.

He continued to hold me while chanting some indistinguishable words, spoken so low I could barely hear them. At last he pushed me at arm's length but still kept his hands firmly clasped on my shoulders.

"You have done well Zed, some of what you've experienced I've seen with my own eyes, and much more of it I've heard with my own ears. For three days and three nights, I have sat 50 feet below you in that sheltering alcove, fasting and praying, going without food or water, the same as you.

"I know of no one that has experienced as many visions, and especially so many visions of great power as you. We will talk of this at length back at the house and I am confident we will discuss it for the passing of many moons, for there is promise and mystery to explore for many days to come. Perhaps for many years to come. My head is reeling and I am sure yours must feel like it will burst.

"Come now, and let us break our fast, and let us speak of just one thing while we do." He sat down cross-legged in the circle and removed the largest leather pouch from around his neck.

I joined him and he removed some items from the pouch. He handed me a small object that looked like a pale sausage.

He saw my questioning look and explained, "Its pemmican … dried elk meat and berries ground and mixed with buffalo tallow and stuffed in a length of intestine. This is warrior food, it will give us energy to take our leave from this sacred place."

He handed me a small container of water that might have filled the inside of an egg shell. I took a bite of my pemmican and drank my water in one gulp. I should not have been surprised by anything by this point, but that small container of water seemed to continue to flow down my throat and I had to keep swallowing to keep it from overflowing my mouth.

Ironbear said, "Finish your pemmican because one thing must not be further delayed and we must talk of the bear."

I swallowed the remainder of my pemmican and relayed the story of my encounter with the great bear that had called me 'Little Brother.' I didn't leave anything out because I recalled it with perfect clarity. When I finished my tale, explaining how the bear vanished leaving nothing but smoke, he exclaimed, "Nanasuwekai!"

I asked him what that meant and he explained in the language of the Shoshone it meant amazing, or awesome. It was a good word for what I had experienced. I wondered what the Shoshone word was for unbelievable.

"Zed, do you know what this vision means?"

I confessed to him that I did not know.

He asked if I had seen an image of him in my vision, and I told him of the inner circle that had encompassed me and how there were faces I recognized, and also faces of strangers I did not know.

I pointed to where he and Snowbird had stood and I told him that she had a stethoscope wrapped around her neck and shoulders. I described how all the people in the circle had extended a glowing smudge towards me until the smoke enveloped me.

Again, he looked astonished and uttered the word "Nanasuwekai! "My friend Zed, it is beyond doubt that the heart of a red man beats beneath your white skin and the Great Spirit has decreed that we will be brothers of the spirit ... brother bears ... a bond more sacred than blood.

"Just as the great bear breathed his spirit into me when the lightning struck us both, he also breathed his spirit into you. He turned this hard stone into mud, and then back again into stone and anchored you, keeping you safe from the winds.

"Today, you will take a third name ... you will be known as Stonebear ... a brother to my heart and soul in all ways.

"Our lives and fate are now intertwined, and we will walk the trail together for the rest of our days. He took his medicine pouch from around his neck and draped it over my head. Welcome my brother, Stonebear.

"Come now, we have much to discuss and we need to return to the house, because some of this must be witnessed by Snowbird."

Without further ado, he went to the edge from where I had first entered this place and began descending backward down the steps carved into the rock face.

I cast a hurried glance around this isolated place and knew even if I never returned, I would not forget anything that had happened to me in this place, not as long as I drew breath. And with one last sweeping glance, I began to follow Ironbear's lead and my own backward descent to the alcove below.

Ironbear waited for me and while I was not eager to repeat my journey down the narrow ledge, I was not as fearful as before. Ironbear took my medicine pouch and moved it to my back, and to my surprise began his spider walk down the ledge that continued opposite from the direction from where we had first come to this place.

This ledge quickly disappeared around a bend and I had no knowledge of what faced me. When Ironbear had advanced six feet from me, I repeated to myself…'Become One With The Rock … Become One With The Rock.' I took my first gliding step and counted off …"One."

Three movements took me around the bend and I could immediately see solid ground awaited me just a few more steps away and it was marked by a faint trail leading downward. I gained solid ground and Ironbear greeted me with these words.

"The way in is a test for those considered our most worthy warriors. The way out is a celebration of victory for a successful vision quest. It is longer but much safer." He took off with a ground-eating stride and we were soon down on a forest floor where the bull elk had fought.

He angled left and I hurried to stay up with him. He wound in and out staying on the trail and we began going up again. He did not slacken his pace and I marveled at his youthful vitality.

We kept on going upward until he raised his hand to halt. He turned to me and said, "We guard this secret trail. From here we will jump from stone to stone and leave no tracks." And he leapt from one stone to another, and I followed suit jumping to the same stone his foot had touched.

In less than a hundred yards, we had gained the original access trail and stood just paces from where Ironbear's hat lay undisturbed. He removed the twigs from the hat and placed it firmly on his head. He began pulling up the cord he had secured to the tree, and quickly retrieved the woven backpack. He removed my clothing and boots and directed me to dress.

He slung the pack on his back, and turned to me with a smile on his face, "Let us run like the wind my brother," and he was off. I struggled to stay up with him. He had to be more than 30 years my senior and he was also burdened with the backpack, but he was incredibly fit and tough which befitted a man named Ironbear.

We ran like the wind and much sooner than I would have suspected, we arrived back at his home. Ironbear greeted the house in a loud voice…"mammakkoi … nykka." He explained to me that the words meant … "Dance the bear dance," and he thundered it out again…"mammakkoi …nykka."

Snowbird came running from the house and wrapped her grandfather up in a loving hug and flashed me a beaming smile. We were all smiling. It was a celebration of a successful vision quest. They began to chant and dance in circles dipping and gliding, round and round, and I joined in the joyous celebration.

Finally, Snowbird broke up the dance, "Come inside, I have fixed a feast to break our fast. We have elk back straps, roasted corn, boiled ground potatoes, pine nut gravy, acorn bread, wild rice cooked with pinon nuts and gooseberry pie.

"I was just about to give up on the only two kissable men in my life and eat it all myself." She began moving towards the house shouting back over her shoulder, "Last one in does the dishes" and she bolted away like a startled deer.

I watched her youthful lithe form disappear through the doorway and Ironbear rushed past me chuckling, "When it comes to doing the dishes, it's every bear for himself," and he too made a dash for the door.

Chapter 10

I watched him go, but I took my time. I looked at this solid home that would have looked right at home decorating a picturesque valley in Switzerland, but I could not imagine a more perfect home for the personalities of the two remarkable people that lived within.

It suited them and it suited me. I resolved to myself I would have a home like this of my own one day, something of my own where one day I could enjoy the feeling of returning to a place that had eluded me most of my life … a place to call home.

I entered the door and was again struck with a feeling of being embraced by the house as if it was a living presence and the logs from which it was constructed were alive. Snowbird and Ironbear were filling their plates.

As I looked upon the scene and looked at all the things that made up this home, it dawned on me that this house was so filled with love, it gave love back in return. Could an inanimate object return love, if it was shown love? An interesting thing to contemplate. The obvious scientific answer was, of course not, but I had just undergone 3 days and nights seeing things with my own eyes, impossible to be explained by science.

My thoughts were interrupted by a squeal of laughter from Snowbird, "Stop grandfather, you are going to eat it all, leave some pine nut gravy for Zed." I decided I had better stop wasting time or I was going to lose out on some of the courses Snowbird had prepared.

I grabbed a plate and began to heap it full with the enticing native dishes that had been prepared by this delightful young lady.

She impressed me more and more, and I found her company pleasant and comforting, and suffered a pang of regret that I would soon be leaving these two. I would be returning to a very different type of life back in Gauntlet, a life I treasured, one that had meaning and purpose, but here with these two fascinating people I felt at 'home.'

We took our loaded plates, moved back to the fire circle and sat down and we waited to begin eating until Ironbear sat his plate on the hearth. He said, "Let us pray."

"Heavenly Father, we offer our thanks for the many blessings you shower us with, this food that comes from nature, harvested by our hands and provided to us from the magnificence and abundance of Your creation. We offer our deepest gratitude for the gift of Stonebear's prophetic vision quest. We ask Your blessing and protection on the hands that prepared this meal, and we seek your guidance in all that we do and think. My heart overflows that you have given me not only a new brother … but also a new son … and a father for Snowbird … Amen"

I raised my head with a stunned look on my face and looked at Snowbird who looked even more astonished than me … if that were even possible.. Both of our mouths hung open and our eyes were wide with shock and surprise. Ironbear gave us gentle smile and explained, "Because of the difference in our ages, you are not only my brother in the spirit, but also now my son. I am proud to claim you, I could ask for no better man."

"The Great Spirit searched your heart and found you worthy to be not only my bear spirit brother, but he answered a prayer of mine when you told me of your vision of seeing Snowbird standing with me inside the sacred circle, and of her having a stethoscope draped around her shoulders."

"Her most cherished dream is to study the white man's medicine and become a doctor. She wants to come back and serve her people knowledgeable in the ways of medicine from both our world and the white world. Your vision clearly shows that she will realize her dream only under your guidance. With another gentle smile, he said, 'now, let us eat'."

I quickly realized the truth of what Ironbear had just said. Not only was I personally to do good; I was to help the others within my circle to also do good and find their purpose. Snowbird had been within my inner circle smiling at me with the stethoscope around her neck and shoulders.

The meaning was crystal clear even to me. I was to help her realize her dream of becoming a doctor. I looked at Snowbird and said, "I am more honored by this welcome blessing than anything that has happened in my entire life. I cannot conceive of a more perfect daughter than you and my heart smiles to know we will share life's path together."

She scooted across the furs on her knees and threw her arms around my neck. Her cheeks were damp and I felt her chest heave a deep sigh, and at last she spoke.

"I never was expecting that. You had said you would bring me a gift from your vision quest, but I did not expect you to bring me a father, but just as my grandfather could not have chosen a better brother and a son, I could not have chosen a better father. Now, father, let us eat before grandfather goes back for seconds."

The smell of the food caught my attention and I lifted a bite to my mouth and chewed mechanically. I don't even know what that first bite was, but it was good. I looked down at my plate and selected a small potato looking object covered in gravy. It tasted spectacular like a cross between a raw peanut and a sweet potato and the gravy was nutty with just a hint of pine.

The combination was perfectly suited and it found taste buds in my mouth that must have been dormant until this very moment. I had never tasted anything like this. It tasted like the air smelled at the sanctuary, pure and earthy straight from nature's bounty.

I pointed at what I had just eaten with my fork, "What is this food called? I have never had anything like and it ... Ironbear, what is the Shoshone word for awesome?"

The word is "Nanasuwekai."

"Thank you Ironbear that is exactly what this food is ... "Nanasuwekai!" "I am so grateful to you daughter for preparing these fantastic dishes."

"Thank you father Zed," and she snickered behind her hand, "That makes you sound like a priest." We all laughed at that, and she explained what the dish was.

"It goes by many names but we Shoshone call it 'hopniss.' It is also known as a ground potato or a wild bean. It has been an important food for the 'Newe' since they stepped foot on this land. It is a bounty provided to us by God, and we dig it from the earth. Our people have lived off this for centuries."

"The gravy is made from the pine nut which is also called a pinon nut. There are many kinds." She paused to take a bite, and I realized I had been busy continuing to eat while she educated me. It is another staple food of 'The People,' I decided it would be considerate for me to talk a bit and let her catch up on the eating. After all, she had been fasting for three days also.

"Snowbird, when I saw you in my vision you were facing me a smudge in your hands. All the others were as well, but I just realized from the time the smudges first appeared, my eyes were focused only on you. I was looking at you as the smoke thickened and faces became clouded and indistinct and right before I could no longer see you, your face changed to my mother's."

"You are very much alike, but her smile was different, a smile I remember from long ago and she looked absolutely radiant.

"I know she was acknowledging her approval of you as a granddaughter. She would be proud to know you. You looked radiant in that circle too, just like you do this very moment. You, my daughter have a beauty that shines from your soul."

Before I could prepare myself, she dropped her plate and launched herself at me with such force, she toppled me over backwards. "I have only kissed two nice old men in my whole life. I have never kissed any another man. I never once kissed my father ... never until .... now."

She was kissing me from cheek to cheek and laughing at the same time and I thought she might go on forever, but we were interrupted by Charlie laughing and asking, "Do you need any help, cause doggone if it don't look like she's got you whupped and pinned?"

We got up to greet Charlie, but not before I told Snowbird, "I have never kissed my daughter until … now," and I kissed her on the forehead. We got up, greeted Charlie and told him to fill a plate and come join us.

"I will, I surely will, cause this gal can cook as well as anyone I've come across in all my days, but I have to ask, how in the world did you become a daddy in three days?"

I told him the story, or at least I started to, but he broke in and asked, "Is this tale going to be like one of those operas that goes on and on, until the fat lady sings, cause I can fill a plate faster than a jackrabbit on a date," and he was already moving towards the food.

I took a bite of my acorn bread. I had expected it to be dense and taste a bit earthy and bitter, but the opposite was true. It was light and sweet almost like a muffin. I knew it would be wonderful with some butter, or a scoop of ice cream on top. It was just fine, more than fine with some pine gravy on it. 'What a unique recipe idea for the cafe,' I thought to myself.

I had another flash, followed by another in rapid succession. I asked Snowbird, "I guess acorns have fed the Shoshones for centuries just like the ground potatoes and the pine nuts?"

"Exactly so, everything we are eating is authentic Shoshone food, true to tradition, but few can prepare it so well as me," she said, as she bunched her fingers, and kissed them like a French chef.

I asked her how she learned to kiss her fingers like that. "From a French chef, of course. We have many men and women that come here to learn different things. Chefs, historians, novelists, filmmakers, herbalists, and nature lovers, and now a sailor that wants to know it all."

"Grandfather says people come to talk, so that makes him a therapist, and he charges them $75.00 an hour. He will talk about anything they want for $75.00 an hour. I also am a teacher but I am a specialist in Shoshone handicrafts like your spoon over there on the mantle."

"I demonstrate weaving and preparing native dishes, food gathering, and storage. I only charge $45.00," and she kissed her fingers again, and gave me a smug grin. "They learn from me but I also learn from them."

Charlie had returned with his plate and was quietly eating and following the conversation.

"Charlie, you are going to have to wait till I finish my food before we get into this tale. At the rate I'm eating, archaeologists will be examining my skeletal remains thousands of years from now, with me sitting in front of this petrified food wondering if I was poisoned, or died of old age".

I didn't say another word until I had finished my food, including a second helping, and a generous slice of gooseberry pie. I made up for three days of fasting or at least tried to, but for now I couldn't eat another bite.

I told Charlie the story of how I came to be Ironbear's brother and son in one fell swoop. After hearing the long explanation, his response was, "Looks like you've been blessed with two fathers, a brother, a daughter, and a new name, all faster than a woman can decide on a pair of shoes.

"Son, if the Great Spirit decides to rustle you up a bride tomorrow, I sure hope she has tolerance for a full grown daughter and a man that changes his name faster than the weather, and I surely do hope she ain't from Kansas."

He jumped up, "I plumb forgot something," and he went out the door and returned bearing two hats identical to the one riding on Stonebear's head. We placed ours on our heads and Snowbird looked at the three of us and said, "I believe I am the first eyes to see the 'Nanasuwekai Three Musketeers' in all their glory. I must smudge these new possessions and Uncle Charlie's twice."

"Why me twice?"

"I will smudge you twice, because I am tired of kissing the same two men. It has become so boring. Once I smudge you, I will kiss you too."

She showed her inalienable right as a woman to change her mind, and she went to him and kissed him unsmudged and he blushed down to the toes of his boots.

She left to get her smudge and Ironbear went over to a chest and removed three feathers. An eagle feather, a Raven, and one from a Hawk. He placed the eagle feather in the brim of his hat, handed me the Raven, and Charlie, the Hawk.

"My friends, we 'Three Musketeers,' are going to need to know how to tell our hats apart." Snowbird returned with the smudge and all three hats with the feathers stuck in the brim were purified while they sat atop our heads.

Snowbird shook her head, "I don't know what you men would do without a woman to look after you. Here you have stuck feathers in your hats. You look like three 'Yankee Doodle Dandies,' ready to mount ponies and ride to town and call your feathers macaroni.

"The Wyoming wind will snatch those feathers from your hats and fly them to Montana, probably to some bald-headed cowboy already wearing grandfather's missing hat. Wait, and I will fix it for you."

She went to yet another chest and brought back a small sealed jar containing a dark tarry substance. She saw my questioning glance and explained, "Its pine resin cooked and purified by filtering and mixed with ground charcoal and maybe a few secret ingredients. It's the Shoshone version of Krazy Glue."

She carefully stuck each quill into the tar and deftly stuck it back in the brim and used her thumb to seal it tight. She had skillful sure hands and she worked with confidence and poise. I thought she would make a very fine doctor indeed.

"Zed, or Stonebear, or whatever the dickens I'm supposed to call you now, Wanda said if I didn't fetch you back with me, she would have me shoed and tattooed, and by that she meant branded."

"It's odd you should mention tattoos Charlie, because that's something I need to let all of you in on. We are all to wear the mark of the bear, and I have been thinking that it should be a tattoo depicting the print of the grizzly bear?"

"Hold on son, what do you mean by "we all?"

"Charlie, I mean you, me, Ironbear, Snowbird, Wanda, Abraham and Consuela, Sheriff Debbie, and some others I don't even know yet. I think Dusty Rhodes, may be one of the others, but I've not even met him yet."

"Son I've never been inked in my life, unless you count Marlon Brando, and I can imagine telling the 'Dust Devil' she's got to get tattooed. Who in tarnation told you we all had to get tattooed?"

"Why Charlie, none other than my Brother Bear, an enormous friendly grizzly with smoking fur. He talked plain as day to me, and he was as close to me as you are now."

"You are telling me you saw a talking grizzly and he said we all had to get tattooed with a grizzly paw on our hides?"

Ironbear broke in, "Charlie, all this is true. I was close and I could not see them, but I could hear them talking perfectly. I remember his words precisely because his voice was deep like a drum." Brother Bear said, "These souls will become part of your bear clan and you will walk your path together. All of you will wear the mark of the bear on your skin."

"Charlie my old friend, our son Stonebear has experienced more powerful visions than anyone in my experience. Even my grandfather never experienced visions of this magnitude and he was widely considered to be the most powerful medicine men of all people that call themselves Shoshone."

"I will wear the mark of the bear on the insides of both of my wrists. Quickly, Snowbird, throw the smudge on the fire, we need fragrant smoke, and bring me the eagle talon. Quickly, my child!"

She scampered away and returned very fast bearing a huge eagle talon mounted on a short piece of carved wood that she handed to her grandfather. He said join me now and kneel together in a tight circle with knees touching the ones next to you. We must all be touching one another. Now, point your right hand towards me and he began to chant…
Wanna hai yanna
Wanna hai yanna
Yanna ho
Yanna ho

He took the eagle talon and pierced all of our palms deep enough to hurt. Ironbear instructed us to put our right hands into the circle and place them one atop the other, and as the blood flowed and mingled, he pronounced, "We are now one family as commanded by God, through the spirit voice of Brother Bear."

Snowbird brought us some clean damp clothes to clean the punctures and a pleasant smelling salve that made the stinging sensation lessen until it faded away entirely.

When she finished she went to the mantle and brought back the spoon wrapped in soft tanned buckskin. "What was to be a gift to a new friend named Zed, is now a gift to my father named Stonebear, who is still my friend."

I was now a man with three names, two fathers, and a beautiful young daughter, a bunch of new friends, and I hadn't been in Wyoming a whole week. I had also been on a Vision Quest of incredible significance. Wyoming was making my head spin, but it was filling me with incredible joy and a sense of purpose like I've never known.

I had found a diamond of great value, become a future godfather, been issued a Wyoming driver's license, started sleeping with a Dalmatian, helped find a lost child, and if that wasn't enough, I was a genuine Deputy Sheriff. Poor old Uncle Bob must be spinning like a top and writing it all down in French.

Ironbear interrupted my thought train. "Stonebear, my son, your mind has been flooded with many powerful visions. You must let the flood become a gentle flow. Together, over many days, you and I will pursue these visions.

"Do not try to understand them all at once. It is too much for the human mind to absorb. Be gentle with yourself my son. It will all become clear through meditation and prayer. You must eat the buffalo one bite at a time. It cannot be swallowed whole. I know you must return to the white man's world. You have much to do to prepare for your daughter to join you." The last statement delivered with a smile.

He must have noted my surprise. "She cannot become a doctor in the white man's world living isolated in the mountains of the Wind River Reservation."

That certainly made sense, but what was I going to do with a 17 year old girl? I knew I would figure it out, but it would take some doing. I needed some womanly advice and the only ones I knew were Wanda, Debbie and Consuela. Just thinking of those three names eased my mind, but only a little. I was sailing some unfamiliar waters without a chart or a map to guide my way.

Charlie burst out laughing, "Son, it looks like you're more confused than a chameleon in a bag of Skittles. Don't you worry none. We'll all get it figured out.

I'll give you plenty of fatherly advice. Look what a fine job I've done raising you. Any man that can talk to a full growed grizzly bear with smoking fur shouldn't have no problems with a little bitty girl like Snowbird."

Snowbird made her presence and opinion known, "Our life paths have joined and I know my new father will be there to help me, just as I will be there to help him.

"He has no experience raising a daughter and I have no experience having a loving father. We shall learn together. We shall teach each other and be patient. I think it will be a journey of discovery for both of us. Love will find a way."

Ironbear gave me some final words, "It is time for you and Charlie to leave us now. There is much for all of us to think on. When you are ready, return to me my son. This home is now your home too. Here you will always be welcome by my fire."

He rose and went to one of his many chests and brought out another leather wrapped parcel. He returned by my side and unwrapped the item. It was a 4 inch grizzly bear claw on a leather thong. He placed it around my neck.

"Stonebear, this is a claw from our Brother Bear who passed his spirit on to me when we were struck by the lightning bolt. The Great Spirit has chosen you as worthy to wear it. Now my son, go with your other father. I shall await your return, we will have much to say to one another when you return."

Chapter 11

I said my goodbyes to Snowbird, grabbed my hat with the Raven feather, and said, "I want to invite you and your grandfather to come to Wanda and Charlie's wedding.

"I will come and get you. I hope to return before then, but it will be no later than that. We will know more about where our path goes by then. I miss you both already, but now we must go."

Charlie and I made our departure and I paused and looked back at the house. I knew I would be coming back here many times. It was now my home too.

"Zed, I reckon you want to practice your driving some more between here and Gauntlet?"

"I'll tell you Charlie, if we are going to make it to Wanda's in one piece you'd better do the driving. I've been awake for three nights and days and attacked by demons. My mind's going in a million directions and I calculate our chances of making it to Gauntlet safely with me behind the wheel at slim to none."

"Don't you worry none Zed, I'll handle the driving and let you just sit there looking pretty in your new hat. I've made this run many a time and it's a heap easier in Wanda's Jeep than in my old truck. You need to rest up anyway, there's a surprise waiting on you back at the cafe. I've got to stop in Lander and call Wanda and let her know we are on the way."

"What kind of surprise Charlie? I've kind of had about all the surprises I think I can handle for a while."

"I can't tell you that. Wouldn't be no surprise if I spilled the beans. Just you keep your powder dry. This here surprise won't trouble you none at all. I think you're going to be as happy as a frisky colt when you know what it is. I ain't going to say no more about it. That big old peach of a woman done warned me to keep it tight to my vest and that's just what I'm going to do."

He cranked the Jeep, put it in gear and we started on our return. We passed under the crosspiece with the hanging metal bear and began making our way back down the winding mountain road. I looked at the passing landscape with a renewed interest.

The land had branded me and made me a part of it. I would forever look at it with changed eyes. Beautiful as it had been when I first came here, it now shone in a different light.

I saw it the way an artist might before he put it to canvas. I saw it all, but I also saw the detail, the colors, the shapes, and how it all connected. It looked so different through the eyes of Stonebear than it had through the eyes of Zed. I saw a shadow cross over the road and I looked up and saw a Bald Eagle riding the updraft. It was magnificent.

"Charlie, you know any folks that do tattoos in Lander?"

"Nope, I ain't ever needed to know before. I don't reckon Bainbridge from the jewelry store would be much help on something like that either. He don't quite seem the type. Maybe, that young feller from the place we bought the 'Double L' might know something about that. If he's a motorcycle rider, he'll know for sure. Them folks that favor those iron horses usually are sporting one or two. You really going to get you a grizzly bear tattoo Zed?"

"Charlie, I've thought about a tattoo over the years. Tattoos are as common with sailors as they are with motorcycle riders. I never could fix my mind on something I was confident I wouldn't regret. When that bear spoke to me, and I said I would bear his mark, I knew I had found my tattoo that I would wear with pride for life."

"You say me and Wanda are supposed to get these tattoos too, along with Sheriff Debbie, and even Connie and Abe?"

"All the people I saw in my circle are supposed to get them, but Consuela needs to wait until after the baby's born. I certainly don't expect everyone to follow my lead on this but I don't have much of a choice in the matter. When a 1,000 pound talking grizzly speaks, it's best to pay attention. There was even an old man in the circle standing with a walker. I think it was Dusty Rhodes, but I've never met him. I heard about him from Debbie."

"Lordy Zed, Dusty must be near 90 years old. How in tarnation are you going to convince a 90 year old man to get a tattoo? If you are that silver tongued, you need to get one of them TV evangelist shows and sell them prayers scarves for fifty dollars a throw and heal them by getting them to put their hands on that TV set and shouting Hallelujah. Maybe even run for political office 'cause that's where the big bucks are."

I started to answer Charlie, but I had a mental flash so strong, it stilled my tongue. I saw a crystal clear image of me wearing my Raven feather decorated cowboy hat and on the back of my neck was the unmistakable footprint of a grizzly.

I had already thought I would get it on my wrist. That thought went right out the window. Wasn't anywhere I was getting inked now except on the back of my neck. After what I had experienced with flashes and visions there is no way I would disregard a flash that strong. I returned my thoughts back to Charlie's question.

"Charlie, I know of no way to convince anyone of this by clever salesmanship. All I can do is tell them the truth of what I saw, but it's going to have a lot more credibility if I am already wearing the mark of the bear. I want to see if I can get it done in Lander, before we return to Gauntlet. It's important and I don't think I can delay this. I just had a huge flash telling me to get it done and get it done now."

"Wanda won't be expecting us back till an hour or so after I call, so I just won't call till we can see if you can get stuck about a gazillion times with a needle. Don't you reckon it's going to hurt powerful bad Zed? Where you planning on getting it done? Someplace where folks can't see it?"

"Nope Charlie, I am going to wear it proud right on the back of my neck."

"Dadblamed if that ain't going to hurt like the dickens. Looks like a tender spot to me."

"Charlie, there's no way, no way at all that it could begin to approach the pain of being shot with hundreds of tiny poisoned arrows by a bunch of screaming demons.

"I never experienced pain like that. It was worse than rolling naked in a field of cholla cactus and then wrapping yourself in stinging tentacles of a 1,000 Portuguese Man of Wars. It was agonizing, I begged God to take my life and I didn't have any regret about asking either."

"My God, Zed, you've endured a trial by fire, that's for sure. Was that the worst of it, getting shot with all them arrows?"

"No Charlie, that was bad, worse than anything I thought I could imagine. But it was not the worst part of that long and horrible night. Charlie, the worst part was feeling like God had turned his face from me. That is the deepest and the darkest despair I've experienced. A dark pit where hope no longer lived and light did not exist. Charlie, it felt like I was in Hell."

"Zed, I got chills all over my body just listening to it. I can't imagine what you've gone through but I ain't got a doubt in my mind that you experienced it just like you told it. I think I would have plumb lost my mind and ended up pure loco.

"I'll wear the mark of the bear on me too. I'll have to ponder where. The back of the neck don't feel right for me. I'll think on it some, but you convinced me. You just tell the others like you told me with your face showing the pure agony you endured, and they'll know the truth of it.

"There's a place up ahead where we can get to a phone. Pay phones are hard to find nowadays, but there a few still around these parts if you can one find working. Folks take a lot of anger out on telephones. Here we go, right up here on the right. I'll run in and get us a soda pop while you make your call. What flavor suits you son?"

"I haven't drank soda in more than 20 years. You know what we used Cola for on a ship? We used it loosen up rusty bolts and to take corrosion off of battery terminals. Tell you what, if they have coke in a plastic bottle with a twist off cap, bring me one. I don't want it to drink, but to show you something when we get home. I'll take a plain bottle of water to drink."

Charlie parked and went inside while I got on the payphone. I got Mike's number out of my wallet and gave him a call. Charlie's instinct was spot on. Mike not only knew about tattoos, he was close friends with the best one in town. He put me on hold while he called his friend. He returned and said his friend could see me right now and we could discuss it. He gave me the address and directions.

Turned out to be close to the Italian restaurant where we ate to celebrate Wanda and Charlie's engagement. Charlie returned carrying two bottles of water, a bottle of coke, and a bag of jerky explaining he had promised Dimmit a treat. I told him where to go and twenty minutes later we pulled into 'Desert Tattoos' and minutes later I was introducing myself to a tall man covered in tattoos going by the name of 'Lobo.'

He was bare chested except for a denim vest festooned with patches. He was also an obvious iron freak. Massive muscles and scarred knuckles indicated a life of conflict. It seemed impossible for a man of his size to have a delicate enough touch to do the type of artwork that was depicted by the many photos adorning his walls. Surprisingly, he spoke with a quiet southern drawl.

"I'm pleased to meet ya'll. Mike said you were a special friend and I put trust in what Mike says. You won't find a better dude than Mike. What can I do for you fellers?"

I explained I wanted a grizzly paw print on the back of my neck.

"Here take a look at this catalog. These are my own designs. Bear tattoos start on page 41, as I recall. There's some there that might catch your eye. You take a gander while I measure your neck. First, see that trophy on that case?

"That's for me placing first at the All-American-Tattoo Convention in Fayetteville, North Carolina. He went over to the wall and removed a framed photo and brought it back. See this grizzly tattoo, that's mine and it won me the trophy."

The artistry was truly incredible. It was in full color and it was a massive grizzly standing erect with a ferocious snarl on his face. It looked as if it could step off the back it was tattooed on and disappear in a puff of smoke. It was incredible work.

"Lobo, you are an superb artist. I haven't seen anything like this, not even in Japan. They have some talented tattoo artists there but nothing the equal to this. Not even close. I can't help noticing your southern accent. May I ask where you're from?"

"I'm from a little old wide place in the road you've never heard of. I hail from Apalachicola, Florida. Little town east of Panama City. My daddy was a shrimper and I had enough of that life by the time I was 21 and I got my happy tail north to the big city of Atlanta.

"You can get in a lot of trouble in that city and I found my share. I used to be quite a brawler till I figured out I wasn't going nowhere with that kind of life. I found me a different way to leave a mark on a man without using my fists.

"A young gal I was hanging with named Ruby connived me into going to a Billy Graham crusade. His words grabbed me and wouldn't let go till I got on my knees. I left that place a changed man."

"Lobo, I not only know where Apalachicola is, I've been there dozens of times. When I was a young man I worked on a shrimp boat named the 'Crimson Tide' based out of Bayou la Batre, Alabama. We docked at Water Street Seafood in Apalachicola, many times to sell our catch."

"Don't that beat all? Two redneck former shrimpers from the Gulf of Mexico, meeting up here in Lander, Wyoming?" How did you end up here in Wyoming? We're a long ways from any ocean and you've got the look of a man that's got saltwater in his veins?"

"Lobo, I got a feeling that I'm going to be telling you that tale around a campfire over a cup of coffee, and you're probably not going to believe it because I am still not able to understand much of it myself. We are rushed for time right now because we have to get back to Gauntlet before Charlie's bride to be turns into a dust devil."

"Wait a minute ... I just figured it out. You're the guy that rescued that little lost girl about a week ago. I saw you on TV with that big lady Sheriff. You invited everybody to the wedding, bless your heart. Folks in Wyoming like an excuse to party, and you might have a 1,000 folks show up for the ceremony."

"Maybe me and my motorcycle club will show up too with our old ladies. Mike's a member and there ain't no outlaws in the bunch. At least none that ain't been reformed by the law or Jesus. Took Jesus and the law to get it through my thick head."

"I would be pleased if you could make it. I'll make you a cup of Diablo coffee and we'll have us a fireside chat under the Wyoming sky. I wish we didn't have to go right now, but I've been up with an old Shoshone medicine man undergoing a vision quest for three days, and we've got to skedaddle."

I pointed to the picture that matched almost perfect with the one I'd seen in my flash. "How much would that cost and about how long would it take?"

"Zed, that's just one color, so that's considerably faster to do and it doesn't require a lot of detail. Most average tattoo artists would take about four hours to do that, but I'm not average and I can do it in two hours. As far as the cost, let me ask you is that Shoshone medicine man named Ironbear?"

"It sure is and he just became both my father and my brother and his granddaughter became my daughter. It's a long story. Come to the wedding and I'll tell you all about it."

"Zed, that medicine man saved my life. I had melanoma on my back and it had spread like wildfire. I was paying the price for all those years shirtless under the Florida sun. It had spread to other parts of my body and the medical doctors here in Lander gave me about an 18% chance to live.

"They wanted to pump me full of poison to kill the cancer. I decided I'd rather go out like a man than let them kill me with chemo. I told them I would have to think about it and got myself out of that place. I was already out to the parking lot when this old white headed doctor caught up with me. He was one of the ones I had talked to.

"He said, 'Don't ever mention my name to anyone about this, but I tell you what I would do if I was in your shoes. Get up with a Shoshone medicine man named Ironbear on the Wind River Reservation. If you can be cured, he can do it. Anybody up there can tell you how to find his place. You can tell him I sent you, but don't mention my name to anyone else. I could lose my license to practice medicine.'

"Zed, that's just what I did. I found that wise old man back in the mountains, and that man cured me with his herbs and ointments along with lots of smoke and chants. Some of that smoke was in a pipe loaded with primo weed.

"He said more people could be saved by the sacred smoke except for the ignorance of white men.
He said chemo kills thousands of people every year and marijuana had never killed anyone. He said God provides man with all the medicines he needs from nature. So with that long winded explanation, it will take me two hours to do the tattoo and it will cost the son of Ironbear ... absolutely nothing.

"Ironbear refused payment from me. He said I had a good spirit and that I should pass the good I received from him along to someone else. I've been trying to do that for 8 years now ever since he cured me. Here, let me show you something."

He stood up and removed his vest. When he turned around, I knew immediately what it was. It was a tattoo, and it was remarkably like the Lichtenberg figure that Ironbear wore on his back from the lightning strike. But there was more.

At the base of the 'Tree of Life' like design sat a grizzly bear. The bear was not snarling or fierce. It was just a large bear sitting on his haunches and it seemed to be looking right at me. It was Brother Bear from my vision!

"Lobo, I swear to you I saw that bear in my vision, and he talked to me. He said my path would be joined with others that wore the mark of the bear. You and I, my friend, are going to walk a path together. You must come to the wedding. We have much to talk about and it will require more than two hours to tell it."

"There's no way I would miss it now. Anyplace around there me and my buddies could pitch about twenty tents? We clean up after ourselves wherever we go. We have some serious hikers in our club and they constantly preach the L.N.T. motto, and that stands for 'Leave No Trace.' Sometimes, we even clean up other people's trash and I've made a few go back and clean up their own."

Charlie decided to join the conversation, "I'm sure Wanda will let you set up behind the cafe. It's got plenty of room for twenty tents and you could use the bathroom in the kitchen. You'll have to be respectful of our neighbors. We have a young Mexican couple that work in the cafe and they live in an apartment over the garage. She's in a family way and we are trying to be extra considerate of her. Zed's going to be the baby's godfather and I'm going to be its god-grandfather."

"We'll sure be respectful. We have two fantastic Mexican guys in our motorcycle club. Couple of brothers that run a paint and body shop on the edge of town. What I can do with a tattoo gun they can do with a paint gun. They are true artists and can turn a motorcycle or anything on wheels into a rolling masterpiece. 'Cisco' and 'Pancho' as we call them are as good as anyone in the country."

"If they happen to be the same two fellows Mike knows, I'm anxious to talk to them. Lobo, for the second time today, I am having to say goodbye before I'm ready to leave but me and Charlie have to get on the road. Could Charlie borrow your phone to call Wanda and let her know we are leaving Lander?"

"Sure, go ahead Charlie. Zed and I are going to step outside. I want to show him something. You come on when you finish up."

Chapter 12

Lobo and I went out the door and he led me to a van that had been painted like a rolling landscape of the Red Desert. There were mesas and buttes surrounded by cactus, a band of antelope and a galloping herd of magnificent horses with their tails and manes flowing ... There was a life-like coyote baying at the moon, but what really caught my eye was the sacred wheel of the Shoshone, painted to match the colors that were still painted on my chest. Sitting in the middle of the wheel looking right at me was Brother Bear.

"This van represents the type work that Cisco and Pancho turn out, but that's only part of what I want to show you. Here, take a look inside."

Lobo slid back the side door revealing the inside to be a rolling tattoo studio. It was as immaculate as a hospital operating room.

"I go to all the big bike rallies across the country. My fee is $300 an hour and I stay busy from sunup to sundown. I had to take a week off after I got back from the Sturgis Rally in South Dakota last month.

"There was close to a million people there and seems everyone wanted to be inked. I'm showing you all this to let you know I can come to you. I sense there is some urgency in your case and I can be in Gauntlet tomorrow. We can talk some while I work. What you think about that?"

"Lobo, that is some welcome news indeed. There is urgency on my part for this tattoo, but I have so many irons in the fire I need two more hands to juggle all the balls I have in the air." I looked back from where Charlie and I had just come.

I pointed to the Wind River Range, "Back on that mountain, something grabbed hold of me, like you described happened to you at the Billy Graham Crusade. I am a changed man and I've got so much to do there's no possibility I can do it alone. You coming to me would be a tremendous help, and I might have a few more customers for you."

Charlie joined us saying, "Wanda's got us on the clock now son so we've got to put some spurs to this Jeep, and get back to the cafe pronto. She's fit to burst she's so anxious to show you the surprise and I can't hardly wait neither."

We said our goodbyes to Lobo and as we opened the doors to the Jeep, Lobo had a final question, "Did Ironbear happen to give you a new name when you became his son and brother?"

"Yes he did. He named me 'Stonebear'."

We rode along in silence until Charlie cleared the city limits of Lander. He got back on the open road headed south to Gauntlet and not until then did he speak.

"Son, looks like you've got yourself busier than a cat trying to cover turds on a marble floor. I don't rightly see how you can ride all these horses at the same time and hope to end up in the same corral."

"Let me offer you some well-meaning advice. You write down all that's going on in that head of yours. Write it all down and when you get through, you mark them in order of importance.

"You put your main focus on the one that is most critical and get that one unsaddled and settled in the stable before you tackle the rest of the herd. You are plenty smart enough to work on all the other things at the same time. You get the main one put to bed and tucked in and that'll free up your mind to go to working on the next one in line."

"Charlie, that's some mighty fine fatherly advice and it makes a lot of sense to me. I've got so much to do there's no way one man can do it on his own, but I won't have to. I'm going to have the people in my circle to help me get it done."

"There's no doubt in my mind that my first priority is to find some way to bring Snowbird into my life where I can look after her and help her pursue her dream of becoming a doctor. That's the most important one and the hardest for me to figure out. Where in the world am I going to put a teenage girl? Where can I keep her safe and get her feet on her path?"

"Zed, you'll figure it out, but you ain't got to do it on your lonesome. As I understand it, me and Wanda along with Debbie, Abe and Connie are all in your circle. Why don't we have a War Council of all us together and put our heads to finding a solution.

"Abe talked to me while you've been gone. He said you told him, if a bunch of people got together and worked on the same problem, it was the same as having a genius working to find a solution."

"Thank you Charlie that is some excellent advice and I'm going to do exactly what you suggest, and if I can get in touch with Debbie, I would like to have that council meeting tonight. I would like to swallow this bite before I tackle the rest of the buffalo. Wise advice from my other father."

"Shucks son, all you need is a few more names to go by, and another pappy or two, and you'll get so much advice you won't know whether to whether to mount from the left or the right. Just so you'll know, you always mount a horse from the 'port' side. I reckon that's the best way to explain that to a sailor."

"Charlie, I do believe you are a cowboy genius all by yourself. I've learned so much from you since we met that day in the Red Desert. I am indebted to you for sharing your knowledge and experience with me. If I could choose who I wanted for my father, I would choose you all over again."

"That goes for me likewise. If you are learning anything worthwhile from me, I sure as the dickens hope it is as useful as what I'm learning from you.

"Well now, here we are back in beautiful downtown Gauntlet. You get prepared to be surprised, and you don't have to worry none about rounding up the Sheriff. She'll be there for sure. Yessiree, she'll be there along with the rest of the War Council."

In minutes, Charlie pulled the Jeep in and parked behind the cafe. "C'mon son, you're burning daylight. Everyone's waiting for us inside. Golly, I'm about to burst for you to see your surprise and I know that little woman of mine is fit to be tied."

Charlie ushered me inside, and rushed me through the kitchen straight to the rock table. Seated there were Wanda, Debbie, Abraham and Consuela, and a distinguished elderly man that had to be none other than the Dusty Rhodes who seemed to be destined to part of our circle. I greeted them all with a smile and a tip of my hat.

"It is sure good to get home and see all your faces. I have missed you, and Mr. Rhodes, I haven't met you yet, not formally anyway, but I've seen you in my dreams and I feel like I already know you."

I extended my hand to Mr. Rhodes, and introduced myself. I'm Zed Bowden, I now answer to another name as well. That name is 'Stonebear.' Seems I've got myself two fathers and two names. I'm proud to be called by either one of them."

"Mighty pleased to meet you, and I'm going to call you Stonebear, and I'll tell you why. I dreamed about you too, at least I believe it was you. The man I dreamed about was naked except for a loincloth and he had the sacred circle of the Shoshone painted on his chest."

I unbuttoned my shirt and pulled it apart revealing the circle still marking my chest.

"That's it. That's it, exactly like it was in my dream. But that's not all; you were riding bareback on the back of a huge grizzly bear. Stonebear, I rarely dream, and the few times I have, it escapes like smoke when I open my eyes. Blown away just like the smoke that was coming off that huge bear's fur."

"Bear with me, because this gets stranger. You got off that bear and hugged me to your chest like we were old shipmates. Then the bear spoke to me. I swear to you, as I'm standing here before God, that bear spoke to me. He said, *'Come my friend. Zed will help you on my back. We shall take a spirit walk together.'*

"You helped me up on that bear's back. I grabbed hold of the thick fur, cause his back was broad as a Brahma bull, and that was all there was to hold onto. That dream was so intensely alive. I can still feel that bear's fur between my hands right now. That ride felt just as real to me as being here in this room."

"The bear started off gently but picked up speed until it seemed like we were flying. We went all around the boundaries of *the Anchorage*, that's the name of my spread, and you ran right beside us. When we got to our starting place, the bear said "ONE". We went around ten more times, and when we got to the jump off point on the eleventh go around, you jumped up behind and we rode that 12th circle together."

"On that 12th go around my boundary lines turned into the sacred circle of the Shoshone and colored flames leapt high in the sky. It was like being inside an aurora. Inside that circle, which stretched as far as I could see, were dogs and horses running free in a green meadow with a meandering creek flowing through it. Some were old and slow, but they all seemed happy."

"We finished that 12th round and you got off to help me down, and there was my darling Debbie, standing there holding my walker. She was smiling at me with pure love in her eyes. She had the Shoshone sacred circle painted on her forehead."

"I don't understand it all from stem to stern, but I've got enough of it figured out. I would very much like for you and Debbie to come out to the 'Anchorage' tomorrow for dinner, and come prepared to stay for the night. I've got bedrooms that have never been slept in.

"Lettie and I had dreams of starting a type of foster home for troubled kids and we built the house to accommodate that dream. We have much to talk about. You can call me Dusty. No one's called me Mr. Rhodes since I was a Navy Lieutenant back in the big war."

"I'm pretty sure I can do that, but first thing I've got to do tomorrow is get a grizzly paw print tattoo on the back of my neck. Now tell me about this big surprise."

My last statement completely caught them off guard and they took a second to digest what they just heard.

Wanda recovered first, "Come sit down Zed. You need to be sitting when you hear this and we are going to need the table as you'll soon see. I took an open chair by Debbie, who grinned at me and punched me on the arm.

Wanda opened a folder she had lying in front of her. "Son, it's amazing what's happened since you came into all our lives. It's like a fairytale come true and I keep thinking it can't be real and that the 'Double L' is going to turn into a pumpkin and Charlie turn into a genuine desert rat, but here we are … all of us sitting together like family, and that most definitely includes Dusty."

"You'll see why tomorrow. Charlie doesn't even know about this part yet because he couldn't possibly keep it a secret. Matter of fact we'll all be there tomorrow because this is going to affect all of you."

"Now, to get back to the first surprise, Charlie and I are old and we have no heirs. We want to formally adopt you as our son and make you our heir. Charlie has his cabin and his granddaddy's old buffalo gun he wants to pass along. He has some secrets he wants to pass along to you, but he'll do that in private in his own good time."

"I have a little more complicated situation I'm facing. I own this property, free and clear. Not a penny is owed on anything I own. I also own the buildings housing the bank and the mercantile and they pay me rent.

"I get royalties from a book I wrote on rock collecting, not a lot, but better than a poke with a sharp stick. I plan to write another one on our extended honeymoon.

"I also own some land and we'll talk about that tomorrow. Since you are well above the age of consent, you have to sign granting approval to be adopted by us."

She started to explain further, but I stopped her. "Hand me the paper and pen Mom. You can explain the rest after I write my name Zed Bowden for the first time in my life."

I signed it, and handed the paper and pen back to her. She took the paper but told me to keep the pen because I was going to need it. She handed me another sheet of paper filled with legalese containing words like 'aforementioned' and 'I do hereby attest.'

"Mom, make it easy on me. I've not slept in three days and this all looks like Uncle Bob's one armed French writing."

She laughed and explained, "Yep, it looks like a bunch of nonsense, plain and simple, but lawyers couldn't charge so much if they wrote like normal people talk. Here's what this paper essentially does. It's a Power of Attorney, giving you the legal authorization to act on my behalf. There's another just like it giving you the same authority for Charles."

I signed those two and handed them back and held on to the pen. She handed me another sheet.

"Zed, this form adds you to my bank account, both checking and savings, and gives you joint access to my box in the vault."

I signed form after form. When I thought I had surely signed the last one. I attempted to return her pen, she stopped me once more.

"Son, there's one more, and it's the last one. While you were gone on your vision quest. Charlie and I were working together on a new dish in the kitchen and suddenly I felt like I had grabbed a live electrical wire. Not exactly like that because it didn't hurt, but I saw a burst of light. I saw with absolute clarity all I needed to do. I'm calling it a flash until someone can give it a better definition.

"I told Charlie about it on the spot, and he agreed we needed to do exactly like I understood it to be. That's what signing all these papers has been about. Remember when I told you to run this place like you owned it? Well, one day you will, and here's where the last part of the flash comes in."

"The last of the flash revealed you were to be a custodial owner and when the time comes, you are to sell the place to Abraham and Consuela.

"Since you now have power of attorney, we don't have to be planting daisies before you can do it either. Without me having any knowledge of the fact, Dusty established an investment account in my name. His wife Lettie was like a second mom to me and she asked him to do it. He's managed to make me a wealthy woman, as I just learned today. Very wealthy indeed. I never have to work another day in my life. He'll explain this all to you tomorrow."

I know I had a dumbfounded look on my face, but nothing could match the looks of astonishment on the faces of Abraham and Consuela. They were frozen statues of disbelief. You couldn't even tell they were breathing. Wanda handed me the last paper assuring that one day Abraham and Consuela would one day be the owners of the cafe. I signed it and handed it back.

"I turned to the stunned young couple and said, "*Mi casa es su casa.* For real my friends … welcome, '*somos familia*' … we are family."

We three embraced, and Consuela finally took a deep breath, "Senor Zed, can this be true? My ears have heard a miracle," and her tears started flowing, "Only God can do a thing like this. Only God can make a miracle like this happen."

"All right everybody, if I could have your attention please. One last surprise and it doesn't amount to a hill of beans compared to your other surprises, but I betcha money it'll make you happy."

I looked at Debbie and said, "You've got a surprise too? Am I head of the F.B.I. now?"

"Not quite yet Deputy Bowden. It'll take you another week or two before you get that far. For my surprise we've all got to go outside. Abe, if you'll fetch the bottle of champagne we discussed and a kitchen towel, we'll mosey outside and get this done. Dusty's got to get home before nightfall."

"You got the smudge Wanda?"

"Right here in my emerald clad hand, but there's one last thing before we go. Zed there is one more paper but you don't have to sign anything. It's already been signed."

I took it from her hand. I looked at it. It was a perfect sketch of Dimmit. It had a print of his paw below an inscription that read, "I LOVE MY DADDY."

I shook my head in a total daze and let Debbie lead me out my arm. She took me right to a bright red Toyota Tundra pickup truck. She opened the driver's door and said, "Hop right on in Deputy Bowden, this is your undercover vehicle."

I did as she suggested, mostly because I needed somewhere to sit down and digest the blur of the last 30 minutes. I was near a point of mental and physical exhaustion. I don't know if you can die from sheer unadulterated joy, but if it was possible, I had to be close to flat-lining.

"Get out now. We are going to smudge and sailor bless this rig. Then you and I are going to take a little ride together."

I got out and joined the others and Charlie proceeded to smudge the truck from stem to stern. Abraham handed me the towel wrapped bottle of champagne.

Wanda spoke up then, "Son, say your piece and bless your truck."

"In the sight of God, surrounded by my friends,
I launch you on your way...now our journey begins
Let this truck help me to do all that I should
Keep us safe on the path and let us seek to do good"

"I now christen thee 'Snowbird'."

I swung the bottle into the massive steel cattle guard that armored the front of the truck. And the bottle broke showering the truck and me in a fine bubbly froth of champagne.

Everyone applauded, except the Sheriff. She laid back her head and howled like a wolf.

"Zed go to the passenger side. I'm going to drive us out of town. I'll explain why when I get us out of town a piece."

I followed instructions. By that time I had no resistance left. I was going with the flow and smelling like a combination of champagne and exhaustion.

Debbie said, "Buckle up tight Zed, I am going to show you something that'll blow your socks off. Bear with me till we get out of town, and I'll explain it to you."

I nodded my head and she cranked the motor and the whole truck shook with the raw power harnessed under the hood. That woke me up a little, and I woke a little more when she reversed us with a squeal of the tires only to stall out. Debbie cranked it up and put it in gear and jerked forward only to stall out again.

I was paying attention the third time it happened and I saw it wasn't stalling at all. She was goosing the gas to squeal the tires, throwing the transmission into neutral and then hitting a kill switch on the dashboard. She was driving the truck the same way a mother bird does pretending to be hurt to distract attention from her babies.

In Alabama we called it playing possum; pretending to be dead, when you aren't. I had no idea why she was doing what she was doing but she sure woke me up from my dazed state.

She reached down and grabbed a microphone. I was so out of it, I hadn't noticed the truck was equipped with a police radio and computer.

She activated the microphone, "Bert, we're out of town. Go ahead and clear the way and holler back if there's any wildlife by the roadway. I'll give you a minute to get on up ahead."

She got a 10-4 back from the other end. Several hundred yards up ahead, a Sheriff's car pulled onto the highway and activated its blue lights and headed north. After a bit, Debbie looked at her watch, looked over at me, smiled and threw back her head and howled.

I grinned at her but I was too tired to howl.

"She said, "You ready Zed?"

I nodded my head and mumbled, "10-4."

She turned on a dash mounted blue light and stomped the gas. Smoke boiled from the rear tires and we shot down the road like a fighter jet rolling for takeoff. The G-forces threw me back into my seat and in a few moments when I glanced over at the speedometer, we were already doing 110 mph and still climbing.

She kept her eyes on the road but she howled again and this time I howled with her. It was exhilarating and I was thoroughly awakened by now. We hit 130 mph and the truck seemed like it had plenty left to give, but Debbie begin to back off and picked up the microphone again.

"Go ahead and pull over Bert, we'll be up with you shortly."

She got another 10-4 from Bert, and she began explaining why she had been driving like she did back in town.

"Zed, this truck was confiscated by me and my deputies. It was hauling 500,000 doses of OxyContin. This truck has been heavily modified to run from the law and we were falling further and further behind. This souped up speed demon might be able to outrun our cruisers but you can't outrun our radios.

"We got this bad boy stopped when we took out all four tires with a spike strip. I am confident that this truck was carrying the final fatal hit for some of its intended recipients. We have over 100 people every day dying from drug overdoses. It is a scourge on our society of epidemic proportions.

"The truck belongs to the Sheriff's department now. It will be offered for sale to the public at next week's Sheriff's Auction. It will be sold to the highest bidder.

"I currently have the county's biggest and most notorious gossip locked up on a drunk and disorderly charge. I accidentally had a conversation with one of my deputies in his presence. I discussed how I thought the truck had been run so hard that the heads were probably warped and the motor had to be pretty well shot.

"I voiced my opinion it wasn't worth anything more than scrap metal. He gets released in the morning and by the time of the auction most everyone in the county will know this is just a pretty piece of junk. You should be able to get it pretty reasonable. I know there's some deception involved in this but it's all for the good.

"As my special deputy, when I need you, I'm probably going to need you to get there as fast as you safely can. You don't have the skill to drive a vehicle this fast but you're a quick learner and I have the just the man to teach you."

She pulled in behind the cruiser on the side of the highway with its blue lights still flashing. She put it in park and hit the kill switch. "C'mon Zed and meet Bert. He's going to be your driving instructor."

I got out and met Bert. He was a compact personable man, sturdily built, and his eyes displayed a man with a lot of confidence in himself. We shook hands and I promised to get up with him when I had time for a driving lesson.

Debbie offered to let me drive back to Gauntlet, but I felt too drained to even think about getting behind the wheel. That was a wise decision, because on the ride back to Gauntlet at a much saner speed I kept seeing pink bunny rabbits run across the road.

I knew it wasn't another vision. I was hallucinating from 72 hours of sleep deprivation. I don't remember getting back to the cafe. I don't remember Debbie helping me up the stairs or her taking my boots off. I heard Dimmit snoring beside me and when the lights went out I drifted away on a cloud of pink bunnies with blue lights flashing in the dark.

Chapter 13

I awoke the next morning well after dawn judging from the brightness of the sun beaming through the window. I was still fully dressed except for my boots and hat and my bed partner had abandoned ship. Someone had thoughtfully opened the door for him go out and left me to sleep on undisturbed.

I looked around the room and it gave me a similar feeling like I had experienced at Ironbear's cabin. A feeling of being at home.

I thought of the things I had to be grateful for. The list was growing in leaps and bounds. I could smell coffee from below and I hit the deck. I got a quick shower and with some regret washed the painted circle from my chest.

I put on clean clothes not even bothering to notice what color my drawers were. I was suddenly famished and I wanted to see the faces of my friends. I bounced downstairs to an empty kitchen except for Abraham working with speed and efficiency.

He greeted me with a cheerful "Buendia mi amigo. The others are at the table. It has been a busy morning but now it comes the time where I can handle the kitchen by myself. You look well my friend. The sleep, she was good for you, no?"

"Thanks Abraham, I do feel well rested and I'm starving."

"Excelente mi amigo, I have taken the liberty of choosing your breakfast this morning. Go, sit with the others. I will bring it to you in un momento. Consuela and I will begin speaking to you a little in Spanish every day you are around. Slow, like a child learns. Day by day until it becomes natural. This is how I learned back in Tres Virgenes listening to gringo music and watching old movies in subtitled in Spanish.

"I watched "Gone With the Wind" and "Singing In the Rain," more times than I can count. Listen … *'Frankly my dear, I don't give a damn.'* Pretty good, no? Just like Senor Gable. Go sit, mi amigo, I will bring your breakfast muy pronto."

I smiled and shook my head. This place was turning into Hollywood. First it was Marlon Brando making his debut and now Clark Gable. I went through the swinging doors and found Debbie and Charlie seated at the rock table.

Wanda and Consuela were flitting about the dining room attending to the few remaining tables. I slid myself into what appeared to becoming my designated chair. Wanda gave me a wave from across the room and the customers turned to see who she was waving at.

She said, "That's my son."

I gave her a cheerful wave in return, and greeted Debbie and Charlie.

"At least you look back to being human again. Zed, by the time I got you back here last night, you were in the twilight zone and mumbling about pink rabbits.

Charlie's been bugging the fool out of me asking if I pulled your britches off you last night, and if I did, what color were your drawers."

"I'm not sure Wanda is marrying a man with a sound mind, but there's no mental fitness test for grooms. Look at most married couples, and you'll find being of a sound mind wasn't a prerequisite for getting a marriage license … not for either of them. Ignorant people marrying other ignorant people keeps the stupid gene flourishing in the human race and gives me loads of job security."

Debbie's monologue was interrupted by Abraham bringing me my breakfast including a steaming frothy cup of Diablo. He placed the food in front of me with a flourish.

"Te presento tu desayuno." I present to you, your breakfast. I call it "S.O.B. Caliente." It is an experiment, no? If you die, I will not make it again."

I looked at the plate and it was an exceptional presentation artistically arranged. It deserved to be photographed and placed in a magazine. He had made perfect cat's head biscuits but they weren't covered in normal sausage and gravy like I was accustomed to. It was considerably more colorful.

It was lighter colored and had an appealing but distinctly different aroma. He had used chorizo instead of our normal sausage blend. The gravy was swimming with chunks of Jalapenos and sundried tomatoes.

The different aroma I realized was cilantro, a standby Mexican herb, and there was something else I couldn't quite place. Atop it all were three slices of ripe mango and three slices of avocado.

It was almost too pretty to eat but I managed to overcome that hesitation quickly. I took a test bite. I looked up and everyone was looking at me to judge my reaction. It was out of sight phenomenal and I smiled while I chewed, enjoying the complexity of the flavors. I grinned at Abraham.

"Mi amigo, it is absolutely 'Nanasuwekai' Truly an awesome dish you have created."

Wanda joined us, "Well Zed, what do you think of Abe's latest creation?" We all love it. Even Charlie finally admitted it tasted like the chorizo went fine in this dish. It's got some bite to it, doesn't it?"

"Wanda I was just telling Abraham that it is 'Nanasuwekai, and that's the Shoshone word for awesome. It's outstanding and I like that bite the jalapenos add to overall flavor. There is something else I can't quite identify. It's very subtle but it definitely enhances the flavor. I recognize the cilantro but the rest escapes me. What is it Abraham, that makes this so unique?"

"Zed, I am pleased you like it and I am happy to see you have not died. I fed it to Senor Charlie first as my 'conejillo de indias' or as you would say in English, my guinea pig."

"I made it exactly like you did when you showed me the first time. I added Jalapenos and sun dried tomatoes for color. I also added in one cup of my green chili that I normally put on the huevos rancheros. I mixed it right in with the gravy. Then I added cilantro, sage and some fresh ground nutmeg. Es bueno, no?"

"Abraham, I think you are a shining star in the kitchen. This is exceptional, and we must add it to the menu. I encourage you to keep experimenting with unique dishes. We won't have Charlie around to test it on to see if he lives, but we can always use the Sheriff as a substitute."

"Hold your horses, Mister! I'm much too pretty to experiment on. I'm not a washed up has been like Marlon Brando here. I think we'll just keep you as the official food taster, while your new daddy goes off to honeymoon in the sun, leaving us poor souls behind to endure a cold Wyoming winter."

The last customers paid up and told Wanda breakfast was fantastic. I had to agree with them. It was an exceptional dish and I would be having it again. I was just finishing up my satisfying breakfast when Abraham and Consuela joined us. Abraham brought me a fresh cup of Diablo.

"I took a sip, it was perfect. "Friends I have so much to tell you, I don't know hardly know where to begin, but I received some wise advice from Ironbear.

"He told me you cannot eat a whole buffalo all at one time. You have to do it bite by bite and allow it to settle before you try to eat more. I have a whole buffalo to feed you but we will take it one bite at a time. This is the most pressing thing on my mind this morning."

"I have suddenly and quite unexpectedly become a father to a teenage Shoshone beauty named Snowbird. She is Ironbear's granddaughter. I have now become both a brother and son to Ironbear. Snowbird's mother and father were killed in a car crash and she has been raised by her grandfather way back in the mountains since she was a little girl."

"I am now charged with her care and seeing she pursues her dream of going to medical school. She wants to become a doctor and then return to the reservation to serve her people. She's extremely bright and has a charming and engaging personality. As surprised as I was to become an instant father, I am delighted that it's happened. She also looks like a teenage version of my mother."

My announcement sat off a flurry of questions coming my way. I was bombarded with a barrage of questions. I waited until they slowed up before I spoke.

"Folks, trust me, we are going to have to take this one bite as a time. First, let me tell you how I became both a brother and son to Ironbear and subsequently father to Snowbird, and we'll go from there."

I relayed the long tale involving my vision and the encounter with Brother Bear and how he had called me little brother. I stayed away from the other visions. Some I knew would have to be discussed alone with Ironbear.

Once everyone had a general understanding of what had transpired I said, "So does anyone have any advice about what I'm supposed to do to fulfill my obligation to care for Snowbird and get her in medical school? Where am I going to put her and make sure she's alright?"

I looked at Charlie and Abraham, but they shrugged their shoulders. They were as clueless as me.

"Why don't you menfolk go to the kitchen and bring us all a cup of coffee. We women think better on our own. Go on. Skedaddle the bunch of you. Go on now son, and take Charlie and Abe with you. Don't you rush back neither.

We "menfolk's' got ourselves out of there without protest, relieved to turn this problem over to the 'professionals' and do what we men do best. Staying out of the way.

The kitchen was our refuge and we took shelter there and made ourselves a cup of Diablo. I heard Dimmit bark and I let him in. He seemed as happy to see me as I was him. I scratched him behind his ears. I noticed Abraham had more biscuits on a cooling rack and another skillet full of his unique gravy.

I had to ask, "Did you expect more customers this morning and ended up with this much leftover?"

"Oh no, Zed, I do not waste food. This was planned and I wanted to do two more experiments. I want to see if the gravy can be prepared and then frozen in containers and used as needed. This I will not know until tomorrow, to see if the quality is the same using the flash freezer ... The second experiment I will show you now. Un momento, por favor." "One minute please."

He left me and Charlie alone to savor our cups of Diablo and to conjecture about what the women were discussing out in the cafe. Charlie ventured it probably involved shock collars and cattle prods since Debbie was part of the conversation. While we were laughing about that possibility, Abraham returned bearing two dishes.

He presented them with his signature flourish and said, "Gentlemen, I present you, Abraham's "S.O.B. Flambé." Try it my friends. If you both die, I will never make it again."

What sat in front of me was a cathead biscuit transformed in a very appealing dessert dish. He had created some type of light colored caramel sauce. It contained diced peaches and what I thought might be pepper flakes. It flowed down the side of the biscuit and pooled on the plate. The concoction was topped with a huge serving of whipped cream sprinkled with cinnamon. There was a slice of raw peach standing upright in the cream like a crescent moon.

"Come a mis amigos," Eat please, and tell Abraham what you think, and please do not die."

Charlie and I dug right in and it was no surprise that it was outstanding. The caramel sauce was a combination of sweet and salty and it carried enough heat to make the cooling effect of the whipping cream most welcome. Hot pepper in a dessert dish was a surprise, but it worked, and it worked magnificently well.

Chapter 14

I was telling Abraham how well I liked it when we were interrupted by a loud scream of surprise from Consuela. We almost ran over one another rushing out to the cafe.

We found Consuela with her arms wrapped around the neck of a short Mexican man, while another short Mexican beamed on from the side. Standing with them was a more than slightly embarrassed Lobo.

Abraham rushed across the room and hugged the other Mexican, then he and Consuela swapped partners and the Spanish began to flow so fast, it would be impossible to follow, even if I knew a lot more than I did. I looked at Lobo and he shrugged his shoulders.

He looked at Wanda and Debbie and said, "I am sorry ya'll, I don't have any ideas what's going on here. Cisco and Pancho followed me down here on their bikes. They wanted to meet up with Zed, about some matter he discussed with our friend Mike. I didn't know they knew a soul here in Gauntlet.

"Sorry ma'am, and good to see you again Sheriff. I appreciate you cutting me some slack on that expired tag a while back. I go by the name of Lobo, and I'm here to give my new friend Zed, a grizzly bear paw print tattoo."

The four excited Mexicans calmed enough for Abraham to explain that the two men called Cisco and Pancho were Consuela's cousins from Tres Virgenes, and they had been all raised together as children. They had not seen each other since they left Mexico. Neither of them had any idea they all lived in Wyoming, not an hour away from each other on a fast Harley.

We had introductions all around. The morning was quickly turning into a combination party and family reunion. I suggested to Abraham we adjourn to the kitchen and make our guests some Diablo coffee and a dish of his "S.O.B. Flambé" dessert. He and I left while they pulled chairs from other tables to take a seat at the rock table.

When we made it back to the kitchen and began preparing the dishes for everyone but ourselves. It went pretty quick. Abraham knew what to do to prepare the biscuit dish and I was an old hand at whipping up a cup of Diablo. We finished in unison like a well-oiled team accustomed to working together. It was plumb natural. I was already learning to do what I referred to as the kitchen dance.

"Zed, shall we take these things into the cafe and see if maybe Papa Noel has arrived in a sleigh pulled by reindeer with a bag full of gifts for everyone. Could this day become more miraculous that this?"

"My friend, God works in mysterious ways, but I think we have enough on our hands without Papa Noel added to the mix."

We carried the laden trays of Diablo and S.O.B. Flambé' through the swinging doors to find everyone chattering away like old friends, but the most surprising sight, was seeing Sheriff Debbie and Lobo engaged in an arm wrestling competition that appeared to have been going on for a while.

Neither was making any headway against the other and when they saw the delicious dessert placed on the table, they jointly agreed to call it a tie.

The 'S.O.B. Flambé was a huge hit with everyone, and Lobo and his crew absolutely raved over the Diablo coffee. Lobo said he drank three pots of coffee a day and if we would teach him how to make this, he would up his intake to four pots a day.

Lobo gave a huge sigh of satisfaction. "Stonebear, this coffee is so good it'll make you want to 'slap your momma from the table'."

"Ay caramba! What is it with you Norte Americanos wanting to slap your mothers' from the table?"

"Now, if I could speak to my son for just a moment. We three ladies have solved your biggest problem. It wasn't hard at all. We know exactly where to put Snowbird.

"First, she will go live in the spare bedroom at Abraham and Consuela's place. Consuela's baby is not due until the end of March, or early April. Abe and Connie are excited about Snowbird staying with them. Connie volunteered this herself; she says she always wanted a little sister."

"Si Senor Zed, it is my hope that the baby will be born on my birthday, April 5th. My birthday is the same as my mother's, and it would be fantastico if this child could be born on that day. It would be a good omen, no? So, I have still many days to prepare this baby's room, and my new sister can help me."

The Sheriff obviously had something to say. "April 5th, is your birthday? That was my mother's birthday too. That's kind of interesting, and it would be pretty special indeed if the baby was born on the same day. Wouldn't surprise me at all if that doesn't take place, like maybe its destiny, or fate ... or something."

"Back to where Snowbird will stay. Once Charles and I go away on our honeymoon, you'll move into our bedroom and Snowbird will take over yours. It's your house now too. Your daughter should live with you. That wasn't so hard now, was it?"

I was surprised, but greatly pleased at how the women had found such an agreeable solution to a problem that had grown to mountainous proportions in my mind. Lot of worry over nothing. I would take advantage of getting women's help more often in the future.

"Zed, what's the next problem, or challenge you are faced with?"

"That is very welcome news and I appreciate all of you for finding a solution. I am glad to ask your advice on the next challenge facing me. Somehow, I have to convince all of you, and that includes Dusty Rhodes, to get a bear paw print tattoo somewhere on their body"

"That's everyone except Consuela. She will have to wait until the baby is born, and longer, if she's nursing, before she can get a tattoo. That's why Lobo is here. He's going to tattoo the back of my neck in his van. He has a rolling tattoo studio inside and he's the best in the nation."

"I know of no way to convince you of this, other than to tell you of my encounter with a huge grizzly that spoke to me in a vision."

I don't remember speaking another conscious word after that. In an instant I was transported right back to that sacred ceremonial rock where my visions had taken place. There was no warning, or time to see the storm approaching. I didn't have any opportunity to prepare myself.

I was immediately thrust back within the stone circle, and right into the ferocious height of that raging storm.

I was being put through the same hell all over again. This time it was with more terrible intensity than the previous vision. I screamed out begging God to save me. I was so terribly cold; colder than at any time in my entire life. It was a bitter, soul killing cold, and so deeply invasive, that I thought I couldn't possibly recover.

Tears were freely running down my face and freezing before they could fall to my chest. I felt my heart become sluggish, and I feared it would freeze solid. I begged God please save me from this icy agony. I was in such utter and complete anguish that I knew I could not endure much longer.

Then Brother Bear was instantly with me and he let the warmth of the stone ease my pain. He told me that I must seek the souls that would become part of my bear clan and that all of them would wear the mark of the bear on their skin. After those words were spoken, the bear disappeared with only a trace of smoke to mark his passage.

I opened my eyes to see Wanda staring wide-eyed at me, her arms clasped around her body and everyone else looking at me absolutely stunned.

"Zed, you had frozen tears on your face. We all saw it with our own eyes. I still have chill bumps. It was spooky and spiritual at the same time. I never in my life thought I would get a tattoo, much less a tattoo of a grizzly bear print. My momma would whip my butt, but I'm getting one on the inside of my right wrist. Charlie's getting one on the inside of his left wrist, so when we hold hands, our prints will be together. Isn't that right, Charles?"

"Why, of course, Honey, I was kind of leaning towards Zed's idea of the neck location, but being I'm the reasonable kind of feller I am, I can sure see the wisdom of doing just like you say. Shoot-fire, my onliest son won't even tell me what color drawers he's wearing. Why, a man would have to be cross-eyed fool not to see which horse I'm going to hitch my buggy to."

Consuela still had her mouth open in disbelief, but Abraham said, "As for me and my little bird, we too shall get the mark on our wrists like Charlie and Senorita Wanda. I will have mine done now, if I can afford it." My bride, she will wait until the baby comes, and then she will get hers. We have seen the miracle of the frozen tears, and it is not something we can ever forget. As soon as you can Senor Lobo, I wish this thing done to me."

"I'm assuming since Cisco and Pancho saw all this happen just like I did, we three are included in this deal too?" Lobo said.

I nodded my head and spread my arms to include everyone in the room.

"Well, I am honored to be a part of whatever it is. It feels good to me and I want to see where this line takes me, and I've already got the mark of the bear on me."

He shed his vest and displayed the tattoo on his back with the *Tree of Life* like design with the large and impressive grizzly sitting there calmly looking everyone in the eye.

"Since this is going to be like a fraternity, or a club, there won't be any charge for any of you. Not one red cent. This sounds like an adventure and I want to be along for the ride wherever it's going. As for Cisco and Pancho, they've been wanting a bear tattoo on their back kind of like mine, only with a grizz showing his teeth, for quite a while now.

"I'll do theirs for free too, and they know what kind of value that represents. I've thought of a way they can pay me back. Theirs can't be done in hours. It will take weeks, but it will get done."

A thought occurred to me, "Wanda, can you call Dusty, and see if we can bring three more to dinner? I think our circled just widened."

"I'll do that Zed, and I can tell you right now, they'll be welcome, and if they can stay the night, they will find a lot to interest them out at Dusty's place. I guarantee that. You wait and see."

"I think I can speak for all three of us that we'd be glad to join ya'll, and we're obliged for the kind invitation Miss Wanda. This has got me more fascinated than a kitten under a leaky cow." Lobo said smiling.

"What you say, Zed? You ready to step out to my van and get you inked up? I'll do Wanda and Charlie next. Their tattoos won't take very long because going on the wrist means a rather small tattoo.

"That's a tender spot for most people and some folks need to take a break from time to time, but I can do all three of you in about 4 hours. Maybe less … this Diablo coffee has me inspired and energized. Let's go get her done."

I got up and followed Lobo out to his rolling office and marveled again at the exceptional artwork that wrapped around the entire vehicle. Truly, Cisco and Pancho were as exceptionally skilled at their craft as Lobo was with his.

Lobo had a paper circle cut out of the size of the tattoo he was proposing to put on the back of my neck. He held up a mirror so I could judge how it would look. It looked good to me and I gave him the go ahead to proceed. He started by drawing an outline of the paw print and then began.

There was some pain, but definitely bearable. It was a rapid vibrational type of pain that seemed to be causing me a release of endorphins. I got to where I found the pain turning to a kind of pleasure, and I could see how some people might get addicted to it.

"Lobo, can I talk while you are doing this?"

"Absolutely, unless you are one of those types that has to talk with their hands while bobbing their head around for emphasis. I would rather be caught riding a Japanese rice grinder than to try and ink up an Italian. It's like trying to put lipstick on a hummingbird."

"I was just wondering do people get addicted to being tattooed."

"There's no scientific proof there is an addiction, but I assure you, it's very close to an addiction for some. About 1 out of every five adults has a tattoo, and it's more like 40% for those under age thirty. It's definitely a big thing with the young crowd. Up to 20% of that group have 4-5 tattoos, and those numbers are growing incredibly fast."

"Most of my customers are repeat, and at my prices, I would say they are definitely addicted. A tattoo like the one on my back can run $5,000, or even double that, from a well-known artist.

"I am at the top of the game, and I can afford to do some freebies for folks with scars and deformities. I get more satisfaction from that these days than anything else."

"Lobo, how long did it take you to get this good at tattooing?"

"This may sound a tad immodest, but I was always good as an artist from the get go. I have a natural, God given talent. I started drawing pictures when I was knee-high to a grasshopper, and I was good at it. My daddy encouraged me because I sketched pictures of the shrimping life and how it was living on the Florida Panhandle.

"I think all children are born creative but it gets killed off by lack of support from adults. Kids need an atmosphere where their gift, whatever it may be, can blossom and develop.

"No telling how many gifted little kids got shoved into Little League, or ballet classes, just to satisfy the expectations of the grownups, and their true potential was never realized. People spend a lifetime as tattoo practitioners and the level they attain is what I would call competent. Not great, but OK.

"You can teach technique but the ability to make ink come alive on skin is rare. I think you're born with it, or not."

Chapter 15

Charlie had been observing and listening from the open door. "You know, Connie is a really good artist too, plus she can sing so pretty it'll make your eyes water up. That sketch of Dimmit, with the paw print. She did that, and it didn't take her hardly not time at all. Just whooped it right out, pretty as you please.

"I watched her do it and it was durn near hypnotizing to watch her work. Of course, Dimmit made the paw print his own self, and right proud he was to make his mark."

"I agree with what you are saying Charlie. It seems like everyone in our circle brings some kind of special God given talent to the mix. We all are going to have roles to play wherever this amazing journey takes us.

"It's like I was telling Abraham … you get a circle of people that work together for a common goal and you can harness a power that is the equivalent of a genius at work. That's true for average people and I don't see our group as anything like average."

"Zed, you doing OK? I've got the outline done and I'm ready to ink it in, if you're ready. It won't take much longer, but the neck is one of the more tender spots and we can take a break if you like."

"No problem for me Lobo. I am finding it quite pleasant, so go ahead, and then we can get Marlon Brando inked up, and then we'll put Wanda in the chair."

"Now, who in the world is Marlon Brando?"

"Don't you worry, I know Charlie will tell you all about it when you get him in the chair, but whatever you do, don't let him show you his Marlon Brando tattoo. I saw it once and I'll never be the same."

"Okie-dokie, my friend, but first thing I want to do right after I finish you, is to get another cup of Diablo coffee. Tattooing might, or might not, be addictive, but that Diablo most certainly is. Best darn coffee I've ever drank and you don't have to say any of that silly Starbucks nonsense, like Grande and Venti. They've got some pretty fair coffee, but it pains me to go in there and have to spout that nonsense."

"Lobo, you can have all the Diablo you can handle and I'll show you how we make it, so you can make it on your own anytime you have a hankering for it."

"That's a deal Zed, and I hope ya'll know you've got a sure enough winner with this coffee. It's pure gold, and in a big city you couldn't make it fast enough to meet the demand. You could sell it from a food truck wherever people bunch up headed into work. You might could sell donuts along with it to make even more money."

"Instead of donuts, how about Indian fry bread with honey, and Shoshone acorn bread topped with that caramel glaze like Abraham had on the S.O.B. Flambé?"

"I don't reckon I've ever had acorn bread. Does Abraham know how to make bread out of acorns?"

"He will once he sees it done just once. I have the perfect teacher in mind to show him how to make it the authentic Shoshone way. He can also show her how he makes the glaze. Maybe together, they can come up with a recipe to make the glaze using honey instead of sugar. Healthier and more natural that way."

"Well look here Zed, I've finished your tattoo up already. I told you that Diablo worked wonders on me. Here, you take a look in the mirror, and don't mind the redness. That'll go away in a short while."

Lobo held up two mirrors, one in each hand and positioned them where I could see his work. It was perfect … plumb perfect, just like I envisioned it would look.

"That's excellent Lobo, that is exactly what I wanted, now let's go get you that cup of Diablo and maybe a snack too. I've got something else I would like you to try, if you're not too full."

"I've been too empty a time, or two, but I ain't never been too full. The Chinese folks that run the all you can eat buffet up in Lander, used to hate to see me walk in the door, bless their hearts. I finally took pity on them, and I pay now like I'm a party of four. I still think they're losing money, but they seem happy with the arrangement."

"I'm going to put a sterile bandage over the tattoo to keep it clean. After 4 hours, you take it off and wash it gently with soap and water. Then put some antibiotic ointment on it for a couple of days, and you'll be good to go."

We went back to the cafe, waved at everyone, and then straight back to the kitchen. "Hola Abraham, if it is not too late I would very much like our new friend to try your S.O.B. Caliente. He's originally from the south like me, and was probably raised on biscuits and gravy. I want to see what he thinks of the Mexican twist you put on an old southern standby."

"No hay problema mis amigos … no problem my friends. It is never too late for Abraham. I am like Speedy Gonzales in the kitchen. Sometimes, even my hair, she catches on fire I move so fast. Go sit at the table and I will bring it to you Senor Lobo."

"Abraham, we will eat it here at the bar. I want to show Lobo how we make the Diablo coffee so he can learn to make it himself."

"Excelente! Por favor, siéntese y estará listo en un minuto. Excellent! Please sit down and it will be ready in a minute."

I showed Lobo how we made the Diablo, and impressed upon him Charlie's kitchen motto …   Doing it exactly the same way, using the same ingredients every time. As I was sitting down our two cups of Diablo, Abraham was placing a huge platter of S.O.B. Caliente in front of Lobo.

"Enjoy my friend, it is a pleasure to serve you, and please don't die. No one has eaten this much before, not even Charlie, or the Sheriff, and they both eat like starving wolves. Ay yi yi, my momma would slap them from the table the way they eat." The last sentence was delivered with a brilliant smile.

Lobo was doing some serious eating and he had already consumed two of the biscuits before he even came up for air. "This is some righteous groceries. It's poking my taste buds in brand new places and making them smile. I do like that spicy bite it has and the avocados and mangos add a lot of color and variety."

We wound up our business in the kitchen and I gave Lobo written instructions for preparing 10 cups of Diablo at a time. He said he might tattoo it on his arm if he could find an empty spot so he would never lose it.

We returned to the cafe where Wanda and Charlie were waiting their turn to get the mark of the bear put on their skin.

Wanda stood up and pulled Charlie up with her. She reached for his hand and gave him a warm smile. "See here, Lobo, how we are holding hands and our wrists touch on the inside? That's how we want our tattoos to be. Touching when we hold hands … two paw prints following the same path in life. What you are giving us is a very special wedding present that will last all our lives. Thank you for this Lobo. We are ready when you are."

Lobo was in the groove. He finished both of them in a little over an hour and started on Debbie. She got hers on her neck exactly like me, only a little larger than mine. She's a big old peach of a woman with a neck to match, but he still finished her up in less than two hours.

That was everyone except for Abraham and Dusty Rhodes, assuming I could talk a 90 year old man into getting a bear tattoo. I really didn't think it would be too difficult not after riding the back of a bear in his dream. I was feeling quite elated with the progress and felt inspired to mimic Charlie's practice of trying to put it in words...

Twelve times the eagle's shadow circled the stone
Twelve times it cried showing I was not alone
I saw the light of those that would journey with me
Their faces like leaves of our family tree
Then came the visions marking my path
Anchored in stone I survived the wrath

Brother Bear spoke on that rock where I stood
Little Brother, your purpose is to do only good
Your circle will grow and they'll all bear my mark
Follow the light, and not the dark.

Lobo said, "Did you make that up yourself, or are you quoting somebody?"

"The words are mine and it's a little trick I learned from Papa Charlie. It helps the brain, or so he says, to give your mind a jump to find words that fit a situation. I am enjoying following his guidance. I can see how Charlie would do that out in the desert to keep himself entertained and his mind active."

"Let's go fetch Abraham away from his wife's cousins and get his tattoo done. Then I'll be all wrapped up."

"Maybe not quite wrapped up, not just yet. The man we are going out to see in a little while is 90 years old, and I've got to get him to agree to be tattooed with a bear print. It might be an easy sale because he had a dream about a bear that made quite an impression on him."

In less than 30 minutes Abraham bore the mark of the bear on his right wrist, while Consuela looked on from the side and said 'ouch' at least a dozen times, and 'Ay' 'Ay' 'Ay' many times more.

We left the cafe in a convoy with Sheriff Debbie leading the way. She was followed by Wanda and Charlie in the Jeep, along with Abraham and Consuela riding in the back. Next came the painted tattoo wagon, followed by the two Mexican motorcycle riders on their flashy rumbling bikes, and finally me in the big red caboose of a Toyota, recently christened 'Snowbird.'

In the passenger seat was my buddy Dimmit and he seemed to be thrilled sitting up in the big red truck. He was ready to get back out where he could run free. Town life was oppressing his free spirit.

We caught a few stares as we drove out of Gauntlet, and I could tell one old cowpoke was plainly asking his sidekick, did somebody die?

It wasn't too long a drive before we made it to Dusty's eastward boundaries and there was no doubt we had arrived. Marking the entrance to his place on either side were two huge ship anchors. It was pretty remarkable to find something like that on a ranch in the middle of Wyoming, but quite appropriate for a ranch named '*The Anchorage*.'

Even in the relative short distance we had traveled since leaving Gauntlet, I noticed the landscape changing. It steadily became greener and the vegetation more lush and varied. The peaks of the Shoshone National Forest seemed tantalizingly close. It was a totally different sight than what I had experienced out at Charlie's cabin.

Both were in Wyoming, and both definitely beautiful, but in totally different ways. It filled me with peace and reverence to take in this impressive view. I stopped the truck to take in the grandeur of the panorama greeting my eyes.

It was the kind of scene that could accommodate and foster big dreams. Looking at nature's magnificence spread out before me, filled me with a sense of being connected to our Creator and that all things were possible.

I started the truck back up and quickly caught up with the rest of the convoy. We drove on for a while until we began to see the structures. It looked much like a small orderly town off in the distance.

Some of the buildings looked absolutely enormous. As we closed the distance I could see a huge two story log lodge that seemed to be the most prominent building.

It had the appearance of an exclusive rustic hotel that would have been perfectly at home in Aspen or Vail. The massive log building was an architectural masterpiece, and it was surrounded by professionally landscaped grounds with numerous well placed flower beds displaying a riot of bright colors.

A small herd of elk grazed unconcernedly on the lawn. Standing tall and proud in front of the main building was a regimental sized flag pole with Old Glory waving in the breeze. It was all perfectly immaculate and would have made a fantastic picture postcard.

The grounds were breathtaking and as we pulled around the circular driveway, I saw Dusty standing with his walker, and at his side was a tall slender woman with long black hair streaked with threads of silver. She had a proud bearing with an unlined, ageless face and her right hand lay on Dusty's shoulder.

We got all the vehicles parked and before I got out, I had a word with Dimmit, advising him that we were guests and I expected him to behave like a gentleman. No stealing and no eating tires off of anything. He gave me his paw and we shook on it.

I got out and Dimmit took off at top speed. I was grateful he ignored the elk. There was an impressive 6 X 6 bull in charge of his happy little harem and their peaceful presence made the place feel like the Garden of Eden, much like Ironbear's place, but on a more massive scale.

I shook Dusty's hand and he introduced me to the woman at his side.

"This is Sirena, my dear and treasured friend. She came to work for me and Lettie more than 30 years ago. She quickly became like a daughter to me and my late wife and I don't know what I would do without her.

"She oversees the house and grounds, everything from the kitchen to the garden and she does a superb job at all of it. She is a trusted friend and partner and I value her wisdom and loyalty.

   Knowing her name, Sirena, is the word for 'mermaid' in the Spanish language, I introduced myself.
   "Mucho gusto Sirena, mi nombre es Zed."
   She replied in perfect and precise English,   "Welcome Zed, to *The Anchorage*. We are honored all of you have come here. Dusty and I have been anticipating your arrival and we are preparing a welcome meal, but first let me meet the others and I will show you to your rooms."

I observed her as she talked and her mannerisms and demeanor indicated a person of cultured bearing and one with a lively intelligence. I still couldn't tell her age but her eyes were kind and wise. She was in every way impressive and she possessed an air of dignity that was both confident and humble.
   Introductions were made all around and Dusty was delighted to meet with Lobo, Cisco and Pancho. Surprised me a little, but I was getting plumb used to surprises.

   "Sirena, let's get our guests to their rooms. I have much to show them before we dine. I can't wait to take these fellers to the barn.
   "Well, pardon me ladies, let me change that to I can't wait to show it to all of you. Wanda and Debbie have seen it before, but it will be interesting to see what Lobo, Cisco and Pancho think of my collection.
   "Sirena, would you please have the boys bring a couple of golf carts to the west deck? Might better make that three carts. I'd like to keep us all together for a while."
   Sirena pulled a small hand-held radio from her pocket and made contact with a man she called, "Red," and he said he would have the carts there in a jiffy.
   We mounted the broad steps leading up to the porch. I'm not sure porch is the right name because it was enormous and it wrapped around the sides of the building. More than a couple of dozen people could have easily sat on the front in the numerous rocking chairs and porch swings.
   It faced east and I knew watching the sunrise from here would be a memorable experience. I decided in my mind it deserved to be called a veranda, and I resolved to myself to watch the sunrise from one of the comfortable swings in the morning.
   "Come on into the house and make yourselves to home. Sirena will show you your rooms, and I'll meet you back here in the main room once you all get settled. Debbie and Wanda have been here before and they already have permanent rooms."

We followed him through the carved doors into a room that was dominated by a towering stone fireplace that could handle eight-foot logs easily.

The main room had an open ceiling with large log rafters from which hung four elk horn chandeliers. The place was a virtual museum of western and Native American art. Debbie's previous guesstimate that old Dusty was worth a couple of million was way off the mark. The house alone had to be valued at many millions and the artwork perhaps even more than that.

The house was warm and inviting and gave me the same sense of wonder that I experienced when I stopped to look at the scenery on the way in. The room definitely inspired awe, but it was also a room of luxurious comfort where dreams could soar to the rooftop and beyond. I felt in my heart that important things would be said here... maybe sooner than later.

"Come gentlemen and I will show you to your rooms. Debbie, if you and Wanda will please show Consuela and Abraham to their room, it would help get us back to Dusty faster. He's got a great deal to discuss with you. They are to be in the Aspen room, right across the hall from your rooms."

We followed Sirena down a wide hallway decorated with paintings and western bronze statues and numerous Indian artifacts, bows and quivers along with war lances were artfully displayed, but what stopped me in my tracks was a square glass case that held an exquisite pair of beaded shin-high moccasins. The intricate beadwork was superb and fit to be worn by an Indian princess.

One by one we were shown our rooms and no one was prepared for the splendid accommodations we were assigned. Easily the most plush and inviting place I would ever lay my head.

The room was fit for royalty, assuming royalty had an appreciation for western motif and rugged hand craftsmanship. My room was appropriately named 'The Bear Den.' I decided to explore my room later and hurried myself back to join Dusty.

The others had the same idea and in minutes we were all gathered in front of the immense fireplace. Dusty was deep into a conversation with Lobo and his crew about something called a Shovelhead Electra Glide.

It was a mysterious conversation to me but apparently of great interest to the four of them. Once we all got there he wound up that conversation.

"I hope everyone likes their room and if you don't speak up now, because otherwise those rooms are yours whenever you come to *The Anchorage*. Just so there's no mistaking my meaning, your room is yours, and you are welcome here anytime as long as you like while I'm still living on the right side of the dirt. I'll have more to say on that in a bit."

Everyone expressed delight with their rooms which caused Dusty to smile and acknowledge our satisfaction with a nod of his head.

"Come on then and follow me. I've got a heap of things to show you and not enough time to fit it in before sundown. Some will just have to wait till tomorrow."

We followed him from the great room down another short hallway that led to a kitchen and what a kitchen it was. It was a completely equipped commercial kitchen designed to prepare meals for hundreds and four women and two men were busily engaged in various tasks.

"I apologize for bringing you through the kitchen but it's shorter than walking all the way around the house. Being on this walker, I like taking shortcuts.

"Now you know where the kitchen is, feel free to help yourself anytime you want something to drink or snack on. There's usually someone here to help you, but make yourself to home whether there's anyone here or not."

We followed him out a side door to the covered veranda, which did encircle the house on all sides. A large round table was being set with plates and silverware for 10 people. There was another outside stone fireplace with a fire already burning. Flowers were in pots resting on the deck and hanging from baskets. Dusty had created a virtual paradise that blended perfectly with the picturesque vision freely provided by nature. We would have the pleasure of dining while watching a Wyoming sunset.

Dusty led us up to a line of three golf carts each with seats for four riders, and he threw his walker in back of the first one in line. "Mount up on these buggies. You mash the gas to go and take your foot off to stop. I have a speaker and microphone on mine and I want Lobo, Cisco, and Pancho to ride with me."

He was off and we followed like ducks in a row. He started talking on the loudspeaker almost immediately.

"There are five of these buildings I refer to as barns on the ranch. They are all built the same and constructed to withstand hurricane force winds and massive snow loads. They are insulated and heated and are powered by a combination of wind, solar, and natural gas.

"We have our own gas wells on the property and we always have one or the other we can depend on. There's a generator big enough to light up half of Gauntlet, and it runs off natural gas too. We are pretty much self-sufficient here except for medical needs.

"We are only going to have time to look at two of these barns before Sirena rings the dinner bell, and we don't want to be late for that. No sir, we sure don't want to be late because she's prepared quite a feast for us."

"Here we are approaching the barn that I call my museum. The boys have opened the doors on both ends, so we'll drive slowly, and I'll let you know what we're looking at."

We passed through into an immense well lighted structure that Dusty said was 50,000 square feet. I did some quick figuring in my head and surmised they were 100 feet X 500 feet. It was large as an ocean going freighter and clean as a whistle. Someone ran a really tight ship.

Dusty abruptly stopped and got on the horn, "Sorry folks, my crew is threatening to mutiny if I don't let them disembark."

I saw immediately what had captured the biker's interest. There was row after row of restored motorcycles. Some obviously antique and others of more recent vintage.

"I guess everyone can see by now I am a motorcycle nut and a lifelong collector of these magnificent machines. I specialize in Harley's but I have models from every American manufacturer going back to the early 1900's and every one of them is in working order.

"I am building me a Harley trike so I can ride again, but it will be next spring before its ready. I can't stick with the handwork like I used to. Arthritis is not my friend."

"There are 286 motorcycles in here and probably one of the finest collections in the world, but we've got to mount up and move along. After dinner, Lobo and the boys are welcome to come back and look all they want."

Dusty led us through puttering along making a comment occasionally over the loudspeaker but he did not stop again. We arrived at the end of the building and drove through the huge doors that had sufficient space to allow a tractor trailer truck to easily travel from one end to the other. Off several hundred yards was another building exactly like the one we just exited. Dusty proceeded without delay towards barn number two.

When we entered I halfway expected to see rows of vintage cars or some other large collectible items, but there was nothing like that. Dusty stopped his cart, dismounted and grabbed his walker out of the back. He stood there waiting for us to join him and we all assembled around him.

"This is a dream Lettie and I shared. We both loved animals of all types, but especially dogs. We had plans of providing a sanctuary for old dogs and dogs that had not had a loving home, or tender care at the hands of humans. We intended for each dog to have his own space."

"You see down both sides of this building there are divided rooms with elevated padded benches. There is a ramp up to the beds and there are automatic waters in each stall. The concrete floors are sloped to the back connecting to a drainage system where each stall can be hosed down with high pressure steam."

"The waste goes into a methane digester. It has never been put into operation, but it was hoped the dogs own waste material collected over the year and converted to methane would provide the heat to keep this place comfortable in our Wyoming winters."

"There is a substantial kitchen and even living quarters at the end of the building where we planned to prepare healthy home prepared meals using meat from our own grass fed animals as the protein source.

"The open center area is intended to be filled with sawdust and become a dog playground where they can exercise and socialize inside during the winter time. This is my dream and it was Lettie's as well. Before I leave this life, I want to see this dream come true. We'll discuss this over dinner."

I started to ask how we all fit into this, but right then someone began vigorously ringing a dinner bell back at the main house.

Dusty said, "That's Sirena calling us to supper and I don't know about you folks, but I'm famished. Let's get this wagon train back to the house."

Just as I started to press the gas, I saw Dimmit coming into the building from the other end, running full speed and he was not alone. Matching him stride for stride was another Dalmatian.

I pointed at the pair and asked Dusty if the Dalmatian was his dog?

"She sure is. That's Daisy Duke and she's my buddy. She's two years old and I raised her from a pup, bottle fed her and everything. She's smart as she can be and a loyal companion and it looks like she's found herself a handsome feller."

Dimmit was smiling. There's no doubt he was smiling and Daisy Duke looked mighty pleased herself. We took off toward the house and they followed seemingly keeping up without effort.

Sirena greeted us as we parked the carts and ascended the steps. "Come my friends and be seated. In honor of having four other Mexicans dine with us, I have prepared a feast featuring Mexican dishes.

"I am confident everyone will like it as well. Come, come, sit where you wish and we will get started. There is much to eat and much to talk about before this night is over.

"Dusty is a vegetarian, but no one else on this ranch follows this custom. Some of the dishes are vegetarian, but most are not, and I will explain as we are served."

I looked out over the horizon and felt a great inner peace. The fire was crackling in the background as the sun drifted lower in the sky. Down by my feet lay Dimmit and Daisy Duke, both tails wagging like a metronome.

Dusty said, "Let's give thanks. Would you all please join hands?" "Lord, we're all here honored to be Your children and covered by Your love for us. Please guide us in what we do this night and all nights forward. Let us work for the good of all, without envy or jealousy among us. Let us become brothers and sisters working together to bring comfort and security to Your creatures. All the gifts of life are from Your hands and we humbly give thanks. Amen."

Sirena started the meal, "First we will start with salsa and tortilla chips served with delicious melted queso blanco and we shall also serve an appetizer of corn tamales with tomatillo sauce. Some vegetarians eat cheese and some do not. Dusty eats a little sometimes. Tonight he seems so happy, he deserves to have a cheesy smile to go with his happiness.

Everyone seemed to enjoy the first round and were eager to see what came next. The corn tamales were quite good with the peppery sauce and the salsa was absolutely first rate. As good as any I've had anywhere.

"Now, my friends, we shall have shredded beef empanadas with mole sauce and there are also empanadas stuffed with chilies, corn, onion, black beans, and green mango. The latter is vegetarian and one of Dusty's favorites. Do not eat too many, because there is more to come."

We ate and enjoyed each dish. The vegetarian empanada was surprisingly good, but so was everything else. I *accidently* dropped a morsel from time to time and I was surprised and pleased to see Dimmit take his nose and push pieces to Daisy. We were all having a good day!

"Now, here comes two tasty dishes. One is vegetarian and the other is not, but I recommend you try them both. The first one is called Tacos De Pappa. It is made of tacos stuffed with cumin-spiced potatoes and fried till crunchy. It is vegetarian and goes very well with the other dish which is called Quesada al Pollo, which is a simple chicken stew made with chipotles, blue corn, and black beans."

We ate and talked and kept our eye on the sunset which promised to be glorious. The meal was superb and I had partaken of every dish.

Dusty and Sirena were wonderful hosts and I could tell everyone was finding the meal delicious and the company congenial and easy going. Abraham was especially complimentary towards the food and I could tell he was sincere and impressed.

Sirena announced the main course which was Mexican braised spare ribs with squash and corn served with a salad made from mango and shredded coconut sprinkled with a spicy red pepper. It was so good you had to be thankful your momma wasn't sitting at the table.

Dusty was served an interesting masa ball soup in some type of tomato sauce and Consuela chose that as well. I noticed she had stuck with the vegetarian meals eating exactly what Dusty ate.

Charlie said, "Would you look at that sunset? Ain't that a fine one? Uncle Bob always said the sun didn't waste none of its beauty on the flatlanders till it crossed over the Rockies. Tell me Dusty, how did a Wyoming rancher become a vegetarian? Somehow, it just don't seem quite natural."

"Charlie, it came about in a perfectly natural way. My Lettie, God rest her soul, had the kindest heart of anyone I've ever met. She was a pure earth angel and no man ever had a finer and more caring wife. She loved animals with a passion and she couldn't stand to see one suffer or be mistreated."

"She said they have no voice to speak for themselves and we have a responsibility to speak for them. She was always gentle in her teachings. She never badgered anyone or tried to enforce her beliefs on another.

"Lettie, talked the talk and walked the walk, and I listened to my heart and I followed in her footsteps. Years ago this went from a working cattle ranch into a totally different enterprise.

"I now raise prize bulls and I sell bull semen all over the world. It's little known, but most prize cattle are now artificially inseminated and I have bulls that have generated over a million dollars in revenue.

"I sold a Hereford bull named Ajax for $600,000 and I still retain 25% interest in him. We continue to harvest a few head to feed the hands and guests, but we sell none to market for meat."

Chapter 16

"That gets me right to a point where it seems the right time to discuss why I have invited you all here. This especially concerns Debbie and Zed, but I have a feeling all present will play some part in this.

  "Like I said back at the barn, it is my dream that this ranch be turned into a sanctuary for animals, especially dogs. I don't have the years or the energy left to see it done in my lifetime. I have to find someone I can trust to see me and Lettie's dream come to life, and sustained even after I'm gone."

  "I know Debbie's heart and her determination, but she can't do it alone and my dream has led me to you, Zed. I think you too have a pure heart and are a man I can trust with my dream. I have prepared legal documents appointing you two as caretakers of my estate, assuming you'll accept."

  "I need people that will hire the right men and women to make this a home and safe haven for all manner of animals. You will be the de facto owners of *The Anchorage*, lock, stock, and barrel for the rest your lives."

"You can live here, build a home anywhere you want on the ranch. I want you both to oversee it and make sure the right people are hired to make this a reality. If you agree, you will be responsible for finding like-minded people to carry on this venture when your time on earth is done."

  "There is more. In addition to *The Anchorage*, which is comprised of a little over 15,000 acres, Wanda is the registered owner of the 43,000 acre *Buena Vista* ranch that adjoins this place. I arranged some time back for it to be bought in her name."

  "Wanda is throwing her land in with mine and both would be under your stewardship. We want the land preserved and the wildlife protected and managed. Essentially, we want it turned into a national park that's not run by the government."

"I have no issue with hunters or other visitors. I've hunted all my life. Hunting is necessary if the number of animals gets to where it exceeds the carrying capacity of the land, then you get disease and starvation, but I am not a fan of trophy hunting.

  "Hunting will be necessary, but I have a stipulation that it be restricted to disabled hunters, especially wounded veterans, and it is not to cost them a cent once they get here."

  "This is their thank you from an old Navy vet and his shipmates that died at Pearl Harbor, in 1941, all 1,177 of them."

Dusty paused and bowed his head. I saw him take a deep breath and bring a thumb up to rub his eye. He looked up at me and saw the respect I had for him, and he bowed his head again. He composed himself after a few moments and continued.

"That was a terrible day I'll never forget. Not many survivors from the USS Arizona on that brutal day in December, and not but a few of us still drawing breath.

Anyway, this is something I want done first class, no expense spared, to make this into a showplace for animal lovers, photographers, people that crave a connection with nature, but I want it kept pristine and uncrowded.

"Set it up on a permit system, or make it a work for stay, where we only get the right people here that will honor our values."

I had been blown away by the enormity of what he was proposing and I could tell Debbie had been rocked back on her heels too. But he wasn't finished yet.

"Zed and Debbie, I am wealthier than anyone here, except for perhaps Wanda, can imagine. Trust funds have been set up that will run both ranches well beyond any of our lifetimes. You will never have to worry about funding this operation. It's on automatic but you both will have access to substantial discretionary funds each year to apply where you feel it can be best utilized.

"Now, I must apologize to the rest of you. I have to borrow Zed and Debbie for a while to introduce Zed to someone he needs to know. Debbie already knows her a little."

"Lobo, if you and the boys would like to go back and see the motorcycles, this would be a good time, but let me ask you to give me your full legal names, dates, of birth, and social security numbers. I know it's a strange request, but I promise, you won't regret it."

Wanda vigorously nodded her head, "I guarantee you won't regret it. Here, write it down on this pad and print it neat and legible. He'll explain it to you in a bit."

Once this information had been collected, Dusty beckoned us to follow him. He moved well on his walker until we came to the stairwell that had a seat attached to a rail that ran up the wall.

He handed his walker to Debbie and took a seat in the chair. The electric lift carried him to the top at the same speed we climbed it. Debbie handed him back his walker and we started down the corridor. He talked as we walked, pausing frequently.

"I am going to introduce you to my niece. Her name is Riley and she's 26 years old. She's been with me most of her life and I have raised her as my daughter. She's my deceased brother's daughter. Her mother was simply no good. She drank and used cocaine while she was pregnant with Riley, and that may be the cause for her condition."

"Her mother ran off shortly after Riley was born, and my brother drank himself into an early grave. We took her in as an infant before she was even walking and raised her here on the ranch."

"Riley is what is known as an autistic savant. It is a condition that causes developmental disorders and she is socially awkward, sometimes in an extreme way.

"She is extraordinarily gifted with numbers and music, but she only likes music without vocals. The exception to that is that she loves Creedence Clearwater Revival and Bob Seger. She says their words are right with the music."

"She sees music as actual words and she sees numbers as living motion pictures. Her brain works much differently than ours. She is not comfortable in many social situations and large groups of people she simply can't deal with. She has compulsive behaviors and mannerisms that you will quickly become aware of.

"I can predict she will like you immediately, or not at all, and I can't predict how that will go. She will also see you as a color and the color will determine her acceptance of you. She can be extremely outgoing at times, or shutdown and be non-communicative for days.

"No way would she have been able to endure our dinner. The holding hands and the talking, nor would she have eaten the type food we ate. She only eats certain things that must be prepared and served the same exact way each time.

"She can go days without eating at all, especially when she focuses in on something that interests her. She doesn't like to be touched, or have people stand too close to her but she will sometimes touch others. Debbie's size intimidates her, but she's getting over it ... gradually. It's a process that has taken several years now.

"Riley has a condition called misophonia making her intolerant of certain sounds like people chewing, or sneezing. Life in a city with all the noises would be a living hell for her.

"With all that said, she is a genius on a computer and she plays the stock market like a conductor at the Philharmonic, and I mean that literally. You'll see what I mean in a minute.

"My precious girl is different in a very unique way and I love her dearly."

Dusty stopped by a door and flipped a switch outside the door three times up and down. "She knows we are coming but I always warn her with this switch before I enter. Let's go in and meet Riley."

Debbie and I followed Dusty into a large room that was a complete surprise. It had a whole wall of computer monitors and a large spacious desk, more like a table running the length of the wall and three different keyboards evenly spaced on its surface. Indian drum and flute music were playing softly in the background and there was a remarkable young lady sitting in a huge rolling office chair that made her look tiny in comparison.

She was exceptionally pale, with hair so blonde it appeared white under the bright lights. I thought at first she might be an albino, but that was quickly dispelled when I got a quick glimpse of her eyes which were artic blue. It was just a glimpse, as she seemed to be totally unaware of our presence and in a world of her own.

She was rolling between the keyboards focused on the monitors on the wall. She was weaving her hands as if she was folding and forming the air into shapes, and then her fingers danced on the keyboard in a blur, typing at a speed that seemed humanly impossible.

She rolled to the next keyboard and again used her hands like a Hawaiian dancer. It was graceful and enchanting to watch. She *played* the keyboard like a concert pianist but at a speed that look like she was being fast-forwarded.

"We'll have to wait until she's finished. She's in the middle of what she calls a 'movement'."

I noticed over in the corner, safely out of the range of the rolling chair, lay a chubby black and tan Dachshund. The dog's eyes followed Riley as she rolled back and forth along the table. Every move she made the old dogs eyes followed.

I looked around the room and it was clear Riley had a fascination with elephants. Stuffed elephants from small to human size were neatly arranged according to size and color, none touching the other. Both color and black and white framed photos of elephants hung precisely on every wall up to within inches of the ceiling.

Riley had stopped rolling from keyboard to keyboard and with a final flourish of her hands, said, "Ta Da!"

She turned her head around and looked our way but never engaged her eyes with anyone except Dusty, and him only briefly.

She was barefoot, nails unpolished, no makeup, and dressed in a simple white shift. She was smiling but immediately began unconsciously tugging at her hair and rocking rhythmically back and forth. She was beautiful like a porcelain doll.

"Hi, Poppa D, you brought me somebody new. What's your name?"

"My name is Zed, but some people call me Stonebear."

"I will call you Stonebear, because it suits a blue man. I like blue men."

Dusty breathed a sigh of relief, "Thank God for that. I was hoping and praying she would see you as blue. That's her favorite color for people. She says Debbie is pink and that's her second favorite color."

"Poppa D, I see Debbie is not all pink anymore. She's changing and starting to turn blue. Her ears are blue and her hands are too."

Riley had stopped tugging on her hair but she picked up a silk scarf and began tying knots in it, four of them evenly space, and when she got to the end, she unknotted it and started over again. Briefly, her eyes looked into mine.

"Stonebear, did you marry Debbie and that's why she's turning blue?"

"No, Riley, Debbie and I are very good friends, but we are not married."

"Then why is she changing colors? People can't change, can they?"

"Riley, I think people can change, and I think they are supposed to as they learn new things and forget old things they learned that were wrong. I have changed a lot over the last few days and I suspect I will keep changing."

"Stonebear, do you like elephants? I mean really, really like them?"

"Yes, I do. I think they are amazing intelligent animals that can teach us humans how we are supposed to care for one another. Elephants and whales are my favorite animals of all."

"Me too, Stonebear. Have you ever seen a real life elephant with your own eyes?"

"I have, Riley. Many times in other countries and they lived mostly a free life. I've never seen an elephant in a zoo, and I hope I never do. They don't belong there and I know they can't be happy in captivity."

"I want an elephant so bad of my very own. A real live elephant, but Poppa D says I can't have one here in my room. Do you think I could have an elephant in my room?"

"Riley, I can understand why you would want one of your own. I really can, because when I touched one and it touched me back with her trunk, it was a wonderful experience I'll never forget. I can truly understand why you would want one, but an elephant couldn't get up the stairs. They need to be able to move about freely on their own."

"But, I want one Stonebear, more than anything."

I looked over at Dusty who seemed amazed at our conversation and how quickly Riley was responding to me, and he nodded for me to continue.

"Riley, since an elephant can't get up the steps to your room, what do you think could be done to make your dream come true?"

I looked again at Dusty and he was smiling and he again nodded his head for me to continue.

Riley continued knotting and unknotting the scarf and I could tell she was considering my words.

Finally, she answered, "Maybe I could move to a room downstairs with a big door where it could come and go when it wanted too, but I know mostly it would want to stay with me."

One more reassuring nod from Dusty and I followed my instincts. It wasn't exactly a flash, but it was mighty to close to one.

"Riley, it looks like I will be spending a lot of time here at the ranch and I think we will do exactly what you suggest. We will fix you a big room downstairs with big doors and we will find you an elephant just as soon as I can. I promise I will do that and nothing will be more important than making your dream come true."

"Really, Stonebear? Poppa D, is he serious? Am I really going to get an elephant? Oh, please say it's true. Please tell me this is real."

"Yes, baby. Stonebear is a man of his word and if he says you are getting an elephant, you are getting an elephant. You have both his and my word on it."

Riley awkwardly walked to Dusty and gave him a brief hug and then turned to me. I thought she might hug me too, but instead, she looked at me with her glacier blue eyes and said, "I love you Stonebear." And then she dropped her scarf on the floor and began to weep.

I looked around the room and we all looked a little teary eyed. I think I had shed more happy tears since coming to Wyoming than in all of my previous life. Happy tears do water the soul and grow the spirit.

"Riley, it does please your Poppa D's old heart to see you so happy. Now, before I forget, here's a list of three new friends I want you to work on. Start them all with $50,000 in their account and shoot for the moon."

Riley took the list and replied, "To the moon Poppa D, to the moon."

She picked up her scarf and unknotted it and returned to her rolling chair, seemingly now oblivious to our presence and her fingers once again flew across the keyboard. The old Dachshund followed her with his eyes all the way but never moved from his spot.

Dusty indicated we should leave and we exited the door and he gently closed it behind us.

"Her room is totally soundproofed and she can't hear us now. I thank the good Lord for how that went. I never in my life would have believed it would go that well. It is an answer to my prayers, because I want both of you to become her guardians when I'm gone.

It's a mighty big thing I'm asking of you. Her genius with the stock market would make her the target of people that would use her like a piece of machinery. She has to be protected from the world and her ability kept a closely guarded secret. Only you two, Sirena and Wanda know about her money making ability and I would like to keep it that way."

I shook Dusty's hand and Debbie did too, and we pledged our word that we would look after her as best we could. It was easy for me to do. I liked Riley. I liked her as much as I had ever liked anyone that I had just met. I needed Uncle Bob's advice. He was the expert in the family on acquiring elephants, but I knew I would figure it out. It was part of my path.

"I want you both to know I've been trying to get that child moved downstairs for years. Even back when Lettie was still alive, we both tried our hardest, but autistic people don't do well with change and Riley can be stubborn as a mule."

"Just goes to show you, what it says in the good book is right on the money. '*A prophet is not without honor except in his own country, among his own relatives, and in his own house.*' You bring in somebody new, especially if he's a "blue man" and durn if things don't make a sea change."

"Stonebear, would you mind if I hugged you? I don't quite know how to say what I'm feeling right now. My old heart hadn't been this much at peace in a while, but I surely know what I'm feeling."

I hugged Dusty. One of those long meaningful hugs that replace words, and when I was finished, Debbie hugged him too. Then she gave me a fierce bear hug that squeezed the breath out of me.

"Stop it Debbie. I just ate a ton of Mexican food, and if you squeeze me any tighter I am going to bust wide open like a piñata. You are a big old pink peach of a woman with Smurf colored ears and hands, but you don't know your own strength."

Dusty broke in, "C'mon you two. I see those new bear tattoos on your neck, and I want to get Lobo to give me one too. Debbie knows where I want it and I'll trust you two, and Lobo, to keep that a secret until after I'm dead and gone."

"My Lettie had a little bear tattooed over her heart and don't a soul know that but us. Debbie saw it when she was trying to revive Lettie. I want my paw print over my heart just like Lettie, and I'd like to get it done tonight because this has been a remarkable day. Yes sir, this has been a most wonderful day and that will be the cherry on top, me getting tattooed."

We made our way back down the stairs just like before. Dusty riding his lift chair and me and Debbie walking by his side with Debbie carrying his walker like it was a toy.

No one was in the main room, so we walked back through the kitchen and found Abraham teaching Sirena how to make Diablo coffee. They were laughing and speaking in rapid fire Spanish.

They gave us a cheerful wave as we passed through. We continued on outside finding Wanda and Consuela alone and peacefully enjoying the fire. Consuela had a bowl of pickles in front of her, and Dimmit and Daisy Duke were still enthralled with each other's company. It looked like love was in the air.

Wanda looked up, "Well Dusty, how did it go with Riley?"

"It went so well I am just amazed. I know you said it might go like this, but I can't believe how quick Riley took to Stonebear, almost right from the start. I thought for a moment she was going to hug him. She came close, she really did. She even told him she loved him. Of course, he told her she was going to get an elephant first."

"Are you serious? That dear child is going to get an elephant at last? How in the dickens are you going to do that?"

Dusty threw back his head and laughed, "I have delegated that promise to Stonebear and Debbie. You know how hard we've tried to get that girl to move downstairs and Stonebear accomplished in minutes what we've tried to do for years. I believe they will figure it out and I expect they will find a way sooner rather than later."

"Guess what? Shucks, I'll just go ahead and tell you. You'd never guess it in a million years. She said Stonebear was a blue man, and even Debbie was starting to turn blue. She said her ears and hands had turned blue, and she even asked if Stonebear and Debbie were married."

"Now, where are my biker friends and Charlie? I've got to get me a tattoo and I want to get it done tonight, if Lobo's not too tired."

I saw the headlights of the golf cart headed back to the house and I assured Dusty, "Don't you worry about Lobo. When he gets back and finds we have Diablo coffee available, he'll stay up all night and tattoo everything on the whole ranch. Of course you might have to feed him again. He's a mighty big man and he told me he's been too empty, but he's never been too full."

The golf cart pulled up with a whine and Lobo shut it down. The four of them made it back on deck and had a seat at the table. There was a distinct air of excitement and enthusiasm that emanated from the four of them that I could feel like a physical wave of energy. The boys and Charlie were pumped up about something.

Before Dusty could ask about the tattoo, Lobo began to speak, "Dusty we found your trike you're working on and it's a fine piece of machinery. Me and the boys don't want to overstep on another man's project, but we'd be happier than a possum eating a sweet tater to pitch in and help out.

Cisco and Pancho both acknowledged their willingness to help and Cisco added, "Pancho and me, we are the best motorcycle mechanics and the best painters in the country, and I tell you this true, without having the big head. La verdad es la verdad, and that means the truth is the truth. Lobo, he will tell you the same and he is the best designer in the country.

Together, we three amigos will have you rolling in style in time to ride with us to Wanda and Charlie's wedding, if you will give us your *permiso* to do such a thing,"

You could tell old Dusty was taken aback by this news, and I was a little blown away by it myself, but it didn't take long before Dusty let us know what he thought of the idea.

"You fellers making that offer is a blessing to this old man's heart. I would be mighty proud to ride with you to the wedding. I truly would, but I want to be sporting the mark of the bear when I do, and I would be grateful if you could do me tonight. It was going to be a secret, but I reckon you all just earned the right to know. Lobo, I want it done over my heart, if you are up to it?

"As for the trike, you men use your judgment and I feel certain I'll be pleased with what you men come up with."

Right then Abraham stuck his head out the door, "Who would like Diablo coffee, the first ever made by Sirena, and I assure you it is autentico, I mean authentic, just the way we make it at the cafe?"

That met with everyone's hearty approval, except for Consuela, who requested a small glass of pickle juice instead.

"Shoot-fire Dusty, you keep the Diablo coming and I could tattoo an elephant before sunup. Let me get a cup or two down and we'll get her done."

I had to grin at the timeliness of that remark. "Lobo, we happen to be in the market for an elephant. I'm serious about that. You don't happen to know where a man might get his hands on one, do you?"

Lobo laughed, "I'll be dadblamed if you ain't about the most interesting man I've run across, and I've run across some real dillies in my time. I'm afraid I can't help you out with an elephant."

"Bout time you folks let old Charlie back into this free-wheeling rodeo. Son, I would have thought you would have knowed to ask your Daddy anything you want to know about elephants. Uncle Bob shared all he knowed about them with me, and I met a feller up in hunting camp some years back. He's from New Mexico, down south of Santa Fe.

"He's got a spread of about 500 acres and he shelters some elephants. I don't remember how many, but last time I talked with him he had four and he said it was getting to be more than he could handle.

You folks go get Dusty all tattooed up, and I'll get on the horn with him and see if I can't round you up some pachyderms. How many of them rascals you reckon you want, what size, and how soon you want them?"

I grinned at Debbie and she grinned right back. She read my mind and threw her head back and howled like a wolf. I jumped right in there and howled too, and old Dimmit and Daisy Duke didn't lag far behind. Pretty soon, the whole table was howling, except for Consuela, who was laughing so hard, she had to go pee.

I had another flash right that exact moment and it struck me with such force, I had to share it without delay. "Dusty, you reckon there's a place between *the Anchorage* and *the Buena Vistas* to put a wolf sanctuary?"

"Stonebear, I think you must be made in the same mold as me. Wolves are near and dear to my heart and I would cherish the thought of a wolf sanctuary being established on this land.

"There's a perfect spot up on *the Buena Vistas* for one. It's as pretty a piece of land as exists in these parts. We could fence in 500 acres, no belay that, we could fence in a 1,000 acres where they could roam and live a pretty normal life. I know they'd much rather roam free but they would be safe from being shot, poisoned and trapped."

Abraham and Sirena showed up with a tray of Diablo and a glass of pickle juice for Consuela, with a dill slice stuck on the rim. We enjoyed our coffee as a mix of conversations went around the table. Everything from elephants, motorcycles and wolves were being discussed and I had to smile at how right it all felt. My heart felt good and I was definitely on my path.

"Now folks, Lobo and I are going to go get me inked up, but before I leave, I need to tell you all something and it's important. I am a very wealthy and blessed man, and what I'm about to tell you, I speak from knowledge and experience. It is often incorrectly said that money is the root of all evil. It's not the money that's evil. No sir, it's the *love of money* that's evil.

"You all put these words in your heart, and remember them, because you all are going to be wealthy. I have established an investment account in each of your names and every one of you started out with $50,000, and it will grow faster than you can imagine. Trust me on this. Use your money to help others.

"That's its purpose. Do not let greed or selfishness taint your heart, because if you do, money will corrupt you. When you leave this world, all the money and property you leave behind doesn't amount to a hill of beans if you haven't left a wealth of good memories.

"Tomorrow around lunch time, my lawyers and accountants and banker will be landing here in a helicopter with some papers for you to sign. It will all become official then, but your money is already at work for you.

"C'mon Lobo, let's get me inked up and you and I can talk some while you work."

Lobo got up in an absolute daze. Dusty grabbed his walker and they headed back to the kitchen on the way out to the rolling tattoo parlor.

After they left we all looked at each other and it was comical the expressions on our faces. I saw dumbfounded and flabbergasted looks which I am sure mirrored my own. Every face was the same except Wanda's. She knew about all this beforehand. You could tell by her smile.

"Let me elaborate a little on what Dusty said. He first off told you the truth. He did Lobo's, Cisco's and Pancho's under their legal names just a bit ago. That's why he wanted that information on that piece of paper.

"Debbie, he sat yours up years ago and you are already a multi-millionaire. Zed, he just started yours, but he set yours up starting at a million because that's what he meant when he said you and Debbie would have access to substantial discretionary funds to apply where you saw fit.

"Dusty is a generous man and smart as a whip. He's taken a liking to all of you. Heed his words, I beg you. Don't let this money change you. It will try, and it will pull at you hard. That's the temptation money brings with it.

"I could buy the fanciest motorhome made, one of those million dollar rigs, with satellite TV and a Jacuzzi, but that doesn't fit who I am. Our rolling honeymoon is plumb perfect for me and my man."

She continued, "Charlie is looking like he swallowed a goldfish and I sure wish I had a camera to get a picture of that look on his face. He's about to look like he swallowed a whole bowl of goldfish, because when Dusty found out we were getting married, he sat up old Marlon Brando here with a million dollar account.

"He's rich enough to attract the interest of some floozy gold digger, but I figure he's plenty smart enough to know better. Like I've said before, in the immortal words of Annie Oakley. '*I ain't afraid to love a man. I ain't afraid to shoot him either.*' He's stuck with me till death do us part."

I looked at Debbie, and said, "Why don't we go get another cup of Diablo and go sit on the front porch. We need to talk."

We excused ourselves and went into the kitchen. Sirena was singing a song in Spanish that I was familiar with. I knew what the words meant in English, at least the last verse, I knew what that meant and it seemed entirely appropriate.

The song was "Guantanamera" and the last verse translated as…
With the poor people of the earth
I cast my lot
Mountain streams
Please me more than the seas

Chapter 17

Debbie and I got our coffee and made it to the spacious veranda and took a seat in one of the cushioned swings. We gently rocked back and forth, sipping our coffee, pleased at the silence.

I knew her mind had to be racing like mine, but we knew each other well enough to let it sit for a spell. I pondered my own situation.

I had wandered into Wyoming, on foot, an orphan that never knew his father. I now had two fathers, a mother, and a bright, vivacious teenage daughter.

I had become a licensed driver, a custodian of a powerful red truck named Snowbird, and I was a genuine badge toting Wyoming lawman.

I had found an amazing diamond that made dreams come true. I had undergone an incredible vision quest that was definitely already changing my life.

I had become a millionaire and I had made friends worth more than all the treasures on earth, and one day in the not too distant future, I was going to become a godfather to Abraham and Consuela's child. I didn't bother to ponder whether I was worthy of all of this.

I knew I wasn't, no man or woman could be. What was expected of me? Was I man enough? I knew the answer to the last question and yes, I was man enough, and I said a well remember verse from the book to myself … *"I can do all things through Christ who strengthens me."*

Yep, no way could Debbie and I do this on our own. We would have to have the help of the Big Boss again, just like when we rolled that stone and rescued the little girl.

I long ago learned you can't out give the Universe. I know I had tried. It reminded me of some more words from the book, and I'm sure I don't have it exact, but it is something to the effect, *to whom much is given, much is expected.*

I switched my coffee cup to my other hand and reached out and took Debbie's big hand in mine. We didn't say a word. I felt her heart beat and it matched mine. After a while, Dimmit and Daisy Duke found us and they lay down beside us, shoulder to shoulder.

I leaned over and kissed Debbie on the cheek and she squeezed my hand. "Goodnight Debbie, I've got to go pray."

"Goodnight Zed, I'm going to pray right here."

I got up and went into the house, followed by Dimmit and Daisy. I made my way to the Bear Den, and Dimmit immediately jumped up on the bed. Daisy gave me a questioning look, and I said, "Go on up girl, there's room for a half dozen of us up there, but you two don't get any ideas from what I just said." She made a graceful leap and nestled herself against Dimmit.

I prayed while I brushed my teeth. I prayed while I took off my boots and removed my clothes. I prayed while I turned down the covers and right before I started to climb in the bed to pray, I changed my mind and dropped to my knees.

I hadn't done that since I prayed for my momma in the hospital when she was dying with cancer. I don't know how to make those flowery prayers like some do. It's not my style. I talk to God, but He doesn't even need the words. He reads my heart. The words are for me.

"God, I love you and I know you love me. You show me every day how much You care for me and you also show me what You expect from me. I kind of think You might be smiling as it's beginning to dawn on me just how much You do expect from me. You know I'm going to try. You know I want to."

"More than anything I want to please You, and fulfill my purpose and do only good. You and I both know my weaknesses, and I am working on them and I know with Your help I can become a better man."

"I want to be worthy of all these blessings and friends You are bringing into my life. I think You have led me right where I'm supposed to be. I don't think I've ever been happier or felt more at home than here with these people."

"I know You don't need these words or these tears rolling down my cheek to know my words are true from the heart. I am before You, with my soul laid bare asking Your guidance and protection on all of us as we follow our paths and find others to help along the way."

"I ask for Your help with Riley. Give me the wisdom to be of purpose in her life, to know what to say, and help me to protect her from any that would take advantage of her. I see my cup is overflowing, and I know goodness and mercy will follow me all the days of my life. Goodnight God."

I awakened early, well before sunrise, and dressed as quietly as I could. Dimmit and Daisy were sleeping peacefully and I didn't want to disturb them because I wanted a few moments alone.

I made my way through the dark and silent house to the front door and opened it without a sound and eased it shut behind me.

I took a seat in same swing where Debbie and I had sat the night before. It didn't take long for my eyes to adjust and I could soon make out the silhouettes of the elk still out there on the lawn. All were laying down except for the bull. He was up and standing guard fulfilling his natural purpose.

I kind of envied him. His job seemed a little less complicated than mine. I tried to think of all the things I had to be thankful for and it was a rolling mass of things that seemed all intertwined in my head. I had a heap of things to be thankful for.

Mind boggling, in fact. I had so much to do, finding a starting point was confusing. I thought back to Riley, and her scarf and I thought back on the advice given to me by Ironbear. It became clear to me, I had to undo one knot at a time and eat this "buffalo" a bite at a time.

I also reflected back on the words of a stern old Dutch captain I had served under. He was a strict taskmaster but fair. I learned a lot under his leadership. I remember his words so well. *"I expect near perfection and the simultaneous execution of multiple priorities."*

The remembrance made me smile. He was a tough one for sure, but he taught me well. Under him I learned to delegate tasks and hold people responsible for duties assigned to them.

I also learned that when you expect a lot of people, give them the right tools to accomplish a task and you treat them fair, they will bust their butts for you. People are always capable of greater things than they think they are when they are helped and get praised for their efforts.

The sky began to lighten just a bit. It was a chilly morning and I could see the steam coming from the bull elk's nostrils out there on the lawn. He was ready to get his busy day under way too. He made a light chuckling sound that I had not heard before. Birds begin singing their morning wake up calls.

I sat there in the swing and made some decisions that felt right. I knew I had to get Ironbear and Snowbird down to *the Anchorage* to meet Dusty, and I needed to ask him if he had enough money to buy a hospital.

Once I undid those knots and swallowed those bites, I would get on the task of finding an elephant for Riley. Piece of cake, I thought to myself; a great big humongous piece of cake, but I didn't have to do it all by myself.

139

I was going to delegate, and I knew who to start with. I needed to meet Red, the foreman whose meticulous attention to detail that showed in the immaculate barns and how efficiently the golf carts were delivered, clean, charged and ready as soon as Dusty called for them.

He ran a first class ship and I was confident he had a fine and well trained crew working for him. I would also seek help from Sirena. She had greatly impressed me with her poise and intelligence and her obvious devotion and loyalty to Dusty was a real plus. I knew she would be eager to help Dusty see his dream come to life.

Lobo was also a leader of a different type, but a leader, nonetheless. I knew men would look up to him, not only because of his size, but also his winning personality and intelligence. The last person that came to mind surprised me a little.

It would take some patience and skill, but I thought Riley's role could be expanded beyond the limits of her self-imposed exile in her little world. I didn't know how I was going to tackle that one, but with God's help, I would give it my best effort.

The bull elk and I greeted the rising sun. Me with deep gratitude and the bull with a huge roaring challenge. He received no response and judging from the size of his harem, he had established his dominance and no one wanted to take him on, at least not for a rematch.

Each Wyoming sunrise was special, but this morning was undeniably spectacular. It was almost like my Creator letting me know all would be well. Just keep the faith and walk my path. It was time for me to go shower and let the dogs out and maybe by then some thoughtful person will have brewed up a pot of Diablo.

Chapter 18

After my shower, and warning Dimmit to leave the elk alone, I let him and Daisy out the door to ramble. I made my way to the kitchen and navigation was much easier now that the sun was up, but after just one day and night here, I was already feeling familiar with the big rambling house.

Despite the grandeur of the massive logs and the impressive artwork, the place most definitely had a "homey" feel to it.

I was finding that everywhere I went in Wyoming, from Charlie's humble desert diggings, to this handcrafted masterpiece, seemed to embrace me and make me feel welcome.

The same feel I had in my room above Wanda's cafe was the same feeling I got when I entered Ironbear's surprising Swiss chalet on the reservation. I think Wyoming liked me and I most definitely liked it back.

Before I reached the kitchen, my nose let me know coffee was ready, or soon would be. You can tell by the aroma when it's right. Use insufficient grounds or too much water, and you can boil it till Doomsday, and it'll never be right. Might as well be drinking tea, not that there's anything wrong with tea. I've drunk my share of it, but it doesn't crank my tractor, so to speak, for morning fare.

I entered the kitchen and it was bustling with early morning activity. Sirena was orchestrating the breakfast preparation, and Abraham was by her side fitting in nicely with the rest of the kitchen crew.

Dusty and Lobo were preparing themselves a cup of Diablo and talking about motorcycles. With them was a man I hadn't met yet, but based on his flaming hair and beard, I assumed he must be the foreman that went by the name Red.

He was much younger than I expected for a man with that much responsibility. I was expecting a middle-aged man, and he couldn't have been much over Riley's age. Late 20's would be my guess.

He was a fine looking man with an honest face and a lean build. He was one of those rare redheads that took to the sun well and he was tanned from a life spent outdoors.

He was dressed in typical cowboy attire; boots and jeans, denim shirt, but instead of a cowboy hat, he wore an Alabama ball cap with an embroidered elephant patch on the front. I thought there is no way there could be another Bama boy out here on a Wyoming ranch.

I introduced myself, "Howdy, you must be, Red. I go by Zed, or Stonebear, whichever one you like."

Red, shook my hand, "Yep that would be me, and I've heard good things about you, Zed, and I'm pleased to meet you."

"I see by your hat you are a Crimson Tide fan."

Red looked a little confused for a moment, then he smiled, "Not exactly Mr. Zed, I wear the hat because I know Miss Riley is crazy about elephants, and I wear it mostly for her."

I understood immediately. This red haired red bearded young man was smitten with Riley. I completely understood and I thought of how frustrating that must be for him to be attracted to someone that would probably run from his presence.

"I met her for the first time last night and I was impressed with her, and she most surely does like elephants. Her room is full of them all different sizes and colors. Pictures all over the wall too."

"I know. I gave her most of them."

"You must be a good friend of hers."

"I would like to be, but I don't rightly know. I've been on this ranch since I was 16, and she's never spoken a word to me. Not one.

"Mr. Dusty, tells me it's nothing personal. It's just the way she is, and I mostly understand that. I wish there was some way I could be her friend and she would talk to me. Just a little would be fine. Did she talk to you last night?"

I almost hated to tell him, but I did. "Yes, we spoke some, not a lot, but more than Dusty thought she was capable of. Mostly, we talked about elephants and I told her we were going to get her one."

"Are you for real, Mr. Zed? You are going to get an elephant for Riley? Is there any way I could help? Anyway at all?"

I had a flash that pleased and inspired me. "Thank you Lord, I needed that."

"First off, unless you want me to call you Mr. Red, I would like you to call me just Zed. Mr. Red and Mr. Zed sound like some kind of comedy act. I had planned to look you up this morning because I do need your help."

"When it was presented to Riley as a possibility for her to have an elephant, I asked her what she would need to do to help make it a reality. She volunteered this completely on her own.

"She said she would need to move downstairs and have a room with a big door where the elephant could come and visit her and be free to leave when it needed to.

"So, the first way you can help is to tell me where we can move her and how long will it take."

Red removed his hat and ruffled his thick hair, "Zed, I reckon we better get Mr. Dusty's idea on that. He's still the boss and he knows more about the possibilities in this house than me. Anything outside of the big house and I'm your man, but I need his say so on anything that goes on in here."

"Fair enough Red, let's ask him right now."

"Dusty, can you spare us a minute or two? Red and I need your help on something."

"I'll be right with you boys, just hold your horses a bit and I'll be over."

While I was waiting on Dusty, I asked Red, "How much do you know about elephants?"

"Not near enough Zed. I've tried to study them some. I've never seen one in person and I can't get to the library in Lander very often.

"We've got Wi-Fi out in the bunkhouse, but I don't know much about computers, so I have to rely on books. I want to know a lot more, but I don't know where to learn."

On cue, Charlie ambled into the kitchen with his customary grin on his face. "Howdy son, who's your new friend?"

I introduced Charlie and Red, and asked about how his call went with his buddy down in New Mexico.

"Zed, I reckon it went right well. He was plumb tickled to hear from me. He's busted up a mite. His old horse got spooked by a tumbleweed and scraped him along a fence, but he'll mend. His name's Homer, but I call him Half Pint."

"He's a little feller but tougher than a $2 steak. He's only about 5 foot-nothing on a good day, but the old boy don't have no quit in him.

"He's still got three elephants. One's not much more than a baby. Her momma died giving birth. Them other two elephants are older and they've looked out for the youngen like she's one of their own, but he had to bottle feed her until last month.

"That baby ain't but 6 months old but already weighs near 400 pounds. He said they was the Indian kind of elephants. You know them littler ones? The grown gals are about 8-9 foot at the shoulder and probably go a good 9,000 pounds each. He said they was gentle and easy to manage."

"That's interesting Charlie, but would Homer, or Half Pint as you call him, be interested in selling any of those elephants?"

"That's what I'm fixin' to tell you son, if you'll keep your powder dry. Hells-bells, boy, I ain't had cup of coffee yet and my brain's dragging like the wagon that's done flung a wheel."

"Now, here's what Half Pint told me and he told it square up. He's done got hisself in a mess with the blamed IRS. Seems folks been donating some here and there for the elephants' upkeep and Half Pint spent it all on elephants and didn't declare it as no income to hisself."

"Swears it all went for them elephants and he didn't make a cent off of it. That old boy is plumb honest as the day is long, and he's kind of lost as last year's Easter egg, dealing with them lowdown varmints at the IRS.

"He's a poor man, don't draw nothing but a disabled veterans pension, and I know that ain't enough to stay in beans, much less bacon.

"So, to answer you direct, he's looking mighty hard for a good place to put his elephants, but he ain't got a nickel left to ship them nowheres, and he's about to run out of feed for them critters too. If money was gasoline he wouldn't have enough to drive a piss-ants motorcycle around a toothpick."

I knew I had to interrupt Charlie, or this might go on for hours before he got to the point. "Dad, how much is Half Pint in debt to the IRS for? Give me a number."

"Well now, best I could figure with penalties and interest he owes them a little over $14,000, and that might as well be a million, cause Half Pint ain't likely to have no good fortune come his way."

Dusty joined us, "What can I do for you boys? Sorry, it took me so long to get free. That Lobo is an interesting fellow but when he gets started on motorcycles, he can talk the horns off a billy goat."

"Dusty, I've got a few things to ask you, and get your opinion on. First, Charlie's found three elephants he can get for free. One's just a baby, a 400 pound baby, but she's only 6 months old.

"The other two are female and kind of look after the little one. An old disabled vet friend of his has gotten into trouble with the IRS. He's been sheltering and caring for them with his veteran's pension and donations. He didn't declare the donations as income and for lack of $14,000 he's about to lose his ranch."

"Stop right there Stonebear. I think I am seeing where you are going. You are wanting to get these three elephants and compensate this man enough money to save his ranch even though he's offering them for free. Do you think that's a sound business practice?"

"Dusty, I can't say I know a great deal about sound business, but I have learned sound heart business is good for the soul."

"Stonebear, the more I know you, the more you impress me. I was hoping you'd say that. I wanted to see how you would respond to having your idea challenged. I am a firm believer in doing business from the heart, so yes sir, I agree completely with that. What else do you want to ask me?"

"I want to fly Red down to Santa Fe, with a certified check in his pocket, let him rent a car and go meet up with this man. I want Red to get all the knowledge he can while he's there and also to make sure the elephants are healthy. I want him to become our resident elephant expert, and maybe even bring this old fellow back up with him to advise on the setup we'll need."

Dusty looked at me and smiled with a twinkle in his eye, "Do you know what you're doing Stonebear? I think I know where you're going with this, but son, you've picked a tall mountain to climb."

"I think I do, and we had a saying back in Alabama, I always liked…"*It ain't no hill for a climber*," I think I can do this with God's help."

Dusty chuckled, "Well you sure aren't afraid of a challenge, I'll give you that." Anything else you want to ask?"

"Two more things Dusty, what room do you think would be best to convert to Riley's new quarters and I want to buy a hospital. I want to buy the hospital in Lander. I don't know what that might cost, but it's part of my path I saw in my vision."

Dusty burst out in the most spontaneous laughter I'd seen him display in the short time I'd known him.

"Now, if that don't beat all, buy a hospital is what you want to do, is it?" Sure, why not? Why don't I just buy a big hospital like in Laramie or Cheyenne?"

"Maybe, down the road Dusty, right now the one in Lander will do fine for what I want."

C'mon Red, let's take Stonebear down to the game room and see what we can come up with by putting our heads together, but Stonebear, you and I are going to talk about this hospital thing. I like it and I am intrigued by the idea.

We'll have a sit down and talk after we get the lawyers and bank people out of here, or maybe even I'll get a couple to stay over. Maybe this evening just you me and Debbie and them, we'll talk this over. Let's get down to the game room and see what we can see."

Red and I followed Dusty down the hall. He moved well on his walker and he surprised me with his mental alertness and how quickly he surmised my plans. Wanda said he was as smart as a whip, and she was dead on target with that evaluation.

Dusty paused by two carved wooden doors, and indicated for Red to open them up.

I immediately saw the potential of the vast room. It was as big as most houses, probably between 3-4,000 square feet and it had the soaring rafters of the main room with plenty of headspace for even a full grown elephant, and another substantial stone fireplace.

The room had a couple of pool tables, a ping pong table and a half dozen other tables where folks could play cards or sit around and talk. Double paned French doors led to the veranda and Dusty walked that way, and Red opened them up.

This was a side of the place I had not seen before. Several hundred yards away lay a pristine man-made lake that had a substantial deck and a swimming platform. Some kind of fish, probably trout were dimpling the surface and a pair of mallards were paddling along the smooth surface.

"Here's how I see it, and I have been studying on this matter since Riley indicated she's willing to make the move.

"The room's too big for Riley the way it's set up. There's two full baths here, one at either end. I propose we build a soundproof room in this corner just like she has upstairs with her work area, bedroom and bath made private from the rest of the room.

"I want to make it as close to identical as what she has now. That's important for her to be able to make the transition as smooth as possible."

"What else do you see that needs done, Red?"

"Mr. Dusty, I'm not sure what the goal is here but I'm thinking you want this room to be able to accommodate an elephant, is that right?"

"Yes, Red, from a baby sized elephant up to a full grown one or two. I don't know how sociable they are but from what I've read the big ones look out for the little ones, so count on two full grown ones and a baby that will eventually become full grown."

"Mr. Dusty, a Wyoming winter is going to be a hard go for them, so they are going to need some kind of heated shelter with a connecting walkway between the shelter and this room.

"We can build a solid ramp up to the deck with pressure switch that will open an outer door when they come up the ramp and then close it behind them when they pass a certain point. That'll keep the cold air out for the most part.

"I know the foundation will hold them no problem at all. The problem is timing. The boys can build the soundproof room and the ramp, and pretty quick too, but a heated shelter is going to take some time and money to build and winter is right around the corner."

"You are right about winter being close at hand Red, but we've got a situation that calls for a temporary solution while we work and plan for the long haul. What would you propose for a temporary solution so we can put a smile on Riley's face?"

Red grinned and blushed a little under his tan. "Mr. Dusty, I'd recommend we put a crew working on the room and the ramp right straight away.

Next, we'd tackle making the doorway where it could accommodate a full grown elephant to come back and forth without having to squat down. I'd pull out those French doors and put in insulated barn doors in their place.

"You'd lose the view, but it could be done in our own shop. Everything we need is at hand and a couple of the boys are better than fair carpenters."

"That sounds good to me Red, but is this going to be enough space for two grown elephants and a baby too?"

"If you two fellows don't mind a suggestion, I wonder if the French doors couldn't be inset into the barn doors, kind of like a stained glass window, so you could keep the view.

"And while I understand the need to make this transition as easy as possible for Riley, I want to make this a challenge for her as well. Her passion for elephants might just work to expand her boundaries."
Dusty rubbed his chest where I knew he'd been tattooed. Mine itched too, and I reached to the back of my neck and gave it a gently rub.

"Stonebear that might work. It just might be what we need to break through that wall she has to keep herself isolated from others. If elephants won't do it, nothing else has a chance."

"I like that idea of keeping the view too, and that's a sailor thinking right there. You have to have a porthole to keep a sharp weather eye while you're below decks. So, where would you put them?"

"What do you think of housing the elephants in the big barn you showed us where the dog shelter is going to go? There's plenty of room in the center for three elephants to roam and not be cramped and elephants and dogs are pretty friendly with each other from what I saw in Asia. You'll also find them very generous 'donors' to your methane digester. They poop considerable more volume than a poodle."

"I like it Stonebear, and it has great potential for Riley to expand her horizons, but we'll have to take it slow and careful.

"We have a deluxe insulated trailer we transport prize bulls in and we can move the baby back and forth between the barn and here, regardless of how bad the weather is. We can tow it behind one of our Snowcats if need be, even in the dead of winter."

"Alrighty then Red, move all this game equipment to the bunkhouse and if there's too much, store it away. We'll find a likely place for any excess, or Stonebear will.

"Let's get a crew to working on the room for Riley, and the ramp right off. Get Sirena to make you a plane reservation to Santa Fe and arrange for a rental car.

"I'll draw you up a check for the fellow they call Half Pint as soon as I get his real name from Charlie, some travelling money and directions to his spread."

"Anything else Stonebear, before we set ourselves down for some breakfast?"

"I would like to try something right now with your permission, of course."

"Go ahead son, and lay it on me. You haven't shown yourself to be bashful so far and there's no need to start now."

"I would like to take Red upstairs to Riley's room and flip that switch three times to let her know I'm there. Then, I want to open the door and ask Riley to come stand inside the door and listen to me talk to Red ... just listen, so she'll know what's going on and she can be thinking about it. I also want her to hear Red's voice and to know how he's involved. What do you think?"

"It could be a start Stonebear, and we won't know if it will work out unless we try."

I handed Red a pen and a piece of paper from one of the card tables and asked him to write his full legal name, date of birth, and social security number down for me. Once he'd done that, I said, "Let's get a start on this, follow me."

We mounted the stairs and as we proceeded down the hallway, I asked Red to respond simply to any questions I asked, and to talk to me like we were alone. He agreed and we proceeded to Riley's door and I hit the switch three times.

I opened the door and stuck my head inside. Riley was sitting on the floor with the elderly black and tan Dachshund sitting serenely in her lap while Bob Seger played quietly in the background. She was unadorned and dressed in the same white shift, or one just like it.

"Hi Riley, I have some news about elephants. If you'll come to the door and listen while I hold it open, you can hear what we've learned. You don't have to talk, but I'm leaving a piece of paper with some information on it. Take it and the number I wrote from my account and take it to the moon. OK?"

She said nothing but gently lifted the dog from her lap and stood up. I could see she had been crying. I stepped back outside her door.

After a moment I addressed Red, "I understand you have found three elephants, is that right?"

"Yes, Zed, we've found three down in New Mexico, on a ranch outside of Santa Fe."

"What kind of elephants are they, Red?"

"They are the smaller ones, the kind they call Indian elephants."

"How old are they Red, and are they boys or girls?"

"Zed, they are all girls, two grown ones and a baby, not but six months old, and I heard she weighs 400 pounds."

"Is one of the girls the baby's mother?"

"No sir, Zed, the way I heard it, the baby's momma died giving birth and the little one's an orphan and the two grown ones look after the little one."

"What do you think we should do about these three elephants all the way down in New Mexico and us up here in Wyoming?"

I winked at Red after I presented him with the last question and he carried the ball like a pro.

"I think I'll get on an airplane and fly down to New Mexico, and see about bringing them back to *the Anchorage* just as quick as it can be arranged."

"Where are we going to put three elephants and how are we going to fix it where Riley can see them and be with them?"

Red and I went through the same discussion as we held downstairs, outlining the plans for altering the game room and where the elephants would be housed. Riley never said a word but I could hear her quick breathing just out of sight. I could almost feel her heartbeat, and maybe I could, or maybe it was just my own.

Once we had gone through it all, I asked Red if he could think of anything else.

"No sir, Zed, I think that pretty much covers it all, so I'll get with Sirena and see about getting myself on down to Santa Fe as soon as I can get on a plane."

I reached to pull the door closed but Riley held on to the knob inside.

"His name is Stonebear, not Zed, and your name should be Blue, not Red. To the moon Stonebear, all the way to the moon," and she gently closed the door.

I put my arm around Red and said, "Son, looks like you just got christened 'Blue' and that's a mighty fine thing. Changing names is not a big thing at all. I do it right regularly."

"Did Riley just speak to me?

"Son, unless you know anyone else on this ranch named Red, she was speaking directly to you and you'd better start calling me Stonebear, and I'll for sure be calling you Blue until it's grown plumb natural to you. If you are the praying sort, you might want to say a thank you to the Man upstairs because that went about as well as could be expected."

"Thank you Lord, and if you keep moving these stones from my way, I'll follow this path You've put us on."

We joined the entire group once again dining outside for our breakfast meal. They were engaged in lively conversation and I got a fine feeling seeing them all together enjoying each other's company. I had lots to do, but *it's no hill for a climber*, especially with a crew like I saw seated before me.

Dusty spoke first, "How did it go Red?"

"Well Mr. Dusty, my head's kind of doing flips, but I reckon everybody better start calling me Blue, because Riley said that should be my name."

"My dear Lord, she spoke to you? She actually spoke to you?"

"Yes sir, and Zed …. I mean Stonebear, heard her too, didn't you Stonebear."

"That's right everyone and her exact words were, "His name is Stonebear, not Zed, and your name should be Blue, not Red. To the moon Stonebear, all the way to the moon.""

Dusty raised his cup and asked for quiet, "My friends join me in toasting Blue and welcoming him to our circle, because a miracle has taken place right here in this house and there's no doubt his path has joined ours."

"Sirena, we've got to get Blue on an airplane pronto, but first I want to ask him a question with Stonebear's approval."

I nodded to Dusty, because I knew where he was going and it matched my thoughts precisely.

Dusty stood up and unbuttoned his shirt and displayed the mark of the bear over his heart and all those already marked displayed their tattoos as well.

"Blue, all of us here are bound on a path with Stonebear to do good in this world. Stonebear had a vision and he was told all in his circle would bear the mark of the bear. Are you willing to be marked like the rest of us?"

"Mr. Dusty, I think that would be a real honor, if you think there's any way I can be of help to you folks, you know I will."

"Blue, you've already done more than I would have thought humanly possible, so sit down and grab some breakfast, and when you're done, Lobo here will ink you up. How about that?"

"Mr. Dusty, would it be alright if I got mine in the same place as yours, but could I have mine done in blue instead of black?"

Dusty and Lobo both looked at me and I smiled and nodded my head. "Son, I think blue ink would be plumb perfect."

Sirena spoke next, "This is a thing I wish for myself, if it is not improper for me to ask. This is an admirable path you are on and I wish to be included, if you will admit me to the circle."

I went to Sirena, and bid her rise from her seat. I joined my hands in hers, kissed her on both cheeks and said, "Welcome to the circle my friend. We are pleased to have you join with us and your skill and talents will greatly aid us as we follow this path wherever it may lead."

Chapter 19

Breakfast continued with stacks of blueberry pancakes and picture perfect cups of Diablo coffee, until even Lobo said he believed that would hold him for a spell.

He and Blue excused themselves to go get the young lad marked with the print of the bear. Dusty left to write a check for Blue to carry down to Santa Fe, and Sirena left to make travel arrangements.

Cisco and Pancho decided this was a perfect time to go work on Dusty's trike and they took their leave with a cheerful adios.

Charlie winked at me, "Look like you've settled into Wyoming fit and proper son. Don't be biting off too much more Zed, or me and this old gal might have to postpone our nuptials just so we can see what's going to happen next."

"Who you calling old? Last night when you bent over to take off your boots you farted dust. This is already pretty near a mercy marriage on my part, so don't be pushing your luck, old timer."

Debbie chuckled. "What are we going to do for amusement Zed, when these two go off honeymooning?" You know that weddings coming up in just six more days, and we'll be on our lonesome while they gallivant down to Arizona. What in the world will we do with all the peace and quiet once Marlon Brando and Wanda vacate these parts?"

"Let's see Debbie, we have a political campaign to get underway, my daughter Snowbird to get moved and housed, a hospital to buy, I have to meet with Abraham's brothers, and get Consuela to a top notch OBGYN.

"Then, I reckon we can get me some high-speed driving lessons, and I can whip your butt pistol shooting.

"I need to have a long talk with Ironbear about my vision. Then, I need to find a restaurant location in Lander, and I need to get me some winter clothes. I have to get a wolf preserve established up on *the Buena Vistas* ranch and I need to find a top-notch person that lives and breathes animals to run the sanctuary for me. In our spare time we can sit by the fire and drink Merlot and look at the stars."

"Whoa, Hoss! What happened to the easy laid back Zed I know and love? How in the dickens are you going to do all of that?"

"Easy my friend. One bite at a time, and you are going to help me, and I'm going to help you. Aside from the political campaign, out of all those things I just mentioned, what can you help me accomplish?"

"Let me think on that a moment. You sure don't ask much of a friend, do you? I do know this gal down in Billings, Montana that just might do for one of those things you mentioned. She's about our age, late forties I would say, but looks a lot younger. She's single and she lives and breathes dogs.

"I don't think I've ever met anybody with a bigger heart for dogs in my whole life. It's not a hobby with her but a burning passion. Last I knew, she had rescued six of them everything from an old Chihuahua to a blind Pit bull, and she wished she could take in more.

"Her name is Prudence St.George, but everyone calls her "Tiggy." If, you call her Prudence, she'll probably howl at you. I don't know how she would feel about moving from Montana to Wyoming, but running a dog sanctuary is her dream.

"She's got things in common with some of our crew already. She's crazy about rocks just like Wanda, and she loves motorcycles and rides a Harley. She eats what she calls a plant based diet like Dusty does.

"She is a nature lover and has dreams for a cabin one day somewhere out in nature. I don't know how she feels about wolves, but they are just big dogs, right. How much would a position like that pay?"

"Tell you what, why don't you get her on the phone and offer to fly her up here to look over the operation and meet our little tribe? Once we've met face to face, and we find we are right for each other, we can discuss salary and where she might want her cabin built. She can stay here in the main house and we'll give her the tour of both ranches."

"You want me to call her right now?"

"That would suit me fine and ask her if she knows where a bunch of dogs can be located that need rescued and given a permanent home."

"Alright then, I'm going to put it on speaker phone so you can listen to her."

Debbie made the connection and I could hear it ringing. Just when I thought no one was going to pick up, a pleasing voice with a trace of a Scottish accent answered.

"Debbie, hello my friend, I was thinking about you last night and thinking it was time for us to have a talk. What's up in the law enforcement world? You and Lucy still doing righteous work?"

"Lucy and I are doing fine, but my call has nothing to do with law enforcement. Have you got a few minutes where I can run something by you?"
"Sure Debbie, I am sitting on the couch having a cup of gunpowder tea after another 11 hour day. The job is killing me, but me and the dogs have to eat and I owe, so it's off to work I go."

"I am with a wealthy friend and a super nice guy. He's the one that helped me rescue the little girl I told you about."

"Oh yeah, the hunk?"

"For your information, he's sitting right beside me and you're on speaker phone. He's laughing his butt off right now."

"Oh my God, I am so sorry."

"You have nothing to worry about. He has a well-developed sense of humor. He can't drink but he can hum "Ghost Riders in the Sky" like a pro."

"Here's what I want to run by you. He and I are going to be managing two ranches with a combined 58,000 acres up here in Wyoming, and it is being set up as a permanent sanctuary for animals.

"There is already a fantastic setup for dogs and there will also be a separate 1,000 acre enclosure for wolves. He's looking for a full-time manager and we want to fly you up here at our expense and show you what we've got to work with and see if you might be interested in the position."

"Tiggy, are you there? Hello?"

"I am so sorry, are you for real?"

"Serious as a heart attack my friend. This is a genuine offer and you are the only one it's been made to. You want to get up here to Wyoming and see if this is the job you've been dreaming of for years?"

"Yes, Debbie, when can I come?"

"How about this week, if you can get someone to keep your dogs for you?"

"Debbie, I am sitting here shaking I'm so excited. I can hardly believe this. I love you to pieces, and tell that man I am anxious to meet him and please tell him I'm not near as ditzy as I am appearing to be on this phone call."

"His name is Zed, but he's been adopted by a Shoshone medicine man and he's also been given the name Stonebear. You'll like him and I guarantee you'll love this place. It's like something out of a fairy tale. The owner of this place also follows your eating lifestyle, so you'll feel right at home at the dinner table.

"I'll call you back in a little while as soon as I have your travel arrangements made. You start packing, because this is going to happen quick"

In the meantime, be thinking where we can rescue a lot of dogs. We are ready for a hundred or more and we'll be interested in getting this project underway right off the bat. No dilly dallying or trying to raise funds. It's all taken care of. It's a dream situation, Tiggy. I'll call back within an hour."

Debbie broke the connection. "What do you think of my friend from what you heard so far?"

"I really liked her voice. I can tell a lot about a person from their voice. Their cadence and modulation along with their tone are quite revealing. I like people that pause, allowing you to interact, and she did that effortlessly, so I know that's her normal style.

"I was also pleased with her enthusiasm and her ability to make a decision without beating around the bush ... That reveals a person with self-confidence, and we need that. Tell you what, let's fly her up here first class and if she's that impressive in person, we'll make her an offer she can't refuse."

"That's super, Zed, and I bet you are going to like her. Did I mention she's gorgeous? I am talking drop-dead beautiful."

"Debbie, I won't evaluate her by her looks. I haven't let your beauty get in the way of our friendship, have I?" I smiled at her, "Nope, I treat you like any other big old peach of a woman wearing a .45 on her hip."

"You say the sweetest things Zed, I bet you'd like me just as much if I toted a 9mm instead of a 45. I am going to get with Sirena, and see who they use to book flights. I see Dimmit and Daisy are headed this way to pay their respects.

"I have to say, Romeo has been acting a proper gentleman up here and he hasn't gotten into a speck of trouble since he's been hanging with Daisy. Just goes to show the right woman can change a man's shiftless ways."

After Debbie left, I began considering the other things that were accumulating on my "To Do List." It was obvious before I could go much further with planning and implementing some of the ideas generated by my vision quest, I needed some serious sit-down time with Ironbear.

So much coming together all at once was somewhat daunting, but just like Riley and her knotted scarf, you had to undo one before you could proceed to the next. How could I get Ironbear and Snowbird down here to *the Anchorage* for a parley?

Then I heard the distinctive whop whop sound of an approaching helicopter. I smiled to myself ... ask and you shall receive. I reached down and hugged both of the spotted dogs and then got up and went searching for Dusty. I needed to borrow a helicopter for a bit.

I found him in the kitchen talking with Consuela, discussing the health virtues of the way he chose to eat. I listened in on the conversation. He knew his stuff and he was articulate and persuasive. The most impactful thing he said was, when he looked at an animal he saw another living soul, that animals were his friends and he didn't eat his friends.

"Howdy Stonebear, just telling Consuela why I eat the way I do. I think it's the healthiest way to eat, as well as the most humane."

He gave me a warm smile, "I believe I have me a convert and I might get me another one or two down the road."

"What can I do for you, son?"

"The men you are expecting are here and I would like to borrow the helicopter for a bit. I need to get Ironbear and Snowbird down here. Much of what I need to do and plan concerning my vision needs Ironbear's input and interpretation.

"The path of our circle involves his people and how we can improve the lives of the people on the Wind River reservation. I have ideas but I need his thinking on the matter and I want him to meet you and I would like to introduce you to my daughter. She wants to be a doctor and that's one of the reasons I want to buy the hospital in Lander."

"You are looking for leverage, aren't you, son? You catch on mighty quick to what money can do for you, if you use it for good. Sure, you can borrow the helicopter. I am pretty anxious to meet both of them myself and I'd like to discuss my dream of riding the bear with Ironbear.

Might be quite interesting. It won't take you long by air, so I'll get the men in suits working on the papers for the rest of our people and save you and Debbie for last. Tell the pilot Dusty said to take you anywhere you want to go."

Dusty and I went out to the main room where six men, not a woman in the bunch, waited. All except one of them had those fancy beaver cowboy hats and carved boots with Spanish heels Charlie had told me about back in the desert.

"Have a seat gentlemen. This is Zed Bowden, but I call him by his new name, Stonebear. He's got to go fetch a couple of other people in the whirlybird, so you'll meet with him later. We've got some new coffee here that will blow your socks off. They call it Diablo, and the folks around here rave about it..

"You go on now son, fetch your family, and we'll see you back here soon."

I waved at the bunch of them and headed out the door. The chopper was parked on the lawn and the elk had wisely given right of way to this noisy beast from the sky and had made a retreat to a quieter locale.

I found the pilot checking over his machine and I introduced myself. His name was Vern, and he looked incredibly young, but, he also had an unmistakable air of competence along with a most agreeable manner.

I was surprised when I told him where I wanted to go and he knew right where I was talking about. He'd flown groups of people in there before, and had even sought treatment from Ironbear. Vern claimed Ironbear cured him of a skin rash that had plagued him for years, that no modern medicine or medical doctor had been able to relieve.

He then asked me, "Have you met his granddaughter, Snowbird?"

"Yep, I met her when I was up there last." I took a closer look at the young pilot and asked him what he thought about her.

"She's so smart, you can almost forget how pretty she is. It makes a man feel good to be in her presence and she goes on about her business like she's just kind of normal.

"First time I saw her, she made me think of an Indian princess. I liked watching her work. She has such skilled hands I know she would make an excellent pilot.

She's got the brains for it too. I don't know how she learned so much living with her grandfather on that mountain, but I would say she the brightest and prettiest girl I've ever seen.

"I daydream about her sometimes. Me and her up in the air and showing her the world from up high like an eagle sees it. Just a dream, I know but that's what foolish men do, dream of the impossible, don't we?"

"It wouldn't be much of a life Vern, if a man didn't have his dreams. We're burning daylight, what you say we get this bird in the air?"

"Mr. Bowden, most folks prefer to ride in the passenger compartment. It's more comfortable and a lot quieter, but I'd be pleased to have you up front with me. It's got a much better view and we are going to fly over some of the prettiest country God made."

"That suits me fine Vern. Let's get saddled up, but I'd prefer you call me Zed. That's what my friends call me."

It didn't take long for Vern to acquaint me with the headset and communication procedures while airborne. I got myself strapped in while the young pilot spun up the motor and we were aloft in minutes.

Vern's voice came over the headset. "I'm taking a wide swing off to the west, so I can show you were *the Anchorage* and *Buena Vista* ranches are separated by a gorge. I like both ranches fine, but for my money, I tend to like *the Buena Vistas* better. More timber, fantastic fly fishing, and full of game."

"Are you a hunter Vern?"

"In a manner of speaking I am. I stalk them with a camera. Everything I shoot gets to walk away, but my daddy loved hunting and he drug me all over these mountains ever since I was a pup. He's the one that taught me to fly. I soloed in fixed wing aircraft before I was 12 years old. I got my multi-engine license before I could legally drive a car."

"Are you in business with your father?"

"He started this business when he got out of the Army back in '72, and he made me his partner when I got my commercial license.

"But he developed leukemia and died two years ago on Christmas day. He served three tours in Vietnam as a chopper pilot and he figured he flew through enough Agent Orange to choke a horse. He was as tough as they come, but he couldn't whip that leukemia."

Vern was quiet for a while and I thought back to my mother's battle with cancer. Seems Vern and I bore some of the same scars on our heart.

"Look off to your right there. That deep canyon is called Bucket Gorge. There's old Indian trails leading down into it and it has some fine trout fishing for a man that don't mind a little walking to get away from the crowds.

"There's some Indian drawings on some of the walls and ancient campsites from long ago. It's one of my favorite places to go to get recharged from nature. It's also the natural boundary line between the '*Anchorage*' and the '*Buena Vista*' ranches. Now, I'll get us up to Ironbear's place and we ought to make it in about 20 minutes. Does he know you are coming?"

"I think he probably does. I don't know how he does, but I'll bet he's expecting us and putting the coffee pot on while we speak."

"I like that old man myself. He's smart and always treated me like I was a welcome guest. He's kind of both dignified and mysterious at the same time, if you know what I mean?"

"I know what you mean Vern. I surely do, and that's an apt description...dignified and mysterious. I am looking forward to seeing him and Snowbird again."

We continued on our flight plan with Vern explaining how his Daddy made a success of the business flying oil and gas geologists all over this part of Wyoming. He said he still did some of that kind of work himself, but preferred not to. He wasn't pleased with what the drilling and blasting were doing to the land.

The twenty minute flying time was right on the dot accurate. I picked out Ironbear's cabin from a long ways off. Vern began his descent explaining there was not a place right by the cabin to put down, but it would be only a short walk up to the house.

In minutes he had put us down within sight of the entrance marker with the distinctive grizzly silhouette hanging from the beams. As Vern began his shutdown procedure I removed my headset and unbuckled my safety harness.

Vern got everything done and he asked if I wanted him to wait by the chopper while I did my business with Ironbear.

I smiled to myself, "Nope, I want you with me Vern. I wouldn't have it any other way."

A brisk 5-minute walk and the cabin was in sight. A tendril of smoke was coming from the chimney and the birds were singing like before. Home...it felt like I was coming home and a feeling of belonging filled me till I felt like shouting with joy.

The door opened and there he stood, just like the first time, except he was wearing my old hat with the eagle feather Snowbird had sealed in the brim with pine pitch.

A broad smile with flashing teeth spread across Ironbear's face.

"Welcome my brother, I have been expecting you and the coffee's ready. Come, both of you and we will talk.

Chapter 20

I had not gotten completely through the door when Snowbird swarmed me with hugs and kisses. "Father, I have missed you so, and have prayed for you every night."

I glanced over at Vern and he looked more confused than a bag of marbles. He looked at Snowbird, and then to me, and back and forth like he was watching some kind of tennis match.

"Sorry Vern, I should have told you, but I've only been a father less than a week, and you are my first attempt at examining a young man's intentions."

"I apologize, sir, if I said anything out of the way. I had no idea she was your daughter, and I meant no disrespect to either you or her."

"Relax Vern, I owe you the apology and you didn't say a thing to me that you couldn't say to Snowbird's face, and you probably should, unless you are a dreamer and not a doer.

"Why don't the two of you go get us some coffee and let me talk to Ironbear a minute, and you can explain to Snowbird what we are apologizing to each other for."

Snowbird grabbed Vern by the elbow, "C'mon Vern, the old folks want to talk and I want to hear what you said to my father that required an apology."

I joined my second father by the fire circle and had a seat on the buffalo hide.

"It's good to see you Ironbear. I have thought of you every day since I left. Many times I have wished I could ask you questions and seek your wisdom."

Ironbear laughed, "We have spent our time thinking the same thoughts. You left here with a heavy load. The biggest burden I've ever seen lain on a man from a vision quest. Snowbird and I have prayed for you that the stars in the sky would light your path and lead you to the sacred circle. Tell me, my son, have you found a beginning?"

It was my turn to laugh, "More than a beginning, father. It is opening almost faster than I can handle, but so far I have been able to eat this great beast one bite at a time. That's why I have come father. I need you and Snowbird to fly back with me."

Snowbird and Vern returned with our coffee and I proceeded to tell Ironbear all that transpired since I last saw him. He listened silently and drank his coffee while I went through the details of my life and how the vision was unfolding.

I explained how I was seeing much of the vision unfolding to involve a path of good for the entire reservation, both Shoshone and Arapaho. I told him about the circle and why we all needed to meet him.

He nodded his head a few times as I talked and mumbled some Shoshone word that was probably the equivalent to a good old Alabama *'bless your heart.'*

When I finished, I asked, "Father will you come back with me and meet the circle and help us determine best how we can work to do good for your people?"

"Yes, my son, I wouldn't miss this opportunity for a herd of paint ponies. A 90 year old man, bikers, a lady sheriff, a Mexican couple, an autistic savant, a Spanish beauty, and a cowboy named Blue? Did I get all of them? How about the young pilot here, is he part of your circle too?"

"You've got it covered pretty good Ironbear, but it's not my circle. It's our circle, and as far as Vern, you want me to tell you what I know, or what I think?"

"Always start with what you know, and then tell me what you think, because before you can truly judge what a man thinks, you need to be aware of where his knowledge begins and also where it ends.

"All men think, even ignorant ones, and they tend to think the most out loud, because ignorance has self-pride and attracts other ignorant people like flies to buffalo dung. Enough of my philosophy, tell me what you know and what you think about young Vern here."

"What I know is that I don't know, but I have a really good feeling. What I think is he could be a very big part if my interpretation of part of the vision is correct. This is something I must discuss with you and then I'll know if Vern fits in this place I have in my head."

"Very well, Snowbird get your jacket and my medicine bag. Looks like we are going to let this young man take us up the sky in the pregnant iron butterfly. Make sure the stove's turned off. It might be late when we return."

Snowbird squealed, "I've wanted to ride in one of those forever. This is incredible. Thank you father for coming to get us."

"You two probably should plan on staying the night, if you don't mind. There's enough room there for a marching band and the glee club too. Fanciest place I've ever stayed and I know you will be welcomed and honored guests."

"Grab us a change of clothing child and bring my pipe and my medicine. If this young man is going to take me in the air, I'm going to smudge him and his machine. Are you wearing the medicine bag and grizzly claw I gave you?"

"Yes, father right here." I took it out from underneath my shirt to show him and he asked me to take off just the pouch. He removed his pouch from around his neck and put it around mine.

"Son, you have traveled rapidly down this path of good you follow, but evil does not fail to take notice of good things coming to pass. They will try to beset you with worries and woes to take you off your path. They won't come at you like the demons in your vision. No, they will come at you in the skins of men and women, smiling in your face and waiting to strike.

"In white man's talk, by giving you my medicine bag, I've doubled your dosage and added a few new meds. Now go put your old bag around Vern's neck. I'm not flying with anybody not wearing a little Indian protection."

I walked over to Vern, "Young man, if you'll allow me, I am going to give you some good luck protection."

"Thank you sir, I wish I had something to give you in return to show my appreciation for this honor. What's in the bag?"

"I don't know Vern, all I know is it's supposed to protect you and you are never to open it or you take away its power."

Snowbird came bouncing back with a small overnight vase and her grandfather's leather mailbag.

"Let's go gentlemen, this girl's ready to go grab some clear blue sky."

"First, my child, we must smudge this young man and the flying beast he arrived in."

The smudging of Vern was accomplished without delay.

We left the house and started making our way down the road, with Ironbear carrying the smoking smudge in his right hand. Snowbird was so excited she skipped ahead of us, but she skipped right back urging us to pick up speed, and we did.

Once we arrived back at the helicopter the first order of business was to thoroughly smudge the flying machine. After that was accomplished, Vern slid back the passenger door and was about to help Snowbird board.

"Hold on Vern, I would like to ride in the back with Ironbear, if you don't mind Snowbird riding up front with you? She could see better from up there couldn't she?"

"Oh, yes sir, she's welcome up front and she'll get a much better view. Thank you sir!"

"One more thing Vern, just so you know, I am a badge carrying, gun toting, genuine Wyoming deputy sheriff. Just so you know, and I also don't mind you taking the long scenic way back. I am in no rush to talk to bankers, lawyers and accountants."

Ironbear and I boarded the plush interior cabin and sat in facing white leather seats. I showed him how the headsets and microphone worked and told him we were on a different channel from the pilots and we could talk freely among ourselves.

"You look a little nervous, have you never flown in one of these before?"

"Charlie and I have flown in plenty of them. I've just never flown in one where I wasn't in danger of getting shot at."

"Do you mean you and Charlie served together in Vietnam?"

"We sure did, didn't he tell you? I'm the medic that dug that Willy Pete out of his butt with his own bayonet. Your other father's a brave man, and he's a modest man too. Did he tell you about getting the Bronze Star over in 'Nam?"

"Yes, I kind of had to pry it out of him after I saw his 1'st Air Cavalry lighter out in the desert. He mentioned your name that day but not in context with you two serving together over there."

"I'm not surprised. That old rascal can keep a secret better than any man I've ever met."

"Did you know Charlie when you were here in Wyoming, before you served together over there?

"Nope, I met him for the first time in basic training at Ft. Benning, Georgia. Being the only two in the unit from Wyoming, we were naturally drawn together.

"Back in those days, the whites and Indians didn't do much socializing in these parts, and that hasn't changed much over the years. After basic training, I went on to Ft. Sam Houston in San Antonio, to be trained as a medic, and Charlie went to Ft. Lee, Virginia to learn how to be a cook. It was a welcome surprise and a great reunion when we got assigned to the same Air Cavalry unit in Vietnam.

"Too many broken promises, and mistrust and suspicion on both sides have led us into an insulated world of our own here on the reservation.

"You combine that with poverty, drugs, violence, poor schools, inadequate health care, and lack of economic opportunity and you have what we face today. Rampant alcohol and drug abuse, mistreatment of women, and a general air of hopelessness."

"Wind River is more of a ghetto than a reservation and that is true for both the people of the Shoshone and the Arapaho alike. It is one of the most dangerous places to live in America. You would think that our shared misery would unite us, but there are too many ignorant people of both tribes perpetuating the hatred of their ancestors."

"Father, that directly connects to one of the main things I wanted to talk to you about concerning my vision."

"I speak of the part where the small horses both black and white galloped around the sacred circle. The horses had handprints on their withers. The white horses had the red handprint, and the blacks, a handprint of white.

"As you will recall my telling, only the white horses had riders on their back at first, but as they rode around the circle twelve times, after each circuit the riders would change from white horses to black horses.

"This vision seems to stay first in my mind as if it's more important and demanding of my attention. Ironbear, I think I may have some concept of what this vision means, but I seek your wisdom and guidance."

"You show great appreciation for your vision my son, and I too have given much thought and prayer to this particular portion of your vision. I agree that it has great importance to your path."

"I have searched for the meaning in my heart and this is my interpretation of your vision. The different colored handprints and the different colored horses tell me that your path involves uniting the red man and the white man in a common cause. In a way that is not clear to me, it will somehow involve horses.

I remember you saying the riders were dressed in loincloths like you, and their long hair was streaming behind them. You referred to them as 'Shoshone warriors'."

"Now, my son, I ask you how you would know the difference between a Shoshone warrior and one from the Arapaho tribe?"

"I answer truthfully father. I would know of no way to tell one from the other."

"Exactly my son, and neither would I. Without symbols or clothing, we look alike. It is much the same as when the whites fought their great Civil War. They looked alike, worshipped the same God, and spoke the same language, but they marched under different flags and one side wore grey and the other blue. Differences created by man, not by the Great Spirit."

"The Shoshone warriors served loyally with the whites as their trusted allies in their war against the Arapaho and the Sioux. The Wind River Reservation was created solely for the use of the Shoshone people. In 1876, the Arapaho were settled temporarily on the eastern portion of the reservation just for the winter.

"It was to be for the one winter only as a temporary measure, and then they were to be moved to their own reservation. Again, a promise was broken and the Arapaho, in much greater numbers than the Shoshone, were left here occupying two-thirds of the best land on the reservation.

The government subsidies my people depended on for survival were apportioned based on tribal numbers. The Arapahos, having more people, received more than the Shoshone. It was a recipe for disaster and 130 years later, we fight the same battles between our tribes.

"That is what I believe the vision is telling me father, that somehow I must seek a path that brings greater unity to the Shoshone and the Arapaho people.

"I have thought on this a great deal and I have some ideas that I would like to discuss with you in front of the circle, because I see places where the talents of the circle can be brought to bear to make these ideas become a reality."

"I am interested in hearing these ideas Stonebear, and I agree it would be better to discuss them in a council setting with the members of our circle. I have an idea about the horses in the vision and I would like to present it to the circle."

"I am excited to share these ideas in front of everyone because I see great promise in them to bring the visions I experienced to reality.

"If they succeed they will bring greater unity to the people of the Wind River reservation and provide job opportunities and economic prosperity for both tribes."

The helicopter stopped its forward motion and it slowly rotated 360 degrees and I could imagine the conversation taking place in the front cabin between Vern and Snowbird.

I was happy that she was having her dream of flying in a helicopter fulfilled in the company of a handsome young pilot.

Now, I had to get her on her path of becoming a doctor, and I had some solid ideas about how to accomplish that goal. I was determined to unravel the mysteries of my vision one bite at a time and as each knot was untangled, I would move to the next and I was confident that with the help of my circle I would fulfill my purpose to do only good.

Vern put the aircraft in forward motion once again and I noticed Ironbear had his arms raised in prayer and his lips were moving in a silent prayer. I joined him.

The return flight to the "*Anchorage*" took twice as long as the initial flight to Ironbear's cabin and Vern took full advantage of his opportunity, but eventually he brought us back home and gently landed the *pregnant iron butterfly* on the spacious well-kept lawn.

Once he had the helicopter shut down and the blades had stopped rotating, Snowbird bounded from the forward cabin and came back and slid the door open to our cabin. She was jumping up and down with exuberance and the smile on her face was a delight to be behold.

"That was beyond awesome. It was totally amazing and I am in love with flying. It's so exciting and Vern says he can teach me to fly grandfather. Can you imagine that?

"A doctor on the reservation that can fly? Is that not absolutely incredible? Please say yes, grandfather that Vern can teach me to fly. He says first he will teach me to fly the airplane with one engine and then he will teach me to fly the helicopter. Please say yes!"

Ironbear smiled and looked at me, and then he broke out in laughter. Snowbird and I looked at each other puzzled, not knowing what caused this spontaneous outburst. He didn't leave us in suspense long.

"I have been dying to have an opportunity to say this to you Snowbird, "Go ask your father."

Snowbird fixed her eyes on me like lasers, "Father, I ask that you consider how important this is to me before you answer. Will you allow Vern to teach me to fly?"

Vern had joined us and he looked at me with same intensity, but with sad imploring puppy dog eyes.

"Daughter, I think a doctor that could fly a helicopter in Wyoming, where some folks have to drive a hundred miles to buy a loaf of bread, would be a wonderful thing. My answer is first a question I must ask. How could you possibly pursue medical school and learn to fly at the same time?"

"Easy question." She gave me brilliant smile, "I learned this from two very wise men, 'I will eat this buffalo one bite at a time'."

I looked over at Ironbear and he grinned and shrugged his shoulders.

"Dear Snowbird, I wish for you a life without boundaries or a limit to your dreams. I say yes, and I have confidence that you can do anything you seek to accomplish in your life. You are destined for greatness and your life is going to make a difference to so many others."

I was surprised she didn't rush and throw her arms around me like she normally did when she was excited. Instead, she stood there and looked me deep in my eyes and held my gaze. I felt transfixed and awed by the intensity of her focus.

"I see before me a man of such great worth. I look into your soul and it's full of thoughts of others. If a woman could create her father in bits and pieces like a puzzle that would create the perfect father, I would choose the bits and pieces that made you, just like you are in every way. You are a complete father with no piece of the puzzle missing."

I didn't wait for her. I gathered her in my arms and thanked God for this chance to be part of this amazing woman's life. She kissed me on the cheek and a gleam came in her eye and she started jumping up and down.

"Father, I had this dream to fly in a helicopter and it came true. I also had a dream that one day a handsome young boy would cross over our mountain and I would have somebody to kiss besides three old men with feathers in their hats like some geriatric outlaw gang. Here comes dream number two."

She rushed over to Vern and threw her arms around his neck and planted a scorching kiss on his lips. Vern was well tanned, but he blushed a bright red that I guarantee went all the way to his toes.

"How was that for my first kiss with a man that is not old and like family? You are the first man I have kissed ever in my life."

Vern was plumb tongue tied and stammered by the events which caught us all off guard. I looked over at Ironbear and both our eyebrows were raised so high we tilted our hats back.

"I imagine I can learn to kiss just about as fast as I learn to fly. I liked it myself, my first kiss, but who am I to judge? I have only kissed old men before and once you've kissed one old man, you've kissed them all. What's the matter Vern, cat got your tongue?"

"I'm sorry, it just took me completely by surprise. That was the finest kiss that's ever touched my lips, and I swear if it gets any better, your daddy is going to shoot me and your grandfather's going to scalp me.

"That kiss was like they write about in novels where people hear bells ring. I didn't hear bells ring. I heard birds singing and I felt a gentle breeze caress my face. It was like I was in a cedar forest. That wasn't a kiss. That was an enchantment, a dream kiss that will ruin a man for life from kisses from any other lips."

I took my hat off my head before my eyebrows pushed it to the ground. Lord, help me that escalated fast. "Hold on you two, before Ironbear and I have to throw buckets of cold water on you."

"Let's get on in the house and we can get this legal stuff out of the way and get on to talking about these other things that are so pressing on my mind."

I escorted our group, including Vern, into the house. Looked like Vern might be in the picture for a while and I was eager, but not in an anxious way, to get to know him better.

I was already pretty impressed with the young man and I wanted to see how he interacted with the others. He had great potential for the plans that were formulating in my mind.

So many incredible ideas were spinning around like a roulette wheel in my mind that I didn't care where it stopped. Anywhere it landed it was going to be a winner because they all advanced something good and positive for others.

Chapter 21

Dusty greeted us at the door and welcomed us all in. "Welcome my friends Ironbear and Snowbird. I have heard much about you from Stonebear. He's spoken highly of both of you and how he's honored to be in your family.

"When he speaks of you, he sometimes says Ironbear, but he usually just says father, and he says it with great respect. Please call me Dusty, and forgive my slowness with the walker or I would have met you outside."

Ironbear grasped Dusty by his forearms and held him while he gave Dusty that same intense gaze into the soul that Snowbird had given me.

After a moment, he spoke, "My granddaughter and I are glad to be here and now that I have met you, I am honored because I have looked into your soul and I see a pure heart like I see in my son and granddaughter.

"Pure hearts are rare and I find them a treasure to add to the ones I know. Greetings my brother, and soon I will give you a new name. I see it clearly before my eyes, and we will need food. You and I have a long night ahead of us and we must have energy. Come, let us dine and let me tell you what we must do and we must do it tonight."

And away they went like they had known each other forever.

I looked at Snowbird and she gave me a supportive look, "What can I say father, he's sometimes a weird old man, but he's got magic in him. I call him my Magic Medicine Man. I am learning as much from him as I can.

"He's an intuitive healer and can diagnose people by touching them. I too have this skill but mine comes from visual clues and his from touch. Remember when he knew you had been bitten by the black widow?"

"Yes, I remember that well. I didn't even realize I had been bitten until he told me."

"That's what I think just happened when he grabbed Dusty by the arms. He felt something, something he thinks he can fix. I've seen it before and don't be surprised at anything he does or anything that might happen as a result. When he's as hyped as he is now, something good is going to happen. I bet my next kiss on it. If I'm right, I'll kiss Vern, and if I am wrong, I will kiss you."

I had to laugh at the audacity of my daughter. "I would never want to bet against something good happening, so why don't we pray for something good to happen, and you can then kiss both of us, if Vern doesn't mind, of course."

"No sir, I don't mind at all and I started my praying as soon as you said it." Vern's eyes twinkled.

"Let's go see what turns up next on this carousel of life. I don't think a talking bear is the weirdest thing that's going to happen on this never ending road I am on. It's starting to feel a little like I'm Dorothy in the 'Wizard of Oz' and we are all following the yellow-brick road."

The men in suits were all out on the veranda having lunch and except for Abraham and Consuela, who were in the kitchen, our gang was all in the great room brainstorming and laying plans for the room's conversion.
The floor had already been covered in a heavy blue tarp and construction materials were stacked neatly in the corner. One card table and a number of chairs remained. All the other furniture and artwork had been removed already.

Debbie spoke first, "Zed you got a call from that Navy pilot renting your sailboat. Your one-eyed cat showed back up and they've been feeding her and she's staying on the boat, but they are being deployed overseas and want to know what to do with her. They say it will cost about $800 to ship her by air."

Charlie chimed in, "Mighty proud of them flying cat houses, ain't they now. Charging $800 for a two-eyed cat might be reasonable, but for a one-eyed cat that's only going to enjoy half the scenery, it's like skyway robbery."

"Mr. Stonebear, if you would consider it, I would be glad to bring your cat back in my airplane. I have a King Air 350 and that's about a 3 hour flight to San Diego. I could be there and back in one day."

"What about fuel Vern, that's a couple thousand miles round trip?"

"Sir, it would take 150 gallons, or less for each leg, and at $5 a gallon, it's the same pretty much as having her flown out here by commercial pet airlines, and a whole lot more less nerve racking for the cat."

"If you could pay for one leg of the journey, I'll pay for the other. I would like permission to take Snowbird. There is much I can teach her in six hours of flight time. She catches on quicker than anyone I've ever seen and this could well serve as her first lesson."

"I've noticed how she catches on to things very quickly, some things too quickly."

"I understand where you are coming from sir, and I wouldn't do anything to cause that girl to disrespect me, or for you to lose trust in me. Those are as true a words as I've ever spoken."

"Vern, I wish I could tell you to go ask her grandfather. I owe him one. Turnabout is fair play, but I believe he's lost to us for the night, so I am going to go along with it and permit her to go, but know that you will never fly with anything more precious to me than her. Keep both her and yourself safe."

"Sir, my father taught me there are bold pilots, and there are old pilots, but very few bold-old pilots. I plan on being an old pilot someday and teaching my children how to fly and maybe even my grandchildren. My father was an excellent pilot and if he were standing here today, he would tell you I'm better."

I introduced Vern and Snowbird to the crew and the conversation just flowed. Vern was intrigued by motorcycles and was a Harley rider himself. He hit it off right away with Lobo and Blue. The name of Blue set me to pondering how many more names we would go through before we escaped our confusing identity crisis. Judging from what Ironbear had said, the next one for a new brand was going to be Dusty.

I headed for the veranda to meet the 'suits' and get something to eat for myself. Looked like it might be a long night for me too, and I might need some energy reserves myself.

I introduced myself all around and there were a flurry of names, but one stood out from the crowd. His name was Devin McIntosh, and he had a tartan hat band on his plain straw cowboy hat matching his tartan tie, and he was a ginger to boot. He looked every bit the Scotsman and he had the most easy going manner out of the lot.

He was an investment banker out of Laramie. He was a little younger than myself, early forties or there about, and he kept himself fit. The rest of them had at least twenty years on Devin, and what hair they had that hadn't turned lose, had turned grey.

None of them were at ease like Devin. They would introduce themselves by their titles and affiliations. I am president of blah, blah, blah or I am the senior law partner of blah, blah, blah. Nothing wrong with being proud of your success. It's all in how you say it. The Scotsman simply said his name was Devin, and he liked to make money for folks and himself.

There was some commotion going on out in the yard and it appeared Ironbear and Dusty were having some kind of canvas tent erected with a wood burning stove in it, and they were both actively involved in supervising its construction.

The men in suits had decided to split me into three sessions, legal, financial, and investment planning. As soon as I had eaten a couple of tasty burritos and had a glass of raspberry tea, we got into the business matters awaiting my attention.

A couple of hours went by in a blur with lots of fancy words, and I signed my name so many times I lost count. Dusty's business empire was far wider than I could have imagined and he was directly responsible for the incomes of over a thousand people spread from Montana to Washington State.

He even owned a substantial vineyard down in the Napa valley and a large marina in Puget Sound outside Seattle. My last session was with Devin McIntosh, and it was the most enjoyable of all and the easiest to comprehend.

He had the ability to explain complex matters in an entertaining and easily understood manner. Captain T used to tell me you could tell when a man was *fluent* in his knowledge by how easily he could explain it to others. Devin had that gift of *fluency.*

I decided to bounce my idea of buying the hospital in Lander off him.

He listened carefully before responding, "Zed, unless you have some other motive, other than making a profitable return, I can do much better for you in other segments.

"Hospitals are a tremendous financial drain and many operate at a loss. Controlling interest in the Lander hospital could be obtained for around $14 million and complete ownership for around another $10 million."

"Wow, I had no idea the costs would be that great. The objective is not about profit but doing some good and obtaining some leverage to do even more good. I'll have to run this by Dusty and get his input."

"Actually Zed, you don't. Dusty anticipated you asking about the hospital in Lander and you are fully authorized to proceed with acquiring the hospital if that is your wish. That's how I know about the costs. I had my office do some checking while you were with the other men going over other matters. Doing good in my opinion is often more valuable than just making money."

"You mean Dusty can afford an outlay of $24 million?"

"To put it plain, it's about the same to him as you or I deciding to splurge and get a scoop of vanilla on our apple pie."

"Excellent, Devin, I appreciate you making things easily understood and you doing the research to be able to respond quickly. Let's make this the first thing you and I engage in our new working relationship. Let's buy that hospital."

"I have another thing that may be out of your field, but I would like your input. My newly acquired daughter is incredibly bright, but I don't know what type of formal education she has, or if she's ever been tested to determine her intelligence level and aptitude. Do you know of anyone that might be able to offer advice and guidance on the matter?"

"I know the perfect man for the job. He's a client of mine. A brilliant man when it comes to the human mind. He's a retired professor of psychiatry from the University of Washington Medical School, and he's a recognized expert in assessing a person's potential. Would you like me to contact him on your behalf?"

"I would appreciate you doing so."

"I will be glad to help any way I can and it doesn't have to be about investment advice. Just like the retired professor, I have many contacts across a broad spectrum of professions and I'll be delighted to assist your various projects by connecting you with experts in many fields."

"Sounds great Devin, let's go meet some folks I think you are going to like. I call them the circle. By the way, are you married?"

"Nope, came close a time or two, but it'll happen one day. I know she's out there waiting for me just like I'm waiting for her. How about yourself Zed, are you married?"

"I am like you. I've never found the right one and I heard it expressed perfectly earlier today. I've never kissed a woman that made me hear birds sing and made me feel like I was in the middle of a cedar forest with a gentle breeze caressing my face."

I kind of think she does not exist for me and that my path will be walked alone. If that ever changes, I will welcome it, but I think that is not meant for me in this life."

"Devin. Could you stay over tonight after the other men fly back?"

"Sure, I believe I would like that. Any chance we could have a bonfire outside and maybe a bottle or two of wine from Dusty's vineyards? They produce some award winning varieties and there's nothing like a bonfire and a glass of wine with friends. You ever notice that yourself?"

"I have noticed that myself. You are not a whistler, are you, Devin?"

"No sir, but I have been known to break out in song when the mood hits me right, but mostly I just hum." He smiled and looked at me, "That was a strange question."

"Well, here's a stranger one, how do you feel about sunflower seeds?"

The last question caused Devin to laugh, "I think about sunflower seeds about like I do a snuff dipper with a drool. Messy things those sunflower seeds. Too much spitting and not enough seed. Give me a pecan or an English walnut any day. My brother and I used to carefully pry open English walnuts and take the half hull and melt candle wax in them. Then we would stick a toothpick with a paper sail into the hot wax. When they would dry we'd race them across the stock pond. He had the red sails and I had the blue. I miss those days."

"What does your brother do, is he in investments like you?"

"No, my brother Ian is not into anything. He developed schizophrenia as a teenager and he's considered delusional. He's in a private hospital in Cheyenne. He's a wonderful man in many ways, but he thinks he can talk to animals and that they talk back."

"He's always getting into some kind of harmless trouble. He'll walk into a grocery store, pick up a bag of dog food without paying for it and go pour it on the sidewalk and claim some dogs told him they were hungry.

"His last arrest was for swimming nude at Guernsey Reservoir. He said the dogs told him the water would feel good against his naked skin."

While Devin talked, I experienced a sensation much like the "flash" I was accustomed to, but it was the voice of Brother Bear speaking in my head. He said, "IAN IS NOT DELUSIONAL."

"He's also crazy about wolves and has been since a child. Wolves and dogs are his favorite. As far as I know, he's never seen a real wolf but he's positively obsessed with them.

"He's not dangerous at all, just very spontaneous in responding to what he thinks he hears without any regard for the consequences of his actions. Sometimes even I think he can understand animals. I've seen wild birds perch on his shoulder and chirp in his ear. He'll laugh and chirp back."

"Devin, I want to meet your brother Ian. I may just have a job for him."

"What kind of job could you have that my brother could possibly do?"

"We are starting a dog sanctuary and a wolf preserve. I need a wolf whisperer and an interpreter for our canine guests."

"Zed, you are serious about this, aren't you?"

"Totally serious my friend, and it will work too. I also can talk to animals. At least one animal and that animal is a grizzly bear I call Brother Bear. I am convinced my Shoshone father can also talk to animals.

"Brother Bear just told me your brother can talk to animals and that I need him here with me to pursue my path. Trust me Devin, this is exactly what your brother needs to fulfill his purpose in life."

"Wow, that kind of blows me away, Zed. Let me check him out next weekend and bring him out here to meet you. I don't want to get my hopes up too high, but this could be what Ian needs. You don't really think he can talk to animals do you?"

"Interesting conversation I had earlier today with my Shoshone father about what a man thinks compared to what a man knows. Trust me, I don't think he can talk to animals, I know your brother can talk to animals and there is a job and a home for him here."

"Zed, I sense we are going to become great friends that is if you don't mind a hummer that prefers walnuts over sunflower seeds."

"I wouldn't have it any other way. Trust me on this too, and remind me to tell you my story about whistlers and sunflower seed spitters one day."

"Let's go meet the crew. I think you are going to like them and fit in just fine. Yes sir, you are going to fit in just fine like a pair of Sunday boots."

Devin and I relocated to the game room and I introduced him around to everyone. He was immediately at ease and he removed his jacket and tie and rolled up his sleeves revealing heavily muscled forearms and one of the strangest tattoos I've ever seen. It was a carabiner with a piece of rope attached.

He saw where I was looking and pointed to his tattoo, "I'm an avid rock climber. I go every time I get a chance. Have you done that before?"

I had to think back to my recent vision. "Not exactly Devin, but I recently went sideways on a narrow ledge, 500 feet above a valley floor so I can say I have rock crawled horizontal but not vertical. It was quite a thrill, but there was no carabiner and no rope. Once I became one with the rock it became more comfortable and natural, but at first it was kind of terrifying."

"Outstanding, you will have to go with me some time. It's an absolute rush and I believe you would find it an excellent way to unwind and recharge.

I might need that sooner than later. My dance card was getting full fast. I had the young lady from Montana flying in, and Blue flying out to Santa Fe in the morning.

Abraham's brothers were coming in to meet me, not to mention the biggest thing of all, Wanda and Charlie's wedding. It suddenly occurred to me ... all of us were here. What was happening to the cafe while we were all gone? I asked her immediately.

"Don't worry about it son. Charlie and I discussed it and we are taking a mini vacation prior to the wedding. I sent Abraham back to the cafe to leave a sign on the door that we are closed until after the wedding. There's too much happening here for any of us to be distracted right now. He should be back anytime now."

"Come with me son. Snowbird and I want to show you something."

I followed them out of the room and we mounted the staircase and I was puzzled what the two of them would show me upstairs. We went straight to Riley's door and Wanda flipped the switch three times and entered with Snowbird in tow. I followed behind curious to see what was going to happen.

Riley was sitting on the floor with the old Dachshund perched in her lap. Same white shirt and bare feet but this time she was facing the door and instead of tears, she wore a radiant smile.

"You've brought my golden woman back to me. Come Snowbird, sit by my side and listen to the music. Do you still see the colors?"

"Yes, Riley, I still see the colors and I still see you as golden. You are the only golden person I have ever seen and you have said I am the only golden person you have ever seen. What we have is called synesthesia and we sense things very differently than most people. We see colors and shapes in music and sometimes in our surroundings. When I say the name Riley, I taste fresh baked bread and you smell like coconut to me. Do you get those sensations from me?"

"When I say your name I see red birds in trees and you smell like grass after a rain. You make me feel peaceful inside like my dog Fogerty makes me feel when I am upset."

I turned my face to Wanda and she was smiling and holding back the tears. "Can you believe it Zed? Look at them talking together. It's a miracle, a dadblamed sure enough miracle. I haven't seen that girl talk that much in two years. Let's you and me skedaddle and leave them alone. I have to tell Dusty about this right away. He's going to be thrilled."

We went back downstairs and met Blue coming up the stairs with another stuffed elephant to leave outside Riley's door.

"Where can I find Dusty? I've got something he's got to hear straight away."

He's out in the yard with Ironbear. They are putting up a tent and are going to turn it into a sweat lodge by covering it with tarps and blankets. They have a bunch of the boys getting it all ready for him and Ironbear asked me to bring one of the Indian drums back to him."

"Some of the other boys are laying a bonfire down by the lake pavilion in a fire pit we use down that way. They've set up lounge chairs for all of you. Looks like an interesting night ahead for sure. I'm going to leave this elephant outside Riley's door and I'll catch up with you in two shakes of a lamb's tail. "

A thought occurred to me, "Blue, did Dusty give you some traveling money for your trip?"

"He sure did. He gave me fifty one hundred dollar bills. Most cash money I've had in my hand in my life. Almost makes me nervous to have that much money on me, and I don't know what in the world I need five-thousand dollars for."

"Let me make a suggestion to you. When you get to Santa Fe, go by a Best Buy store and purchase two things. Get a pair of sound cancelling headphones and a good digital camera that is Wi-Fi capable. The headphones will probably cost as much or more than the camera."

"Get the good ones and don't worry about the cost. If we are ever going to get Riley out of her isolation, we need some way to protect her hearing from being overloaded if she ventures outdoors."

"Get the store clerk to show you how to use the camera and how to send the pictures by Wi-Fi to my email. Once you get down to the ranch, take lots of photos of the elephants.

"Get Half-Pint to take some of you with the elephants. I'll have them blown up and show them to Riley. Make sure you get some with you and the baby elephant. I think she'll like that."

"Thanks Stonebear. I'll do that and I appreciate the advice. Anything else you recommend?"

"I know winter is coming soon and I'm sure that bushy beard helps keep your face warm but its hiding a lot of blue, and Riley likes blue.

"Remember, that's how you got your new name. I think the more blue she can see, the more comfortable she'll be around you."

I put my arm around the young man, "You can always grow it back if it's covering up a lot of ugly. We'll just put a sack over your head and cut you some eyeholes until you're decent again."

He grinned at me, "I'm pretty sure I'm not any uglier than Mr. Charlie, and Miss Wanda seems mighty fond of him, so I'll shave it tonight and when I send back those pictures of me and the elephants my face will be bare as a baby Smurfs butt."

Chapter 22

The next person I encountered was Vern. "Stonebear, it's time for me to fly the gentlemen back to Laramie, but with your permission I'd like to come back and be at the bonfire tonight."

"I would be happy for you to return and be in the circle tonight. There is much to discuss and you can be very helpful in formulating our plans, but remember you and Snowbird are flying to San Diego tomorrow to pick up my cat. I want you well rested and go easy on the wine."

I'll be fine sir, and I rarely drink, and never the night before I'm going to fly the next day. My daddy told me aviation fuel and alcohol was a bad mix and led to many hard landings that people didn't walk away from."

"Funny you should say that. A wise man told me much the same thing about alcohol and diesel fuel many years ago when I was a young man just starting making my living on the sea. It is a good thing when we can learn while young those things that help us all through life."

We made it back to the break room and Abraham was back but he was not alone. He had an elderly man with him wearing a battered green felt hat.

The man had a long silver-grey ponytail and he was wearing a backpack with a violin case strapped to the back. He had a beautiful yellow lab by his side wearing a harness with a handle that the man was gripping with his left hand.

In his right hand was a white cane. I didn't need to see the wraparound sunglasses on his face to know he was blind.

Abraham explained, "This is Senor Wolfgang Menchner, but he prefers to be called just Wolf. I found him and his dog Gretchen standing outside the cafe when I arrived to put the sign on the door.

"Some people had given him a ride and dropped him off. They thought he might be able to play some music as payment for food for his dog. I did not know what to do Zed. I could not leave him there alone, so I brought him with me. I hope it's ok with everyone."

"You did fine Abraham and I am proud of you. Welcome Wolf, my name is Zed, or if you prefer you can call me Stonebear. We are pleased you have graced us with your company. There is a chair four feet to your left that is empty. Please set your pack aside and sit with us. We will bring food and water for you and your dog. You are welcome to stay here for the night and rest from your journey. Have you come far?"

"It's been the journey of a lifetime friend. I left seeking where I belonged many years ago and I have never arrived, so yes, it has been a far journey. Is this a church or religious retreat? I cannot see but I can feel exceedingly well.

"Just like you can feel the heat from a fire, I can feel waves of kindness washing over me from the presence of the people in this room. What is this place where I have been brought by my friend, Abraham?"

"Wolf, it is called the '*Anchorage*' and it is to be a sanctuary for animals, dogs, elephants and wolves."

Wolf threw back his head and laughed. He had a deep baritone voice that was rich and pleasing. His laughter was so genuine, we joined with him.

"It is no wonder I feel welcome here. The Wolf has been brought by the kindness of a stranger to a wolf sanctuary. It's almost like fate, and like you were expecting me."

Sirena had left as soon as soon as she realized there were mouths to feed. She returned with a platter of beef burritos and a glass of raspberry tea for Wolf, and a bowl of brown rice, peas and carrots, with chopped chicken, for Gretchen.

She said, "Senor Wolf, my father was blind and I will do for you what I did for him."

She raised the glass of tea and tapped it twice on the table and tapped the plate with the fork letting him know where things were located in front of him. She then tied a large napkin around his neck.

Wolf smiled, nodded his thanks, and proceeded to eat with a precision and delicacy that was surprising. Gretchen followed suit after looking at Sirena with grateful brown eyes.

She also ate with deliberation, and seemed to savor each mouthful, unlike Dimmit, who inhaled his food like a shop vac sucking up Cheerios. Speaking of the rascal, he and Daisy were pawing at the French doors eager to get in and check out this newly arrived bundle of scent.

I waited until Gretchen finished her meal and asked Wolf, "How is Gretchen with other dogs?"

"As long as they mean me no harm, she is a perfectly well behaved lady."

I went to the French doors and allowed the Dalmatians in the room. Gretchen stood and patiently allowed them to sniff her thoroughly with no signs of impatience on her part. She even gave a courtesy sniff in return.

I asked Wolf, "Does Gretchen get to run outside on her own?"

"It is seldom that she gets the opportunity and when we are in a place where she can, she enjoys it very much. Are we in a place where she can do this?"

"Yes, this is such a place and with your permission, I will let her go outside with the other two dogs and run and play."

"May I meet these other two dogs first?"

"Of course, first is the dog that we call Dimmit. He is a Dalmatian and he is a rascal, but a lovable one. Come Dimmit and meet Wolf."

Dimmit seemed to immediately comprehend what was expected of him and he came and lay his broad head on Wolf's knee.

Wolf didn't pet Dimmit in a classical sense. He caressed him with both hands and I realized he was reading Dimmit's features and 'seeing' him through his touch.

"Ach, he is a fine and noble animal this Dimmit, and the other one?"

"Her name is Daisy, and she too is a Dalmatian, and I think she and Dimmit are sweethearts."

"My Gretchen is spayed, so she is no threat to the happy couple. She just wishes to be friends."

Wolf stretched out his hand and said, "Come Daisy."

She went immediately to the outstretched hand and licked it. She patiently allowed herself to be 'read' by Wolf's gentle touch and her tail began to wag.

"Daisy is a most beautiful lady and she and Dimmit are well paired. I think now Gretchen would like to go out and have some time away from her duties to me. She richly deserves it, but do leave her harness on. She will not stray far from me as long as it is attached."

I opened the door and all three dogs rushed to the opening, crossed the wide deck, down the stairs, and went bounding across the lawn like kids let out at recess.

Wolf took a plastic grocery shopping bag from his coat pocket and began placing the remaining burrito inside. Sirena placed her hand on top of his.

"Wolf, in this house no one goes hungry, not ever. No human or animal ever has to worry about an empty belly at the 'Anchorage.' There is no need for you to save food. If you are still hungry, please eat until you are full."

"I am saving it for Gretchen. We have not eaten in two days and she needs more food than me. I have learned to get by on very little, but she looks to me to provide for her needs and sometimes I am a poor provider.

"When there is an abundance, we share and when there is little, her needs comes first. It is the way God commands my heart to be, to show my gratitude for her loyalty. Without her to guide me, I would be stuck in some charity place depending on the kindness of others. I would not be free to feel the sun on my skin and the wind in my face. I could not partake in the beauty of the world if I was shut off from my connection with nature."

"It is a hard thing to explain to a sighted person, but if I could see like you, but had to give up my sense of feel for the world, I would choose to return to being blind. It is all I've ever known and I have come to love the way the world feels to me. I see it as clearly as you but in a totally different way.

"The only way I can communicate it properly is through my music. Allow me to play for you to thank you for your kindness to Gretchen and myself."

He unfastened the violin case from the backpack and soon had the instrument in his hands. Without any hesitation he began to play.

I recognized the song right off, "What Child Is This." He didn't just play the violin. He made it sing with such clarity and beauty that it transcended any music I had ever experienced before. He played from the depth of his soul with such consummate skill and mastery, that he also touched my soul through the notes he played.

He had that same effect on all of us. We sat enthralled by what our ears had just experienced, and Sirena and Wanda had tears of joy running down their faces. It was music played like I had never heard before.

The notes penetrated into my very being and my soul seemed to vibrate with the intensity of his playing and I felt lifted almost to a state of rapture. It was incredible and somehow he made me see the world the same way he saw it.

Music was his eyes and his face was filled with joy. I am sure he was not aware of our presence when he was playing. He was totally lost in the beauty and purity of the enchanting sounds coming from the strings and his bow.

"Wolf can you play "Hallelujah?"

"Ach, yes, it is one of my favorites and I often play it to myself at the end of the day when Gretchen and I stop to make camp for the night. Would you like me to play it for you now?"

"Can you manage stairs without Gretchen at your side?"

"Yes, if you will help guide me, I can manage fine. Where do you wish to take me?"

"I want to take you upstairs to let a young autistic girl hear you play. She sees music like you, in colors and moving pictures, and I feel that you can touch her spirit in a special way. She is very shy about meeting people, but with her door open she can hear you play."

"That sounds like a worthy task and I will do my best to bring my vision to her eyes. I am ready my friend, and I will call you Stonebear because it is pleasing to my ears. Will you carry my violin and bow so I can hold onto your arm and use my stick with the other hand?"

"I will not do as well as Gretchen, but we will get there my friend and I will keep your violin safe as a babe in arms."

We negotiated the staircase without any difficulty and arrived at Riley's door. I explained to Wolf that Riley's room was soundproof as she was very sensitive to certain sounds.

"Ach, this I understand well, and already I understand this young girl better. There are some sounds that are painful to me as well. That is why I prefer nature. I am ready my friend to play my best for her."

I flipped the switch three times and opened the door. Riley and Snowbird was sitting across from each other and Snowbird was laughing and Riley had a shy smile on her angelic face.

"Hello girls, I've got something I want you to listen to. You can stay right where you are. Just listen."

I nodded to Wolf and he began playing the beautiful notes of "Hallelujah," with the same amazing skill he had displayed downstairs.

The girls reacted as I had expected and half way through the piece Riley arose from her seat on the floor and began swaying with the music. She raised her hands and began forming invisible figures with her hands just as she had when she was working with the computer screen when she was involved in a 'movement.'

Slowly she made her way to the open door and Snowbird rose and followed her.

She had her eyes closed and I knew she could see the music in her head in living colors and shapes much like Riley. Wolf reached the end of the song and the notes still seemed to play on even when he his bow was stilled. Oh my dear God, it was so incredibly beautiful.

"Who is that Stonebear that can make angels dance around my head and the air turn to a rainbow?"

"His name is Wolf, and he is blind, but he sees the music like you and Snowbird. Music serves as his eyes and that's the way he sees the world."

"He cannot see me at all?"

"No, but he can feel you in some way much like you see people in colors. He senses people by their feel and by touch."

"Will he come in so I can see him?"

I entered the door followed by Wolf and we approached were the girls stood.

"Can you teach me to play like that?"

"Ach my child, I will not know unless I can touch your hands. May I?"

Without any hesitation, Riley extended both of her hands to Wolf.

He reached out and took her left hand in both of his. He gently traced her delicate fingers and did the same with her palm.

"May I touch your face?"

She stepped closer to him and tilted her head back. Wolf caressed her face, every line of it much like he did with Dimmit and Daisy.

A pleased smile crossed his face. "No my child, I cannot teach something you already know, but I can show you how to unlock what is already within you. "You were born to play and are only waiting for someone to provide the key. This I can do. Stand behind me and put your hands on my shoulder and feel what I feel while I play for you."

Once Riley was in position, Wolf began playing another piece I recognized. It was "The Rose" and it was a song perfectly suited to the violin. It was a song that touched me deep and when Wolf played it I felt transported and I thought of my mother, and the words to the song…

It's the heart afraid of breaking, that never takes the chance
It's the dream afraid of waking, that never takes the chance
It's the one who won't be taking, who cannot seem to give
And the soul afraid of dying, that never learns to live

When Wolf finished, I wiped the tears from my face.

"Did you feel it child, the music that lives within you?"

"Yes, I felt it. Can you come back tomorrow and play more for me?"

Wolf looked at me for my approval, I nodded my head as if he could see me and caught myself. "Yes, he can. I too want to hear more from this incredibly gifted and sensitive man. I think I could listen to him play forever and I only hope heaven has music half as meaningful and beautiful as his. I think Wolf is on loan to earth from God's orchestra."

Chapter 23

We backed our way out of Riley's room and Snowbird joined us, telling Riley she would come say goodnight later. We eased the door closed and turned towards the stairs. The entire crew, including Dusty and Ironbear had followed us upstairs and they had been silently listening to Wolf play.

Dusty spoke for all of us. "I have never heard the violin, or any instrument played like that before. My name is Dusty Rhodes and this is my home. I extend to you an invitation to stay here as long as you wish.

"I would be happy if you stayed forever and made this your home. You belong here. You have brought with you a magic that will give Riley another form of expression and I consider you a blessing from God."

Wolf placed his violin neck and bow in one hand and held the other out to Dusty, "I thank you for your kind invitation Mr. Rhodes, I have never been in the presence of another group of humans that has generated a feeling like I am receiving from this collection of kind souls.

"I know not how you all came together to be as one heart with many beats, but I know you are all on the same vibrational level and the harmony is unmistakable. I can hear its effect on my music and I can say with complete honesty, I have never played better than I have played today.

"I know without a doubt, God has led me to this place just the same as He has brought all of you together for some good and worthy purpose. I know He wants me to stay here.

"Standing here before you, I can't see you, but I sense you, and it is as if I am standing at the open gates of heaven and being asked to put my wandering ways to rest. I feel like I have found the home I have searched for all my life.

"I will abide with you as long as you will have me, and as long as I fulfill my purpose. My music is my prayer, and here in this sacred place I have found hearts that listen beyond what the ears can hear. This is truly a place of sanctuary and I am richly blessed."

Everyone warmly and genuinely welcomed Wolf to our circle, and I saw clearly the design and purpose for each of us having been brought together as one. Just as Wolf had described it, we were now one heart with many beats, but we now had a conductor that could unlock the music in our souls and help us rise to even greater heights by blending our talents into a symphony of good with each of contributing to the mix.

Snowbird had her eyes fixed on Consuela, "Grandfather, can you see what I see when I look at Consuela?"

"No my child, I cannot see what your eyes can see but my hands can feel what you can see."

"Consuela, I ask permission to touch you and Abraham, I will do so with the greatest respect."

"Si Senor Ironbear, is there something wrong with my wife?"

"Wait my friend, I must seek the answer from within."

Ironbear took Consuela's hand in his and closed his eyes. I could hear him chanting very softly, almost like humming. His body began to rock back and forth, barely perceptible, but it was contagious to Snowbird and myself. To my surprise, Wolf was also gently rocking back and forth and his rich, deep voice joined in a hum that was a chant.

Ironbear opened his eyes and looked at his granddaughter, "You see three, do you not?"

"Yes, grandfather, I think Wolf's music has unlocked a greater potential within me for intuitive sight. I see now with a clearer vision I never had before this moment."

Abraham had listened to all of this with growing anxiety. "Please tell me what is wrong with my little bird?"

"Be at peace my friend. There is nothing wrong with your wife. What I feel, and my granddaughter sees is three. There are three hearts beating as one.

"First, Consuela's strong steady one, and two tiny ones, beating steadily together in perfect harmony. Abraham, your wife is going to have twins."

Spontaneous joy erupted in the hall and congratulations were heaped on the happy couple. No one doubted the accuracy of the diagnosis just rendered in the presence of all of us. The circle of Brother Bear was growing in leaps and bounds.

Sirena asked me to take Wolf's bow and violin. "I will take Wolf to his new home within the walls of this house. He belongs nowhere but in the 'Nightingale' room.

"It is smaller and will suit his purposes perfectly and it's beside my own and I wish him to listen to something. It will be my purpose to introduce him to this place and help him have the confidence to go where he wishes without being guided by anyone. We all seek our path. I have found mine."

She kissed Wolf on both cheeks, took him by the arm and led him away counting the steps to the stairway.

We followed closely behind. Dusty had his arm around my shoulders, "Son, did you see Sirena's face? I have never seen her look more radiant or happy. I think pretty soon, you and I will be the only ones in this crowd unattached."

"Well Dusty, we might be paddling our canoes solo, but our dogs love us and yours smells a heap better than mine. I believe I will do both Miss Daisy and myself a kindness and give the rascal a bath. It's probably going to be a rodeo but I'll have no 'son' of mine courting your 'daughter' in his current smelly state."

"Guess I'm lucky in that regard. Daisy loves her bath. Why don't you try bathing them both together? They've already seen each other naked, so I don't see no harm in communal bathing. If it's good enough for the Japanese, it should be good enough for a couple of Dalmatians."

"Dusty, you are a genius, that's a great idea and I think that will work."

"Son, I've definitely lost a step or two, but the old noggin works just fine. You eat healthy, clean food and your body functions like it was intended to. I just wish it worked on my legs as well as it does on my brain."

"By the way, according to Ironbear, I am going to be wearing the same loincloth in our improvised sweat lodge that you wore on your vision quest. He says the loincloth is lucky because it was blessed by the presence of his bear brother. What do you make of that?"

"Dusty, if you experience even a small portion of what I did on my vision quest, your life will be forever changed."

"Stonebear, you would be welcome to join Ironbear and myself in the sweat lodge."

"No thank you, Dusty. This is an experience for you and Ironbear to have together with no one else present. Some other day I will join you and the others in the sweat lodge, but this is a journey for just the two of you."

"Good enough for me, and straight spoken like a man of the salt. I do like plainspoken men and woman. I see you locked in on Devin McIntosh as being a man of that caliber."

"He impressed me Dusty, not that the others weren't thoroughly competent in their fields, but Devin stood out as a man whose counsel I could understand and trust. Like you say, there is much to be said for being plain spoken. If he has not had a chance to confide in you yet, I instructed him to proceed with the purchase of the hospital in Lander."

"Excellent, I like men that are plain spoken and I approve of men whose actions reinforce their words. Debbie was correct estimating that you were just the man I needed to get the spurs put to my dreams while I'm still above ground."

"I handed you the helm and you've taken charge of this quest of mine with enthusiasm and confidence. Look at the crew you've accumulated in such a short time. What a fine bunch they are and how well they are coming together is a sign of inspired leadership."

"Stonebear, I meant every word I just said, but the thing you have done that warms my heart the most is the almost miraculous effect you've had on Riley.

That girl has made more progress in the short time you've been here than we've been able to achieve in years of determined effort."

   "Wait till the elephants get here, Dusty. I believe we'll have that young lady stepping way beyond the boundaries she and fate imposed on her life.
   "The appearance of Wolf and his incredible skill playing the violin is going to give her another mechanism for expression and interaction with others.
   "Snowbird and Riley appear to be well on the way to developing a true friendship. I knew my daughter was quite special but I did not know that she too sees people in color. They see one another as the color gold, and neither of them have ever encountered another golden person before."
   "Remarkable things are happening my friend. I'll be mentioning Snowbird quite prominently in my prayers tonight and your name won't be far behind. I'll catch you later Stonebear, your father and I have some serious sweating and drumming to do and I'll confess I'm eager to find out what he's so excited about."
   "Good luck my friend, may the spirit of the bear be with you and may God watch over you. We'll all be down by the lake having a bonfire and brainstorming ideas. Come down and join us if it works out that you finish up faster than anticipated."

I found Dimmit along with Daisy and Gretchen, all stretched out on the tarp in the former great room, doing what dogs do best; sleeping and waiting for their next meal.
   I called for Dimmit and Daisy to follow me and Gretchen decided she would join in the parade. We made it to my room and I removed Gretchen's harness and the collars of the other two. I stripped down and turned the shower on and adjusted the temperature until it felt warm without being too hot for the dog's comfort. I called for Dimmit to join me and he looked at me like I had lost my mind.
   Gretchen stepped right in like she had been showering daily all her life and seconds later Daisy followed suit.
   Dimmit still held back.
   "That's alright old son, you won't mind sleeping on the floor tonight while me and Daisy enjoy the comfort of a fine mattress and clean sheets."
   That did the trick and in stepped Dimmit. His attitude quickly changed when he realized he wasn't getting washed in a hollowed out log, but being exposed to something more like being in a warm spring rain.
   With three full-grown dogs it was a mite cramped and I had to sit on the floor to be able to wash the dogs. I may have missed a spot here and there, but I got what I could as each dog came within arms reach. It was like trying to paint the

ponies on a moving carousel. A lick here and there, but overall I was pleased with the experiment of making it fun instead of something to dread.

I used every towel in the closet to dry us as best I could and anticipated some hen clucking from Sirena about washing the dogs inside and using all the towels.

It was the same old story so many others followed. I would ask for forgiveness having failed to ask for permission in the first place.

I found some US Naval Academy sweatpants and a matching hoodie in my closet that fit me perfectly. Quite proper attire for a bonfire and I bet Dusty had these items stocked in various sizes to accommodate guests that unexpectedly stayed overnight. I figured we might look like a bunch of midshipmen clustered around the bonfire that night.

I noticed a quality white fleece robe with *the Anchorage* logo hanging from a hook on the back of the bathroom door. The perfect touch I thought to myself. Classy, but not ostentatious.

I knew how to run a ship but this was a different vessel I was in charge of now.

Of all the things that had been thrown at my mind by the men in suits, the thing that stood out most was that Dusty was rapidly approaching billionaire status, and he was turning it over to me and Debbie, to pursue his dream of a sanctuary for animals and to follow our path to do good. I wish my mother could see the man her son had become. I think she would be proud.

I decided to make some notes, not that I would use them at the bonfire. Just organizing my thoughts. The last thing I wanted was to conduct it like a formal meeting.

Nothing could kill a good idea faster than a business meeting with one person in charge, except possibly a committee or a focus group.

I didn't want to just think out of the box … I wanted to throw the box into the fire and for us to be inspired by the flames. I wanted to see passionate free thinking and thoughts flow like a river. I wanted to churn the depths of human creativity and see what rose to the top.

Help me dear Lord to set the right tone, and awaken the fires that rest within all of us. No sooner were those words out of my mouth than I knew exactly how to prime this get-together to where it kicked off on the right foot.

I grinned to myself. Not much of a hill for a climber, no sir, not much of a hill at all. I continued with my notes and lost track of time until I heard the dinner bell ringing. I took a last look at my pages of notes and left them on the bedside table.

I put Gretchen's harness and the dog's collars back on and we skedaddled out our door onto the veranda and around to the outside dining table. The fire was lit and it was a cheerful sight as I greeted my friends, several of whom were attired just like me, in Naval Academy sweats.

Gretchen went right to Wolf's side and nudged his hand. "Ach, my darling, you smell very nice. Some kind soul has bathed you. I too have bathed and dear Sirena is washing my clothes. I feel like a new man. Tonight our bellies will be full and our prayers of thanks will be long and heartfelt."

"Just so you know Wolf, a number of us here around the table, are dressed exactly like you, in Naval Academy sweats."

"Ach, that is marvelous. I have often dreamed of sailing. Even blind men dream of the impossible. I know many sailing songs for my violin and they are my way to live my dream through music."

Chapter 24

The dinner was remarkable and not surprising since Sirena, assisted by Abraham and Consuela, had strived as a team to make it a memorable occasion and they had pulled out all the stops to make it so. It was a feast absolutely fit for royalty.

We finished at last, and we settled into a relaxed state with most conversation centered around Consuela's pregnancy, but there was plenty of motorcycle talk too.

Lobo and his guys had great plans for Dusty's trike and a well thought out game plan for having it ready for the upcoming wedding.

They kept their cards pretty close to their vest but they were confident they were going to make Dusty a mighty happy man. Sounded good to me. We all owed Dusty, Debbie and me most of all.

Snowbird heard it first. The sound of a helicopter approaching. She jumped up from the table and she was so excited she knocked over her tea glass.

"Vern's back," and she was gone in a flash like a hummingbird.

"Reckon somebody better make that young feller a sandwich cause that pretty little filly is going to have his head so turned around he won't know if he's coming or going."

"Well Charlie, my meals settled and I think I'll mosey on down to the bonfire site before the sun sets. Why don't you join me?"

Devin spoke up, "Let me join you too, there's something I need to let Stonebear know about. I've been thinking about what you said about my brother Ian, and the possibility you might have a job for him. I can't wait till next weekend to bring him. It's got me fired up to think of getting him out of that private hospital and out in nature where he belongs. I am going to catch a ride with Vern and Snowbird in the morning and bring him back tomorrow, if you have no objections."

"No objection at all. I think it's a wonderful idea, and let me clarify something just in case there's a misunderstanding, it's not I *might* have a job for him ...it's I _DO_ have a job for him.

"I'll start him out at a ranch hands pay, and if his talents are what I expect they are, I think I will move him into a management position fairly quickly."

"I won't put him in the bunkhouse with the other hands. I'm going to put him next door to Wolf. Ian will probably need looking after for a bit until he's settled and comfortable and Wolf is the perfect man for the job."

"Thank you Stonebear. You can't possibly realize how much this means to me. You asked me if I was married, and Ian's the main reason I'm not. Any woman that marries me gets my brother in the bargain. Takes a special kind of woman to accept that."

"Many say they will, but the first time they see Ian naked out on the lawn collecting bugs to move to safety out of the way of the lawnmower they are going split and sue for alimony.

"It gets hard sometimes, but I won't abandon my big brother. I remember him before he got sick. He was my hero and he treated me like I was his best friend. I don't forget and I don't cut and run. Not on a brother and not on a friend neither."

"I respect that Devin. Loyalty is an admirable quality and all the more so when it's tested and demands sacrifice. I don't cut and run neither, not from a friend and not from the brother of a friend."

"I can't help noticing that you frequently mention Ian attracting notice because he's naked."

"That's when he most commonly comes to the attention of the police and that's when the courts get involved. There's a psych evaluation ordered and he's held 72 hours and then released. We've been through that a half dozen times.

"The last time it happened the judge threatened to find him guilty of lewd and obscene behavior and sentence him to a year in prison.

"My God, Stonebear, you know what that would mean? Ian couldn't survive any prison. It would be a virtual death sentence so I had to put him in a place, much like a prison, only kinder and safer. He's not happy there. There are no trees and very little grass. Birds seldom come there. Ian says it's because they feel all the misery and loneliness coming out of this place."

"You know, the most excited I've seen him since I put him there, he told me one day a yellow butterfly flew over the far wall and flew on towards him dropping down and then catching itself and rising up, only to sink down again.

"He said it flew right over his head and he asked it to land and rest. She replied, Ian says it was a girl butterfly, she said, 'I can't I'm too far behind the others.' He says he told her they will wait for you. They always wait for the slow ones. She said she couldn't because she was so tired that she feared if she landed before she caught up with the others she would never fly again."

"That's Ian for you, harmless as a yellow butterfly and fascinating to talk to as long as it's about animals and you don't mind talking to a nude man."

"Devin, have you ever tried putting a kilt on Ian?"

"A kilt?"

"Yes, hoot mon, yer Scottish ain't ya. Try putting a tartan kilt on that Laddie and tell him as long as he wears his kilt he has a job here."

"A kilt? Surely, it can't be that simple, and why haven't I thought of that?"

"What made you think of a kilt Stonebear?"

"Well, I always kind of had a hankering to wear one myself but never got the gumption to actually do it. Why don't you get all three of us a kilt. Might be kind of fun when that Wyoming wind kicks up a ruckus or when we do cartwheels on the lawn."

"Stonebear, or should I say Stoned bear, have you and your Shoshone daddy been smoking medicine in his pipe?"

"He probably has but I haven't. I'm just shifting my mind into the type mode I want to communicate with tonight. Borderline silly is what I want.

"When people get relaxed enough to be silly around others, it opens up avenues in their mind to ideas and thoughts that may have been kept hidden because they seemed so silly they were embarrassed to tell it to anyone else."

"Let me tell you a story that came up in a situation where some folks in a little town in Alabama on the decline where they got together in a local church to try to come up with ways they could save the town and create jobs.

"They threw all kinds of the standard things out like festivals, and concerts, but they were out in the sticks, pretty close to the middle of the sticks, and nobody's going to drive forty miles through pine trees and kudzu to hear some banjo picking and watch folks clog. Idea after idea got discarded until people started making silly suggestions like…

"We could say a UFO landed and stole a cow."

"Legalize marijuana, most of you are either smoking it or growing it anyway."

"That's right, let's declare ourselves a sovereign state and open a bingo parlor."

"Why don't we open up a cat dairy and get us a herd of Siamese and we can take turns milking them."

"Why that is a silly idea. You can't milk no durn cats, but it would make a really cool T-shirt."

"That's what they did Devin, from a silly idea, they started a small T-shirt printing company and they made a quality product for a fair price."

"They got lucky and got a contract with NASCAR and soon they were printing T-shirts by the thousands. Then they landed a couple of country-western stars and they are now the biggest vendor of custom T-shirts in the country."

"I mean no offense by asking this, but is that a true story or some kind of flashback to your vision quest?"

"Well, since we are not at either of the official Liar's Lounges, although this would make an excellent one, I'll admit to making most of that up, but I did see a T-shirt once that had printed on it…*'Maxine's Cat Dairy'*…*'Our cream is Purr-fect'*."

The rest of the gang started arriving and Devin lit the preset fire and began uncorking a couple bottles of wine. He poured two glasses and brought one to me.

Debbie hollered, "Don't let him drink a drop of that. Alcohol does to that man what salt does to a snail. He just falls to the ground and starts humming 'Dust In The Wind' and calling everyone a 'big old peach of a woman,' doesn't matter if it's man, woman, or fence post. Everything's a 'big old peach of a woman'."

"You give me that full glass and go pour him about half that much. Anybody that gives Stonebear any more than that gets arrested for intoxicating wildlife."

I looked around at everyone, tilted my cowboy hat back and said, "C'mon everyone gather round, get a glass of wine or whatever suits you, and find a place to sit. Charlie started telling me a story one time about Kansas birth control he heard from his one-armed Uncle Bob, but we got interrupted and we never got back to telling, much less finishing. How'd that go Charlie?"

"I recollect which a one you're talking about. Uncle Bob claimed this poor Kansas clodhopper, he and his wife was fixin' to be having their twelfth child and they didn't see no way they could take on another mouth to feed."

"Twelve was their limit. Husband and wife spit in their hands and shook on it. That's a perfect legal binding contract in Kansas. Twelve was it and there weren't gonna be nary more.

"They went to town and seen their doctor, who they already owed a sizeable amount from their last four children and asked how they could stop having babies. The old doctor saw this was a waste of his time and he suggested they go the low cost route and perform a home vasectomy."

"How in tarnations do I perform this here home vasectomy?"

"Simple, you take a cherry bomb, light it and drop it in an empty tin can and hold it up to you ear and count to ten."

"Now, I ain't too smart, but I don't see no way that's going to keep us from having babies."

"The couple left and drove to another doctor up in Nebraska for a second opinion on the matter. They asked the Nebraska doctor the same thing. How could they stop having babies? Only they brought along the two littlest ones with them, and their diapers were a couple hours past their due date.

That, combined with them being from Kansas, made the doctor want to get them gone pronto."

He told them, "Take an empty tin can, light a cherry bomb, drop it in the can and hold it up to your ear and count to ten."

Charlie paused briefly, and picked up a soda can to pantomime the rest of the story.

"The husband and wife pondered that all the way back home to Kansas. Two different doctors in two different states, and both with the same solution, so it just had to be right.

"They got back to the farm place and the man got him an empty tin can and dropped a lit cherry bomb in it and held it up to his ear and began counting 1-2-3-4-5, then he stuck the can between his legs and began counting on the other hand 6-7-8-9-"

After the laughter died down, I had some information to share.

"Devin's brother will be here tomorrow. His name is Ian, and there's also a woman coming in from Montana named Prudence Campbell. She's coming up to see if she's a good fit for being the head of our dog sanctuary."

Debbie smiled as she said, "She'll be here tomorrow Zed. I already got her on a flight to Denver, and she'll overnight there and catch a connecting flight tomorrow. I'll pick her up in the morning in Lander, bright and early."

"Excellent news Debbie, now let me tell you more about Ian. There's some stuff you need to know about him before he arrives.

"Ian is schizophrenic. He's not dangerous. He's considered delusional because he talks to animals. Sometimes he gets naked and goes swimming with dogs.

"The problem is he does it sometimes this in public places and that brought him to the attention of the law and courts. Devin had to put him in a private hospital to keep him from being sent to prison.

"I have a job for him here. We are going to see if a kilt will give him enough of the freedom he seems to crave to remain decently clothed. I need him here to manage the wolf preserve and act as a dog interpreter."

"Ach, my friend, you do not think this man Ian, can really talk to dogs, do you?"

"Wolf, I do not think he can talk to dogs, I know he can talk to dogs because a talking bear told me so. Furthermore, Wolf, I want to put Ian, right in the room next to yours, and I want you to act as his mentor and guide."

Wolf burst out with a rumbling laugh, "You choose a blind man to be the guide. Are you delusional too?" He started laughing again, "Maybe you too will be running naked and Wolf will not see either one of you. Why would you choose me?"

"Because your lack of sight does not prevent you from seeing deep within a person. Once you touch his face, you will know your path with him, and his with you.

"Another reason it is you, and no one else, Devin says his brother is fascinated with wolves. It's almost like an obsession with him, and right now, you are the only wolf we have. Imagine the possibility of you being able to relate to Gretchen on an entirely new level.

"Wolf, you have had the perfect companion all these years with Gretchen. You had a female by your side all this time, and you never heard what was really on her mind. Now, you may get an earful."

"Ach, my friend, if such a thing should come to pass, I have no fear that Gretchen will have no words to say to me that will not be ones of love. Those are the only kind of words she has ever heard from me."

"Very well my trusting friend. I am pleased you would think me capable of such an important assignment. I will try not to let you or Devin down. Thank you for making me feel I have a contribution to make to this circle. Am I to be honored to wear the mark of the bear too?"

"Yes, I would like all in the circle to wear the mark of the bear, including Vern and Devin."

"Ach so, that sounds wonderful to me. May I ask if I may have a bear playing a violin as my mark?"

I checked with Lobo, and he grinned and said, "Not a problem, my man. I can even make that bear dancing and wearing a kilt if you like."

"I know you are joking, but that is exactly what I want. A dancing bear wearing a kilt playing a violin. That is perfect for me."

Devin chimed in, "For me, I would like a grizzly bear climbing a rock face. Can you do that Lobo?"

"Man, if you can dream it, I can ink it. I can even strap a chalk bag and climbing harness around his waist that helps to convey the message. I can already see it in my head. I'll draw you a picture after a while and see what you think. That's a killer idea, man. Best one I've heard in a while."

"Ach my new dear friends. I have one song to play for you that suits the mood of this group. Just one and then I think Stonebear wants what we called in Austria, der Geistesblitz, or to brainstorm in English. Now, I play for you..."

Wolf picked an appropriate song for the mood I wanted us to share. It was "Drunken Sailor," a great tune for a lively violin and an easy song for a group to sing. Wolf sang as he played and pretty soon we all joined in.

What will we do with a drunken sailor?
What will we do with a drunken sailor?
What will we do with a drunken sailor?
Early in the morning
Way hay and up she rises
Way hay and up she rises
Way hay and up she rises
Early in the morning
Shave his belly with a rusty razor
Shave his belly with a rusty razor
Shave his belly with a rusty razor
Early in the morning

By the time Wolf stilled his bow we were all laughing and the mood I sought had been found.

"I'm going to throw out an idea to the circle and see what you think? How about us opening up a cat dairy and providing our own cat cream for our Diablo coffee. We could say, our coffee is better than good...it's Purrfect."

"Folks, I think even that half glass of wine was too much for Stonebear. I believe we have us a genuine Drunken Sailor in our midst. I don't know about a cat dairy, but Diablo coffee sure has some potential because it's the best coffee I've ever had."

"You've got that right Sheriff, I've never had better myself and I've paid $4.00 a cup for Starbucks plenty of times and it doesn't come close to Diablo. Durn if that stuff doesn't help me to finish tattoos almost twice as fast. It's like rocket fuel for a man like me."

"But where would we sell it? You need volume and lots of customers with a heavy traffic flow."

"Father, we could sell it on the reservation from trucks, like taco trucks. Grandfather could get us permission from the council. We could also sell fry bread with the coffee. It would be easy to make on the trucks, and we could provide small containers of local honey to go with the fry bread and maybe even sell jars of local honey from the reservation too."

"That's purrfect Snowbird, absolutely PURRFECT, and maybe even acorn bread too? Abraham has an awesome sauce he created for his SOB Flambé which would go really well with your acorn bread. He can show you how to make it and you can show him how to make the acorn bread. Once you show him one time, it will be his to know forever."

"Are there enough people on the reservation that would pay $4 for a cup of coffee?"

"We would not depend on the locals. There are two main highways that come through the reservation, Hwy. 287 from Lander, and Hwy. 26 from Riverton. After about 30 miles they join."

"This is a major route for millions of tourists each year on the way to the Grand Teton National Park and Yellowstone National Park. It drops off to just local traffic in the winter but during tourist season it can be bumper to bumper."

"We might even be able to set up coffee bars in the casinos. No alcohol is served in any of the casinos and Diablo coffee is an energizing drink. There are four on the reservation and they are the closest casinos to Yellowstone. Lots of potential customers, father, and Ironbear has great influence with both the Shoshone and the Arapaho."

"Excellent idea and one we will pursue with Ironbear, and see if we can hire and train people from the reservation to operate the trucks and sell the coffee, and obtain permission from the council to set up in the casinos on a mutual cooperative business proposition."

"Stonebear, with your appointment to manage Dusty's vast business empire, you now control two major office complexes, one in both Laramie and Cheyenne. You could put drive-thru coffee bars on your own property. Your ability to grasp what vast capabilities are now within your control will become more clear in the days ahead. You and Debbie have reserves vaster than all the coal barons in Wyoming combined. It's going to take a long time for it all to sink in."

"One bite at a time my friend, one bite at a time."

"We are also needing 100-150 dogs for our dog sanctuary. I want to find dogs that are in danger of being euthanized, those that are old and sick and need medical care. The ones that have had a difficult life and need a forever home. A permanent place where they will be loved and cared for and given any medical treatment they need."

"Where can we find these dogs? I already know where I'm going to get our vet. Right there in beautiful downtown Gauntlet. Doc really impressed me with his integrity and devotion to animals. He is a truly good man, and I know the business we could provide him would do much to answering some of his problems. We will set him up with a fully operational clinic right here on the ranch, and he could still keep his town practice."

"Zed, as County Sheriff, the county's animal control activities fall under the auspices of my office, and this is true throughout Wyoming, and most other states operate the same. I could send out a request from my office to all the other Wyoming sheriff's offices requesting an immediate halt to euthanizing, and advise we have facilities to house and care for dogs in their facilities."

"No one I know likes putting healthy dogs to sleep. We could probably get some of the closer counties to deliver them here. Most people that work at facilities like that have a heart of gold, and to be able to give a good life to dog that is about to have its life taken away will answer more than a few of these people's prayers. We would probably need to transport the others ourselves."

"Excellent, Debbie, can you get that ball rolling from here?" When you talk to them, ask them if they would be interested in helping us set up a free program offering spaying and neutering to the public. It would be funded by something you and I will set up as a non-profit corporation. Think of the good we can do if we can take that idea nationwide."

"Zed, I'll call the office and a message will go out first thing tomorrow morning. It will be a welcome message, I assure you. Be ready to be deluged with 'guests' because I think we can get your numbers pretty darn quick, but how are we going to feed them all, and lots of them will need medical care?"

"Snowbird, see if can we hire people from the reservation to help feed and care for these dogs? Abraham and Consuela can teach them how to prepare the food. Is that not true, Abraham?"

"Oh si, mi amigo. To cook 100 pounds of beans is the same as to cook one pound of beans. You just need a bigger pot, no? This I can do for you and I have seen the kitchen in the huge barn. You could feed a 1,000 dogs or more from there."

"Yes, father, many people on the reservation need work, but how will we get them here to this place?"

"We will buy a comfortable bus and transport them back and forth and consider them on the clock from the time they board the bus until the time they are returned to the reservation and we will have a comfortable place for those that show the most potential to stay here, especially when the roads may be impassable from winter snows. We will need some that stay here full time as resident caretakers."

"Abraham, it seems we have the possibility of making extra food we could sell to pet owners that want healthy, quality foods for their pets. Can we do that?"

"Yes, Zed, we could do that and Sirena can help us train the people. We will need a walk in freezer to store it, vacuum sealing equipment to package it, and some way to deliver it to the customers."

"If you don't mind a suggestion from a pilot, you could ship it via UPS like they do those fancy steaks from Omaha, in a sturdy Styrofoam cooler. Get people on a subscription type service where they get a weeks' worth of food at a time, in the right proportion for the size of their dog."

"It wouldn't be cheap, but some folks have no limits to what they'll do for their furry friends. Some people like Wolf, will even go without for themselves, to make sure their four-legged friends are taken care of first..."

"That idea sits well with me and I like the Diablo coffee idea too. What else can we as a circle do? My vision says much of what we are supposed to be involved in is to benefit the people of the Wind River reservation and try to bring about closer unity between the Shoshone and Arapaho peoples. Considering the talents of the people here, which are many, what else could we do to accomplish this?"

Lobo had an idea, "This is kind of wild, but it might just work. Actually, I have two ideas. The first one is to run an art contest on the reservation with some really attractive cash prizes.

"We can learn who on the rez has true artist potential, and you show me a natural born gifted artist and I can make a first-class tattoo artist out of them."

"If they ain't interested in inking folks for a living, we could help sponsor and promote their art in other ways. Maybe, like an art outlet on the rez featuring the works of local talent. We probably could get the casinos to let us hang some of the works in their building and have them available for sale."

"That's an outstanding idea Lobo, and you'd be willing to do that?"

"Sure I would Stonebear. I owe Ironbear my life and he wouldn't take any money from me. He just told me to find a way to pay it forward, and I think he would like the idea."

"What's your second idea, Lobo?"

"It's kind of wild, so stay with me on this until I get it all laid out. Cisco and Pancho are two of the most gifted motorcycle mechanics and painters I've ever encountered. They can build a motorcycle from the ground up and paint it like it's a masterpiece of rolling art. You've seen my van. That's their work my design.

"Now, here's where it's a little crazy because it would be expensive to set up. We could open a motorcycle training school on the reservation. Teach them everything from the ground up. We could pair them in teams, one Arapaho and one Shoshone to each team and it wouldn't make no difference if it was a mix of boys and girls.

"They'd have to learn to work together while they built two individual bikes with both of them working together as a team. We could treat it like an apprenticeship and we could pay them a salary while they learned. At the end of a yearlong course, they would get to keep the bikes they built, plus they would have been paid while they learn."

"That's a super idea Lobo, absolutely inspired, I would say. What do you think Cisco and Pancho, would you be willing to do this?"

"Yes, this is something we would both enjoy, and Pancho has had a dream for a long time to start a customized motorcycle company. We could start another business on the rez using only our very best students from the training school to start a separate business making custom motorcycles to sell to the public."

"We could get all the business we could handle by riding with all our students on the bikes they built to the big Sturgis rally next year. I can see it in my head now and we would make quite an impression as we all rolled into town.

"There's big money to be made from custom motorcycles. We could call it something like Brother Bear Customs, and we could set it up as an employee owned company. Arapaho and Shoshone working together and earning together. The sacred circle could be our company logo."

Everyone started talking at once and the energy level was electric.

Debbie gave me a grin. "Look at you go Stonebear, I'm proud of what you are doing, and I believe you deserve another half glass of wine. Any more tricks up your sleeve, my friend?"

"Wanda responded to her, "Shucks, Sheriff, our boy hasn't even gotten started yet, have you Zed?"

"I think we all have lots more to add." I pointed back toward the house, "But what are those two ghostly figures running towards us?"

The group all looked at where I was pointing, and once we realized what we were seeing, we were all speechless. Stunned into absolute silence.

It was Ironbear and Dusty wearing *Anchorage* bathrobes and running barefoot towards us matching stride for stride and wearing looks of triumphant joy on their faces.

Dusty broke the silence, "Look at what a miracle Ironbear has accomplished with me in the sweat lodge. I haven't felt this good in years and I can't remember the last time I could run.

"He said I had been doing so much good in my life that I had attracted the attention of evil spirits called Nimerigars, and they had shot me in my knees and legs with their tiny poisoned arrows to slow me down."

Dusty did suddenly look a good twenty years younger and his energy level was remarkably high. He was so filled with enthusiasm at that moment; he could probably sell umbrellas to turtles and hip boots to ducks.

"I tell you Stonebear, we chanted and prayed until I thought I was going to pass out from the heat. I bowed my head and prayed for endurance to last a little longer and when I raised my head and opened my eyes, there was a magnificent albino buck standing in front of me.

"Then its side began to glow from within, and tiny arrows began being pulled from my knees and legs."

"There were hundreds of them and they flew like a cloud of darts right into the side of that deer. I can hardly believe it, even now, after I have run down here with no pain. I know it happened. It was not a dream. Both Ironbear and I saw it with our own eyes."

"First thing tomorrow, under Ironbear's supervision, we are going to start construction on an authentic Shoshone sweat lodge big enough for all of us to sit in at once."

Chapter 25

Words of congratulation and praise were heaped on the shoulders of both men. Ironbear seemed greatly pleased, "My son, it worked faster than I would have thought possible. I anticipated us taking most of the night but I knew it was possible, soon as I touched Dusty, when we met.

"I attribute the speed of the healing to Dusty wearing the same loincloth you wore on your vision quest, but equally, I credit that so many people with good hearts are here, that the evil spirits were overpowered by the forces of good."

"You have quickly assembled a powerful circle my son, and now let me tell you Dusty's new name. My friends, I present to you my brother, Seawalker. Since he is now my brother, he also becomes brother to Stonebear and Charlie, and another uncle for Snowbird. Now, she has another old man she can kiss."

Snowbird promptly did just that and welcomed Seawalker to her rapidly growing family.

Dusty grinned and said, "If someone will bring me and my brother Ironbear a glass of wine, I would like to hear what has happened while we've been in the sweat lodge."

"No wine for me Seawalker, I much prefer the medicine in my pipe, but out of respect for the presence of the sheriff, I will just sit and listen to what has happened."

Debbie looked up and raised her glass, "Ironbear, the sheriff went off duty as soon as I drank Zed's second glass of wine. I reckon I'd better get used to calling him Stonebear, like everybody else seems to be doing, except when we are on duty, and tonight ain't neither one of us here as law officers.

"Besides we have no jurisdiction over Native Americans and my personal opinion is that what you smoke in your pipe is a whole lot less harmful to society than what's in my glass. Please feel like you are at home in a circle of friends that love each other, because I certainly do."

While Debbie was talking, I had an intense flash of significant magnitude. It actually rocked me back on my heels. I had to explore it right away.

"Dusty...I mean Seawalker, your vineyard is in the Napa Valley, in California, right?"

"Yes, it is 2,000 acres of fertile rich land and there is room to expand the operation as several hundred acres remain unplanted."

"Seawalker, California is a state where the cultivation of cannabis is allowed and I would like to plant marijuana on some of your untilled property."

"You want to sell marijuana?"

"Not at all. I want to grow medicinal quality marijuana and provide it free to people suffering from disease and sickness that can benefit from this God given medicine. Especially people like my mother who was in such agony from cancer in her final days.

"Only in areas where it's legal, of course. It would be a non-profit organization solely to provide comfort to people in need, especially those that can't afford it from a retail location."

"I understand even though legal, it is quite a financial burden to many. It is a path to do good just as the albino deer took the pain from legs without cost, marijuana can relieve the pain of many according to Ironbear, and it should be without cost as well.

"You make a very good point Stonebear, and I see both of your fathers nodding their heads in agreement, but are you going to just pass it out to people that say they're sick?"

"No, that would be a recipe for disaster. Either I, or our lawyers, can examine the prospect of providing it directly through their doctor or from face to face contact with the recipient.

"The recipient must have a photo I.D. and a doctor's official diagnosis of their need for the product. We could have rolling delivery vans that arrived at set locations on a regular route for folks that had doctors that would not participate. We could include a request, but not a demand, that the people being given it, allow us to follow up with them so we can build a database of how it helps, or does not help, their particular need."

Seawalker laughed, "You can't see, but even Debbie is nodding her head yes now. I think that's a highly unusual approach to doing good, but so is an albino deer for helping a 90 year old man run again.

"Take it to the moon Stonebear ... TAKE IT TO THE MOON!"

Devin said, "I doubt very much you will find many doctors willing to keep medicinal cannabis in their offices, but a rolling delivery van would be a doable thing with the right setup and the proper precautions.

"I don't suppose you would want Lobo, Cisco, and Pancho to paint marijuana leaves on the side and have words like..."The Canna Van," or "Bongmobile," would you?"

Almost like it was an involuntary reflex, every woman present rolled her eyes ... Wanda – Debbie –Consuela - Snowbird, every one of them rolled their eyes like they were on the same axle.

Charlie said, "How about me. Why don't I get one of them fancy Indian names too? I'm a brother too, ain't I, or ain't I not?"

Ironbear gave Charlie a serious look, "Worry no longer my dear old butt scarred friend. I have thought long of what to name you. Some kind of wise animal but with a distinctive flair to it and I have the perfect Indian name for you. It will be M.B. Coyote."

"What kind of Indian name is M.B.? I've never heard of an initialed Indian before."

"This is true, but there is no Shoshone word for Marlon Brando. The Apaches have a word for it, but its pronunciation is like a cat hacking a hairball, so unless you want to be called Haacccck Coyote, it must be M.B. Coyote."

Ironbear adopted a sorrowful expression that barely hid his smile, "I am sorry, but it is an Indian rule, part of your name has to come from you."

"I'm not real sure that's even funny at all. No sir, you could have called me Willy-Pete Coyote, or something a little more creative than plain old M.B."

"What do you think Miss Wanda, you want folks calling your husband Willy-Pete, or M.B.?"

"Hold it right there Mr. Ironbear, you had me at Willy, and M.B. it's going to be. Ain't no other woman going to be calling my husband Willy-Pete, not as long as Winchester keeps making cartridges for my .44.

"I'll just call him Mellow Butt in private and it'll grow on him, trust me. Just gives him a new story to tell or poem to write."

"Now that you mention it Wanda, I believe I do have words to say..."

There was this old desert rat and Charlie was his name
He had an Indian brother cause they treated each the same
They served in a far away place across an endless sea
Hoping to survive each day and get back to Land of the Free
They looked out for each other, and watched each other's backs
Till one day Charlie got his butt wounded in a mortar attack
Oh Lord it burned him something fierce and he feared he would die
He never had nothing that hurt no worser, I ain't tellin you no lie
But his Indian buddy dug metal from his butt using his own knife
If that sucker had burned any deeper, He wouldn't need to be taking no wife.
My Indian buddy went a probing deep and cutting both left and right
He left one of the finest cowboy butts in Wyoming looking such a sad sight
Now Ironbear has called me brother and wants to give me an Indian name
My second name is Coyote and I like it fine, but the first one's kind of lame
He could have called me Willy-Pete, but instead he picked out plain old M.B.
Guess I'll wear it proud, because of him I made it back to the Land of the Free

We applauded Charlie for his impromptu performance and for his new name M.B. Coyote.

Devin got my attention, "Stonebear, what do you know about growing marijuana?"

"It's a weed, right? Can't be too hard to grow a weed can it?"

"Ah, my friend, you have no idea of the complexity with which modern day cannabis cultivation has evolved into. No worries my friend, once more I have just the man you need. I went to school with him in at the University of Nebraska, and he has a Ph.D. in Botany.

"His name's Tommy Thompson, III. He's what we call a Half-Loonie. American mother and Canadian father. He has dual citizenship in both countries, which is really neither here nor there.

"Somewhere around 2003, he was hired to manage a large commercial marijuana growing operation in the province of Manitoba. The growing facility was situated underground in an abandoned copper mine, and operated under license from the Canadian government, in order to provide a regulated and consistent supply for medicinal marijuana patients

"He loved that work passionately, and he developed cutting edge techniques while there for cultivation under artificial lights, but some years later, the government would not renew the lease, and he reluctantly moved on to different work. I know he would love to get back into it, and he's sick to death of Saskatchewan winters. He'd probably pay you for a chance to go work in the Napa Valley.

"He's also an internationally recognized expert in cultivating and genetically producing new strains for medicinal needs and has written three books on the subject. Medicinal marijuana is his passion.

"I'll get him down here to talk to you. You'll be quite impressed. He can talk genetics in such a way even I understand him, but he's a certified egghead, no doubt about that. His socks probably won't match and his shoelaces might not be tied, but he's not a whistler, and unless he's fallen in to a pit of depravity, he's not a sunflower seed spitter either."

I was finding Devin's company to be a fine mix with my personality and sense of humor. I respected his devotion to his brother and I felt he and I might well become the best of friends after having gotten off to such a promising start. He had already shown how useful he could be for the achieving the aims of the circle with his broad range of connections.

I was bound and determined to find a fit for his brother, Ian, at the 'Anchorage' and keep him in a kilt, even if Lobo had to tattoo one on his hide.

I listened in on my friends various conversations. They were lively and silly, and the suggestions were coming without being considered about how foolish they might sound to the listener.

Ironbear was telling Seawalker they should make a cannabis wine and Seawalker was giving it serious consideration

Snowbird was telling Abraham how to make acorn bread and pine nut gravy. Abraham was telling her how they could take two thinner rolls of fry bread dough and make it into a Shoshone Empanada by making a filling of native favorites, like pine nut gravy. One with meat, and one with just vegetables, something like fried masa balls and 'ground potatoes.'

Wanda was figuring up profit margins on Diablo and fry bread, and fretting about how messy honey could be, and figuring we would need to provide those moist towelettes with each order like in a southern BBQ restaurant.

Blue and Debbie were discussing getting police escort through the major cities the elephant convoy would pass through to keep the animals exposed to as little stress and delay as possible.

Sirena had brought her guitar with her to the bonfire. I surmised that must have been what she wanted Wolf to listen to when she guided him to his room.

She was playing soft soothing notes much to the approval of Wolf, and the fascinated attention of three dogs ... two Damnations and a harnessed Golden Lab, all three seemingly enjoying the music.

Chapter 26

Sirena had a skill with her guitar that helped me understand how quickly she had seen her purpose with Wolf. One pair of gifted hands had found a heart that was in sync with her on.

Sometimes people know immediately. I envied them, but I was not jealous. Just happy for the harmonious confluence of personalities adding to the happiness of both. I hoped they would play beautiful music together for a very long time.

Wolf raised his violin to his face and asked her if she knew a certain song. She said she did, but not all the words. He told her to play along and he would sing the words and for her to sing what she knew.

They began playing and it was my favorite sailing song, "Southern Cross," performed by Crosby, Stills & Nash. Wolf's voice was magnificent and when Sirena joined in, it was seamless, like they had been practicing for years…

When you see the Southern Cross for the first time
You understand now why you came this way
'Cause the truth you might be runnin' from is so small
But it's as big as the promise, the promise of a comin' day
So I'm sailing for tomorrow my dreams are a-dyin'
And my love is an anchor tied to you (tied with a silver chain)
I have my ship and all her flags are a-flyin'
She is all that I have left and music is her name
Think about
Think about how many times I have fallen
Spirits are using me, larger voices callin'
What Heaven brought you and me cannot be forgotten
I have been around the world (I have been around the world)
Lookin' (lookin' for that woman girl)
(Who knows love can endure)
And you know it will
And you know it will

I saw Seawalker's head rise sharply while listening to the tune, and his eyes took on a faraway look. As the notes faded away, his face was so dreamy and peaceful that I suspected he had just experienced some intuitive flash that gave him great peace,

"Stonebear, you have a sailboat berthed at Coronado Island, do you not?"

"Indeed I do, and it she is a fine British made, blue-water capable craft. She is christened 'Genevieve' in honor of my late mother."

"I just had an intense desire to get back on the sea once again with a deck beneath my feet and feel the salt spray in my face. I actually felt that happen just now and I can still smell the scent of the sea lingering in the air.

"I want to go with Vern and Snowbird in the morning and visit your boat. I want to hire a couple of competent deckhands and bring *Genevieve* back to our marina in the Puget Sound. Crazy idea for an old man, isn't it?"

My heart felt full, I recognized what Seawalker had just experienced was a flash and it was his destiny to follow it and seek where that path would take him.

"What welcome news that is to my ears, Seawalker. I have had some concerns about her being so far away berthed and forgotten in a slip. She is a racehorse and is happiest when she has the wind filling her sails and water flowing smoothly under her hull.

"You will only need one other person to help you bring her north. She can be handled quite well by one experienced captain, but having a deckhand is a wise precaution."

"Then that's what I'll do. It might be a month or more before I get back, and I will be excited to see what's happened in my absence; but this seems like a gift to me from the Creator, and I feel it would be a mistake for me to ignore this opportunity. Do you understand my friend?"

"I fully understand Captain Seawalker. When the Creator shows you your path, the only wise course is to weigh anchor and set sail where your heart and soul leads you. I assure you no one can understand that better than me."

Snowbird bid us all goodnight, saying she had promised Riley she would see her before she went to bed.

Next to leave were Lobo, Cisco, and Pancho, on the way to the 'motorcycle barn' via the kitchen first to get cups of Diablo coffee. They seemed very excited about something, but they were keeping it a secret from the rest of us.

Charlie extended his hand to Wanda, and with their bear print tattoos touching at the wrist, they walked hand in hand back towards the lights of the big house.

I turned to Debbie, "Well, that went really well and you are truly one big peach of a woman. Now, I'm going to take my two Damnation dogs and make it to my own bed. Thank you Debbie, for being the marvelous human being you are. You bring much joy to my life and thanks to you I won't be lying here in the night looking up at the stars in the sky. If one falls this way, catch it for me, would you, and put it in your pocket and save it for a rainy day."

I waved goodbye to the ones still left and accompanied by the two faithful dogs, I headed 'home.'

As I made my way across the grassy lawn, I heard Sirena playing and singing a touching song. It was "Tears in Heaven," by Eric Clapton. I reached the house as her talented voice finished the last few lines…

Beyond the door there's peace I'm sure
And I know there'll be no more tears in heaven
Would you know my name
If I saw you in heaven?
Would it be the same
If I saw you in heaven?
I must be strong and carry on
'Cause I know I don't belong here in heaven

For some reason the words touched me deeply. Since I had arrived in Wyoming, I had noticed my emotions had grown ever more tender and increasingly easier to touch. Especially after my experience with my vision quest and I really hoped it grew no worse.

"Weepy people, even people shedding happy weepy tears, still made me a little uncomfortable but I was learning that our circle was a place where deep emotions could be safely shared with one another.

I hummed "Dust in the Wind" until it made my lips tingle, and I had to smile. I lost the tune but not the smile as I opened the door and stepped into the light.

Chapter 27

I awoke the next morning feeling refreshed and my mind was instantly alert as soon as I opened my eyes. No morning fog or Merlot haze to deal with in my head today. I felt pressure on my legs and looked down to see Dimmit and Daisy, heads touching, lying across my leg.

Dimmit was doing some serious snoring, and Daisy was twitching like she was chasing rabbits or maybe she was chasing Dimmit in her sleep. I eased myself slowly from underneath them to keep from disturbing their sleep, but Dimmit opened one droopy eye, sighed, closed his eye and went back to sleeping and snoring.

A twitchy female and a snoring male seemed odd companions, but they looked quite content. I felt great warmth for them both as I looked at their spotted faces and thought no one is truly alone if they have a loyal animal friend.

I drifted towards the kitchen and my nose informed me someone else was not only up and about before the sun rise, but bless their hearts they had already brewed coffee. In the kitchen I found Snowbird, Vern, Seawalker, and Devin, all grabbing some breakfast with Charlie and Debbie busily making pancakes.

"Good morning Stonebear, the young folks and I plan to get underway as fast as we can after first light. Vern is going to deliver Devin to one of his other pilots, turn the whirly bird over to him. He'll take him to pick up Ian and fly him back here. With luck, they should be back before lunch."

Debbie spoke next, "I'm headed in to pick up Tiggy at the airport, and I have Bert meeting me on the way back with Lucy. I miss that old dog, and Tiggy has a special fondness for her. I want to borrow your big red truck and I'll be back before lunch too. Tiggy likes speed and '*Snowbird*' ought to put a smile on her face when I show her what she's got under the hood."

I tossed Debbie the keys to the truck and wished her a safe journey.

They finished their breakfast and I followed them out of the kitchen and out to the helicopter. Charlie stayed behind and assured me that once I saw them off he would have a stack of pancakes waiting on my return, as long as I didn't dawdle.

"Seawalker, I wish you fair winds and following seas. Keep a weather eye and pull into port when conditions warrant.

"Snowbird, I await your return as soon as you can, and my prayers for everyone's safety go up with you as you take to the skies."

With the exception of Seawalker, I would see them all again before the day ended and to him I gave my most lengthy farewell.

"Your dreams for the *'Anchorage'* will get underway during your voyage. I am confident when you return, you will see that Debbie and I will be making great headway in achieving the steps necessary for them to become a reality. Rest easy in your heart, nothing will be more important than Riley's happiness and well-being.

"That's a solemn promise Seawalker, sailor to sailor, and man to man. You are going to love *'Genevieve'* and I predict she will love you back. I know my mother would have loved to have known a man like you, and it's her spirit that fills the sails.

"Farewell my family and friends, go with God. Ve con Dios, mi familia y amigos."

I returned to the kitchen after letting Dimmit and Daisy out to ramble, and found Charlie talking to Wanda about the wedding.

Abraham and Consuela, along with Sirena, were making plans for preparing huge quantities of healthy food for our anticipated canine guests, some of whom might even arrive today.

Wolf was eating my pancakes saying, "You shouldn't have dawdled, but Charlie assures me he can whip you up some more, didn't you Charlie?"

"Keep your britches on son, grab you some Diablo coffee. Sirena made it today and it is plumb perfect. I'll have you a stack of cakes directly."

"Ach yes, Dieser Kaffee ist wunderbar. Best coffee I've ever tasted and I will write a song in its honor soon. Sirena will help me and we shall call it 'Wolf's Diablo Waltz.'

Captain T. would be amazed seeing the grand plans being lain to introduce Bayou la Batre genuine shrimper's squid ink to the great state of Wyoming. The 'Wolf's Diablo Waltz' sounded like a hoot, and maybe even the proper theme song for our circle.

Charlie brought me a plate of steaming pancakes and another plate for himself, along with a small jug of melted butter and a quart jar of amber honey with the comb still inside. It's my favorite way to eat honey since childhood, and I remembered my mother used to chew it like it was gum.

I smiled at the sudden memory. It had been years and years since I had thought of that. That and a million other thoughts all buried in my head just waiting for the right moment to surface.

Some memories brought a smile and others like remembering the agony she endured at the end of her life, still brought a stab of pain, even after all these many years.

Memories of love and loss might dim, but they never died. Maybe, when the soul left the body, the painful memories died, and you traveled onward, only with the good.

As a ship's doctor once told me while sharing a table in a crowded Dutch sidewalk cafe, "My friend, all pain ends eventually … all pain."

It is my belief that all pain does end, but that good does not, and I told him so. The doctor asked me if I could prove that scientifically, and I asked him if he could prove scientifically that it does not.

He pondered and shook his head no, so I asked him what was the favorite food his mother made as a child. He was Polish, and he smiled back at me and said, his mother made the best pierogis in the world. They were his absolute favorite, and she made them for him quite often. When he was older, she brought him into the kitchen, and patiently showed him how to make them himself.

So, I asked him, if he still ate pierogis, and if so, who makes them for you? He said they were still his favorite, and he was now recognized as the undisputed pierogi maker in his family, because his tasted just like his mother's, and everyone in his family loved them.

Have you taught this recipe to anyone else I asked him, and he said he had taught his young daughter the same exact technique and she could now make them almost as well as him, and maybe even better, according to his wife.

I told him, it's not scientific, but that is an example of good passed from your mother to you, and now from you to your daughter. Most likely, your daughter will pass that skill on to her children and the good that his mother passed to him would live on in her family one day. Hundreds of years down the road, his descendants might well still be sharing the good passed to him from his mother.

He agreed it wasn't scientific, but he knew his mother had learned how to make pierogis from her own mother, and although he never knew his grandmother, he still benefited from the 'good' she left behind.

He thanked me by picking up the tab, and months later, he made me some of his family's prize pierogis and they were indeed outstanding. Good lived on in something as simple as a family recipe passed down through the generations.

I think you do leave good behind when you go, in memories and knowledge you passed on to others, and I believe you also take it with you.

I can't prove it scientifically, but you can't prove to me it doesn't.

"Son, you haven't eaten half of your pancakes, and you've been sitting there with a faraway look in your eyes like you're on another planet in outer space."

"Not another planet, Charlie, but I did have my head way up in the stars."

"Have you ever had genuine Polish pierogis before? A friend taught me how to make them years ago, and I can show Abraham how to make them, and once he sees it one time, it will be his to know forever, and good from a long deceased Polish grandmother will live on through the hands of a talented Mexican cook."

"I can hear him now, "Eat this and if you die, I will never make it again.""

Charlie laughed at how well I could mimic Abraham's voice and accent. "You've got him down right good, you surely do, but he hasn't kilt nobody yet, has he?"

"No he hasn't 'kilt' anyone yet, and I expect he never will, but this might be the day when folks remember I 'kilt' my first man."

"What in tarnation has gotten into you son? You are making about as much sense as Wanda explaining why we should still be spending our honeymoon in another dadblamed desert, with all the money we've got, instead of resting on some white sand beach in Hawaii, drinking out of coconut shells.

"Am I'm the onliest one in this family with the common sense the good Lord gave a goose?"

I put my arm around this thoroughly lovable and unique man, "Don't you worry Charlie, it'll all make sense after a while … I hope."

I hadn't seen Debbie's cruiser outside and I asked Charlie if he knew where it was since the big red truck was also missing.

"I don't know a durn thing, so go on and git, and stop worrying an old man with all these infernal questions."

I left the kitchen shaking my head at Charlie's odd behavior, and made my way back to my room, after Charlie assured me he would handle feeding Dimmit and Daisy.

He said he might not have a cool Indian name like Seawalker, or Stonebear, but he reckoned even a M.B. Coyote could dish up a plate of vittles for a couple of love sick Damnation dogs, as good as anybody, even if they had a cool Indian name like Sitting Bull or Geronimo.

I closed my door and spent some time in prayer before I took up my notepad to write some of the myriad of things stampeding through my mind.

Good Heavens, I had a lot to keep up with. I was totally focused on my tasks, and time passed without my notice, until I heard the sound of a siren rapidly approaching the house.

I quickly put notepad aside, and hurried outside to see what was going on.

It was Debbie, because even at that distance, there was no mistaking that big old peach of a woman, and she had her cruiser coming under a full head of steam.

Her siren and blue lights were flashing like she was leading a Presidential motorcade. I was amazed to see the passenger, obviously not buckled in, stuck halfway out the window.

Her long black hair was streaming behind and she appeared to be howling with joy. She immediately reminded me of the loin-clothed warriors from my vision that were riding bareback around the sacred circle.

Debbie brought the SUV to a stop in a professional controlled slide that boiled smoke from the tires. She hopped out and howled like a wolf and her rider did the same. It had to be Prudence from Montana, but where in the world was my truck?

Prudence came exactly as advertised and just a little bigger than life. She certainly knew how to make an entrance and she was definitely drop dead gorgeous, but that's not what caught my eye.

What caught my eye was the plaid kilt she wore and the fancy cowboy boots she had on her feet adorned with the silhouettes of a howling wolf.

She walked right up to me, looked me square in the eye and said, "Howdy, my names' Tiggy, and from the description I've been given, you've got to be Stonebear. I don't know how you interview people for a position here, but if you'll tell me who I've got to kill to come work here, I will dispatch that varmint forthwith, and we can get on to my immediate hiring. What you got to say to that, boss?"

I surprised her with my response. "Is that a genuine Scottish kilt you're wearing?"

"Yep, sure is and these are my clan colors. You don't have anything against the Scots, do you now?"

I heard a familiar sound and I looked off to the east and Tiggy followed my gaze.

"If you're expecting another job applicant on that helicopter, you just tell them the jobs been filled already. There's not a chance you'll find anybody better suited to honcho a dog sanctuary than me. I am the right woman for the job. I am guaranteed bomb proof and super adaptable, and can't nothing shock me."

I smiled at her, "Tiggy, you've got the job, if I can have your kilt."

"My what? My kilt?"

"Sheriff, did you hear this man just now? Already trying to get me out of my clothes. I thought you said he was a fine gentleman."

Then she gave me a smug smile and twirled herself in a full revolution. When she twirled, I look down at her legs. I didn't mean to. Something about a girl twirling and most men will look at their legs.

My eyes almost bugged out of my head and she laughed at me.

"What's the matter, haven't you ever seen a cowgirl twirl before?"

"I've seen a few twirlers, but I've never seen one with a tattoo on her leg of a bear hanging from a climbing rope."

"Well, I like to climb, it's my passion so I got myself inked with a bear on a rope. I love wolves and bears. I'm getting another tattoo one day on my back with a wolf howling at the moon. I've been saving up years for that one. A full back tattoo cost an arm and a leg."

"That helicopter that's about to land has a man onboard named Ian. He is going to become a central part of your life and expand your knowledge of dogs and wolves, but sometimes he gets naked and I need your kilt. Not only do you have the job but I'll guarantee a full back tattoo in exchange for that kilt."

"Counter offer Stonebear, since you are the first employer to ever ask for my skirt before I got the job. How about the other kilt in my suitcase? It's the one I hike in, and this is my fancy one. This is the kilt I wear to job interviews and the kilt I wear for getting hired on the spot. Deal? My hiking kilt for the job and I don't care what the salary is, I'll take it. Shake?"

I shook her hand and it felt like she could crush coconuts. "That's quite a grip you have Tiggy. You get that from rock climbing?"

"Rock climbing doesn't hurt, but I'm from Montana, and I've shoveled enough snow in my life to fill up the Grand Canyon with a cherry on top."

"Well, here comes Debbie with your suitcase, so fetch me that skirt. There's a man on that chopper just asking to be 'kilt' and I reckon the sooner I've 'kilt' him, the sooner we don't have to worry about any of the hands taking viral videos with their cell phones."

She took the suitcase from Debbie, dumped it on the ground and soon had the kilt outstretched to me… "Here it is boss, now give me your hat."

"My cowboy hat?"

"Well, unless you've got a tam o' shanter hidden under that brim, yes, the cowboy hat. I can't give you a piece of my clothing unless you give me something in exchange. It's the Indian way. Aren't you named Stonebear? I am Cherokee on my momma's side and my daddy was full blooded Scot"

I surrendered to this dynamic female force before me and reluctantly handed her my hat. I'm sure if Ironbear had been standing right beside me, he would have shrugged his shoulders, and handed his hat over too.

She wasn't my star fallen from the sky. I knew that right away, but she was a peach of a powerful woman. Just not the peach for me; but I knew she had the kind of personality along with a brash confidence that would take charge of any task put before her and stick with it till it was done.

The helicopter settled on its skids, as Dimmit and Daisy, came loping across the lawn to see what all the commotion was about. They rushed right up to Tiggy, because strangers always have to be inspected first.

She dropped to her knees and spread her arms to welcome their approach. They obviously approved and within seconds began cavorting and playing around her.

Vern got the helicopter shut down without delay and opened the pilot's door. Devin slid back the hatch from the passenger cabin and disembarked first, followed by a tall lean man that bore a remarkable resemblance to him. But he looked like the younger brother, not the older.

They came right to where I stood with Tiggy. When Devin got within reach I handed him the hiking kilt. "This is courtesy of Ms. Tiggy here. She has kindly donated her hiking kilt to your brother Ian, in exchange for a job here running the dog and wolf sanctuary. She will be Ian's boss."

"A great pleasure to meet you Tiggy, and I hope you don't mind a McIntosh wearing your clan tartans."

"Och aye, Mr. McIntosh, don't you know your tartans Laddie? I'm a Campbell, and your people and mine fought side by side at the battle of Glenlivet in 1594, against the Earl of Huntley's men."

"That's a bit before my time Tiggy, and please call me Devin. Mr. McIntosh was my father, but I'm pleased to know we were allies. Did we win?"

"Nope, they beat us like red headed stepchildren. No doubt, there were many on the field of battle were that day, redheaded like yourself, but enough McIntosh and Campbell's survived to insure there was a chance for you and me to exist today."

Then she gave Devin a pretty twirl exactly like she had done for me, and every man present looked at her legs, even Charlie, who got a sharp pinch from a vigilant 'dust devil' right on his Marlon Brando, to help him mind his manners.

"My apologies Tiggy, I forgot my manners. The man kneeling down to greet the Dalmatians is my brother Ian, and he'll say hello in a minute, or so. With him, greeting the animals always comes first."

Ian looked up with a smile and spoke his first words, "Dimmit and Daisy want to get married the same day 'The Elders' do.

That utterance shocked us all but no one more than Wanda and Charlie who looked at each other and said, "Elders?"

Devin rolled up his sleeve displaying his *climbing* tattoo, "Are you by any chance a rock climber, because that's my passion?"

"Tiggy linked her arm with Devin's, and replied, "Rock climbing is my passion too. How about you being the one to show me around this place?"

Devin smiled and looked at me for approval. I smiled back and nodded my head. Bless his heart, she was a peach of a woman, and they did seem to be enveloped in a shimmering circle of approval when their arms linked.

Finally, Debbie showed up with Lucy plodding along beside with her ears dragging in the grass and the Sheriff was grinning from ear to ear.

"Hey, Debbie, where's my truck?"

Debbie pulled out her cell phone and hit one button. "Let the big dogs eat! Boys it's time to let "Snowbird" fly free."

Debbie pointed back to the west, and way off in this distance I saw my truck with blue lights flashing coming out of the motorcycle barn. It rolled at a fast pace and soon made its way right across the lawn, until it was stopped in front of us.

Ironbear was driving and he waved at me. The red truck had changed since I last saw it. On both doors was now painted the Sacred Circle, and within that circle, a smaller circle with a white background with a bright red Cardinal, the *snowbird* of the Shoshone.

"Come closer everyone and see what is written beneath the window sill."

The gathering grew closer until we were joined into a tight semi-circle around the truck. Tiggy linked her other arm to Wanda's, and giving her a smile, said. "You pinch your man again for me, and tell him I told you to. You and me got to talk about rocks later, girlfriend. Little shiny rocks are my second passion. I like to find the little ones and climb the big ones."

Following their example, the entire circle linked arms except for Ironbear, who was still behind the wheel. He hit the siren when we all linked together and everyone had time to read the words printed in gold.

Lucy, with her huge ears was first to respond the siren. She raised her head and howled, and almost immediately Dimmit, Daisy, Gretchen and Ian joined her.

Just like in my vision, the people in the circle all turned their faces and smiled at me, but this time, instead of vanishing in smoke, they lay their heads back, and howled together like a bonded pack of wolves. I joined them and howled too because I was on my path.

Beneath the window sills, and painted in gold script were the words....

"To Do Only Good"

THE END

Made in the USA
Columbia, SC
12 May 2024

35603883R00120